Return of the Sphynx

An A. J. Hawke Legal Thriller

Nail-biting legal thriller

*A scrappy lawyer must use sophisticated science,
and his fists, to aid a client.*

Sharp-witted lawyer A. J. Hawke uses an unusual genetic condition to defend a client against rape in this sequel to The Sphynx Murder Case.

Author Donald E. McInnis mines his years of experience as a trial lawyer to bring a high level of reality to the trial prep and courtroom scenes. He has a talent for making the minutiae of trial work interesting.

While most of the suspense centers on the courtroom, the finale shows Hawke can also be an effective action hero—and, fortunately, leaves open the possibility for more Hawke adventures.

Great for fans of Scott Turow, Phillip Margolin.

—Booklife Reviews Editor's Pick

Return of the Sphynx

An A. J. Hawke Legal Thriller

Donald E. McInnis

J&E Publications
San Diego, California

Published by
J & E Publications
www.donaldmcinnis.com

ISBN-13: 979-8-9865516-0-9

Library of Congress Control Number: 2022913895

Cover design by Timothy W. Brittain

Printed in the United States of America

Existing in man from the dawn of the human species is an evil that thrives whenever there is a lack of a nurturing, forgiving love.

Acknowledgements

Completing a project of this nature and scientific complexity would not be possible without the able assistance and contributions of a number of people, including advance readers, legal and medical experts, and those with editorial and graphic design expertise.

I particularly wish to thank Dr. William N. Devor, MD, neurologist and fellow legal scholar, for his insight and expertise in assisting my description of Chimerism and its unique characteristics.

I thank my editor, Larry M. Edwards of Polishing Your Prose—an award-winning author in his own right—for his patience and diligence in the development, revision, and polishing of the manuscript for this book. I could not have completed it without his honest and forthright critiques and his recommendations for improving this work.

And, once again, I thank graphics guru Tim Brittain for his magic touch in designing yet another compelling cover for one of my books.

CHAPTER 1

Early Sunday Morning

A THIN RAY OF SUNLIGHT TRICKLED into the dark room. At a snail-like pace, the light traveled across the room, widening as it went until it illuminated clothing strewn about the floor in a narrow path toward a large platform bed. A man, nude, lay prostrate on the king-size bed, legs spread-eagled across the width of the silky blue bedsheets.

A hand reached toward the head of the bed, grasping the sheets as though he was trying to find something until his hand touched one of two large, three-foot-long pillows. He pulled the pillow up against his chest, burying his face, blocking out the rising sun. Instinctively, he drew his legs up to the pillow as though he were still caressing the body of the lovely woman from the night before. There the man lay on his left side, fully asleep, nudging his groin from time to time against the pillow as if he was still with her. The increasing morning light bathed the man's body, revealing a youthful physique with a small waist, a V-shaped back with well-defined muscles and a patch of brown hair at the small of his back. A thin trail of the hair went down the groove between his buttocks, emphasizing his tight, athletic butt and narrow hips. He lay hugging his pillow for a good forty-five minutes until the warmth of the growing sunlight caused him to stir.

A low, melodic male voice quietly echoed in his head:

Love and devotion
Deep as any ocean
Don't play by anybody's rules
With your carousel of horses
And your unforeseen forces
You're running with the
Caravan of Fools

Slowly, he rolled over onto his back, clutching the pillow to his torso.

Caravan of Fools
Caravan of Fools
You're running with the
Caravan of Fools

Over and over again the song's words repeat in his mind:

Caravan of fools, caravan of fools,
You're running with the caravan of fools.

He finally spoke, "Tami, what time is it?"

"It's seven-forty. Good morning, Hawke."

Still half asleep, he softly queried, "Tami what happened to your Southern accent?" There was no response. Again he asked, "Tami, where's your Georgia drawl?" No response. He stared at the loft ceiling. *I thought I correctly changed the computer voice program to answer in a Southern accent.* Hawke turned his head to the right, toward the desk with his voice-activated computer and the stacked tower of audio equipment on the floor next to it. Rubbing his eyes so his morning vision could clear, he saw a woman seated next to the audio equipment.

Startled, the man swings himself up into a seated position onto the edge of the bed, the pillow clutched by both hands covering his groin.

"Who are you? What are you doing here?"

"Good morning, Hawke."

"Estrada . . . Silvia Estrada? What are you doing here?" Before she could answer he demanded, "How did you get in?"

"My boyfriend let me in."

"Boyfriend! Shit, did I leave the security system off again? Is that how you got in?"

"You will have to ask him."

"Who's 'him' and what are you doing here?"

"Oh, dear, aren't you a demanding one. The cranky type in the morning, is that it Drew Hawke?"

"Cranky? Shit. You break into my home, what do you expect? Again, what are you doing sitting there watching me sleep?"

"You gave me no choice. You wouldn't return my phone calls. That secretary of yours keeps putting me off with the lamest excuses. So I am here, and we need to talk."

The woman reached over to the audio/video receiver and turned down the volume of the song "Caravan of Fools" by John Prine.

Observing how familiar the woman was with his audio equipment, Hawke demanded, this time more forcefully, "What the hell do you want from me? Why have you broken in?"

"I didn't break in. I told you that already. Let me try to explain. My boyfriend and I followed you when you left that woman's apartment early this morning."

"Who's your boyfriend?"

"Jacob."

"Well, you tell Jacob I will kick his ass if he tries that again."

"I doubt that will happen."

"Oh, you do!"

"Drew, let's move on to more productive things."

"No! Who's your boyfriend? What's his name, uh, last name I mean, and where do I find him?"

"His name is Jacob Wellington and that's why I am here. Jacob wants you to represent his twin brother. And before we continue on, getting nowhere, yes, his name is Jacob Wellington. The Aussie I labeled the Sphynx in my news broadcasts."

"The Sphynx rapist?"

"Yes."

"Are you shitting me?"

"No. I love him and I've been living with him for several months."

"Holy shit! What in the world is wrong with you? The rapist! Have you gone crazy?"

"I know. I never thought I would do anything like this. But I did. I love him and he needs your help."

"Here's how it is Silvia. No! I'm not going to help him or you or his brother!"

"Please, Drew. His brother has been arrested for the crimes Jacob committed."

"You mean for the rapes and murder the Sphynx committed."

"Yes, the rapes. But Jacob swears he didn't kill that girl."

"God! You will do anything for a story. You're the most egotistical, selfish, driven female reporter I know. And all in the name of love you say. Bullshit."

"Driven, yes, but so are men. So what's wrong with wanting to be the best? Besides, what do you know about love? You can't think past a boner. If you were a woman, you'd be called a slut."

Drew's mouth fell open. Shocked as he sat there, nude, staring at the woman, not knowing what to say. His face flushed red with anger as he began to speak, but Silvia wouldn't let him.

"Hawke, it doesn't matter what we think of each other. You can call me all the names you wish. But Jacob thinks you are the best one to help his twin brother. The only one who can save Joshua."

"Well tell Jacob to turn himself in. That should clear everything up."

"He can't. They will send him away for life. I won't let Jacob do that. I told you I love him. I . . . need . . . him, Hawke"

"Look, you created this mess. You clean it up."

"Please, Hawke. Joshua isn't at all like Jacob. He'd never hurt anyone."

"Listen to you. Are you totally out of your mind? You know exactly what is wrong with Jacob and yet you live with him. You even let him fuck you. Woman, you need help."

"I couldn't help it Drew. I fell madly in love with him. He's told me everything about his past. What he's done and why he did it. The bottom line is, will you help Joshua? Will you save an innocent, God-fearing man? I will help you. Jacob said he will pay you. Money is not a question. Jacob has information the police don't even know about—proof that Joshua isn't the Sphynx rapist. He wasn't even in the country at the time some of the rapes occurred. Please, Drew. Do the right thing."

Drew Hawke looked into the pleading woman's eyes and forcibly asked, "Is Jacob outside?"

"No, he left. He said the two of you would fight again if he stayed."

As Drew looked at the loft door, Silvia stood as if to prevent Drew from standing and moving toward the door. "He's gone, Hawke. Packed his things hours ago and is now in Mexico."

"Where in Mexico?"

"I don't know exactly. He has a secluded place somewhere in Baja and another across the Sea of Cortez, north of Culiacan on the Mexican mainland. I've never been to either. Once you agree to take care of his brother, I'm to call him on a phone he gave me. We can do it together; if you wish, you can talk to him. Please do the right thing."

"So you think the cops have the wrong person?" Hawke asked, his voice more curious than argumentative.

"I know so! Once you meet Joshua, you will also know—he is not the one who raped all those women."

Drew paused in thought. *If Joshua isn't the Sphynx, maybe I could use Joshua to smoke out his rapist brother, Jacob. This could help David Caine's recovery from his guilt over the rape and death of his girlfriend, Claire Rewake.* Silvia stood there, her face wracked with emotion as if she was about to break down and cry.

"OK, OK. I will go and talk to his alleged twin brother, but no promises. You understand, I haven't agreed to defend the man."

"Oh, thank you, Drew. Thank you. We are both counting on you. Joshua is the only one in Jacob's family that has ever loved him. Jacob says he can't live with himself if anything happens to his brother."

"Now do you mind? I'd like to get dressed. You obviously know where the door is."

"You needn't be shy, Hawke. I saw everything already."

With that, Drew stood up, threw the pillow on the bed, and, naked, walked past her to a dressing screen.

"Don't let the door hit you in the ass on the way out."

ooooo

Later Sunday morning

Drew Hawke sat at an outdoor table of his favorite Gas Lamp bistro, the Barleymash Café, reading the Sunday edition of the San Diego Herald newspaper. He slowly sipped on an extra-strong cup of cappuccino in hopes of fighting back the urge to close his eyes as he read about the arrest of the Sphynx. With one leg on the metal table, Hawke flipped through the paper to page eight as he continued to read, slowly rocking back and forth on the hind legs of his chair.

An overweight, sixtyish man with balding hair approached the young lawyer.

"Well, this had better be important Drew Hawke. The missus is upset that I once again ducked out of church services this morning."

As the young man looked up at Pat DeLuca, his trusted investigator, he playfully replied, "I'm sure Father O'Connor will be asking her where you are. Has he stopped wanting to know when I will be attending Sunday services?"

"Drew, he gave up on you going to church years ago."

"Ha, Ha. Very funny, Pat."

The detective pulled back the second chair and sat down. "Now, what is so urgent that you had to get me in trouble not only with Mrs. DeLuca but Father Joseph O'Connor as well?

"You heard about the Sphynx?" Drew asked, holding up the front page for Pat to see.

"Yes. In fact my old partner Sergeant MacNeil called me last night."

"What for?"

"He said the police chief had basically ordered Detective Clayton and his special crimes unit not to ask the district attorney to issue murder charges against the Aussie rapist for the death of Claire Rewake."

"Really. That's interesting. The D.A. is quoted in today's paper as saying he is considering filing murder charges. Why would the chief take such a strong stand?"

"Don't know. MacNeil and I used to take cases with less circumstantial evidence to him all the time, and he would tell us to ask for murder charges. It just doesn't make sense."

"Here's something else that doesn't make sense," said the young man as he leaned forward and whispered in a low tone. "I woke up this morning with Silvia Estrada watching me sleep."

"At the loft?"

"No shit. She said she had been watching me for several hours. I demanded to know how she got in and guess what she said—'My boyfriend let me in.' When DeLuca frowned, Drew continued. "It gets better. Estrada said she has been with the Sphynx rapist for the past several months!"

"You needn't be so dramatic, Drew."

"Oh, yeah. Believe me, it is justified. Let me be more specific. She's the girlfriend of the Sphynx rapist—Jacob Wellington."

"Really?"

"Unbelievable isn't it. And Estrada claims the guy in jail isn't the Sphynx rapist. She says the police have arrested Jacob Wellington's twin brother, Joshua Wellington. On top of everything else, Estrada wants me to represent the twin in jail. She said Jacob Wellington thinks I'm the best attorney to help his brother. Estrada said money was no object. The Sphynx would pay anything to free his brother."

Pat sat back in his chair and brought his hand to his chin.

"I know, Pat, I know what you're thinking. Use the jailed twin to bring the Sphynx out of hiding and get him arrested."

"Yes. But something is wrong. Why wouldn't the police ask

for murder charges? Are they thinking the same thing we are? Do they know they only have the twin brother?"

"Not according to the paper. The chief of police and the D.A. say nothing about a twin.

The Feds were the ones who arrested him when he entered the U.S., and the Feds don't usually make identity mistakes. Not with their rabid use of DNA."

"Are you going to take the case?" Pat asked in a cautious way.

"I don't know. But Estrada presents and intriguing opportunity. If the guy in jail isn't the rapist, and I can lure the real one out into the open, it might help my ex-client David Caine to recover from his guilt of not being with his girlfriend when the rapist struck."

"You know, Drew, you can't trust a person in love. Silvia may say and do anything if she is indeed the girlfriend of the rapist. You know the real rapist might be the one in jail and Estrada is lying through her teeth. Something's fishy. Why would the Sphynx rapist tell Estrada you are the best attorney to represent the guy in jail? There are other more experienced defense attorneys. You've been practicing on your own just a few years. Be careful."

"You're right. I think the best thing to do is go visit the guy in jail and see if he is or isn't the Sphynx. In the meantime, I've got to get some sleep. This double shot of cap hasn't helped at all."

CHAPTER 2

Early Monday Morning

DEEP WITHIN THE BASEMENT of San Diego's City Hall, four men sat around a long table in a dimly lit room. Known as the Sanctum, the long-abandoned Cold War bunker was favored by this select group of city leaders because of its seclusion and the fact that the room's thick steel walls made it secure from outside electronic surveillance.

Seated on the right side of the table was San Diego Mayor Sam Sandelson, to his left William Brodsly, his political strategist but officially the mayor's Deputy Chief for Innovation and Policy. Across from the mayor sat San Diego Police Chief James Shaughnessy, and to his right Morgan Mayfield, one of San Diego's wealthiest men and owner of the hotel conglomerate M&M City Built, Inc. Purposefully absent was the mayor's chief of staff, who also served as the mayor's official spokesperson. All four of the men agreed it was important she be kept clueless of their decisions until absolutely necessary. At the head of the table was an empty chair.

"Mayor, who called this meeting?" asked Morgan Mayfield. "I had to leave my golf game to come here."

"We've all interrupted our Monday morning plans Morgan. Just hold tight."

"Well, it had better be important."

At that moment, all heads turned as the big steel door was pulled open. In walked a six- foot, six-inch, 240 pound man, Presiding Judge Brian O'Shea. The imposing figure paused and made eye contact and nodded to each of the gentlemen at the table. In his left hand, he held a rolled newspaper. As he stepped to the empty chair, he gestured for the police chief to close the heavy door.

Once Chief Shaughnessy returned, the judge placed the newspaper at the head of the table. As he unrolled and smoothed out the newspaper, he rotated it so all could read the paper's front page, four-inch-high headline, "Rapist Caught," and underneath, in smaller print: "Who Killed Claire Rewake?"

As the judge sat down, he gestured to the headlines. "Gentlemen, I called this meeting so we can decide what to do with the Sphynx rapist. He's to be arraigned Tuesday afternoon. As you know, one of the Sphynx's rape victims was murdered nearly two years ago. Now, we already have a young man sentenced for that murder, thanks to the handy work of defense attorney Drew Hawke. But our enterprising district attorney says he wants to charge the Sphynx with not only all five rapes but also that very same murder. This could open up a can of worms which you, Chief Shaughnessy, and you, Mayor Sandelson, do not want to answer for."

"Damn right, judge," piped in Chief Shaughnessy. "That fuckin' Hawke made a fool of my detectives, claiming they manipulated a false confession from the dead girl's college boyfriend. Then new DNA evidence identifies the Australian Jacob Wellington as the real rapist. The D.A. panics and dismisses the charges against the boyfriend since a jury would probably find the rapist killed the girl. Later, Hawke talks the D.A. into a manslaughter plea bargain because the boyfriend kept saying he killed her. Now, if the district attorney charges the Aussie rapist for the very same murder, it will make us look like total fools."

"I know, chief," replied the judge. "I was as surprised as anyone when Hawke told the court his client insisted on pleading guilty for the murder. Hawke blamed the whole mess on the police brainwashing the kid into believing he killed her."

"It's worse than that, James," spoke up the Mayor. "Judge, I'm getting huge pressure to defund the police department because of its supposed abuse of minorities in the city. For the district attorney to turn around and prosecute another man for the death of Rewake when that college student has already pled guilty, and Hawke earlier ripped the police department for forcing a false confession—shit, it makes my administration look inept and the police department out of control. There are already calls for me to fire the police chief over this whole Sphynx mess."

Morgan Mayfield chimed in with his two bits. "We can't allow these beach rapes to be front-page news any longer. It's been almost two years now. People are beginning to wonder what kind of a city we have here. When the rapes first became known, my tourist business suffered. Hundreds of people cancelled their reservations. Now to say we never had the rapist in custody to begin with, and even possibly convicted an innocent college kid . . . my god, who's watching the kettle boil here? We are supposed to be a family-oriented vacation city with the perfect weather, the perfect beaches, and a great restaurant and entertainment venue for the young and old alike. Not a place where we can't police crime and young kids are being convicted on trumped-up felonies. No wonder there are calls to defund the police."

The mayor looked at Shaughnessy, and they both turned

their gazes downward, well understanding what Mayfield was saying.

William Brodsly pointed out the obvious. "Gentlemen, we've got an election coming up this November and the beach rapes are endangering the mayor's re-election."

"I think we all understand the problem we are facing," surmised the judge. "So what are we going to do about it?"

The mayor spoke up. "Judge, can't you talk to the D.A. and persuade him not to charge the rapist with Rewake's murder?"

"Every time I talk to that idiot, he says he is an independently elected county official and I shouldn't be talking to him about any of his department's decisions or how he should prosecute. The audacity of the son-of-a-bitch! He just won't play ball. Nope. It's got to be you, Sam."

"But what can I do?"

"As mayor, you have to tell him this whole rape mess is making him look foolish and is absolutely damaging the city and its reputation. In the strongest words possible, tell the district attorney if his office convicted an innocent young man for murder, the voters are going to want blood. Pointedly inquire who in the hell evaluated that case and the flimsy evidence the young man's plea was based on. Look him right in the eyes and tell him you are not going to take any responsibility for this mess. Remind him the 'buck stops with him' even though one of his subordinates rushed to judgement and helped sentence an innocent man to a living Hell."

Mayfield added, "Sam, feel free to mention that the business community is all up in arms. Say we businessmen want a wrap to this whole messy rape fiasco—and now. It's bad for business. Frankly, I think he should let sleeping dogs lie. Call me when you need the Chamber of Commerce to get involved."

"I think you've hit on something," the mayor said, adjusting himself so he sat higher in his chair. "I can be demanding and not be accused of interfering with his constitutionally mandated duties. But I will need you, Morgan, and others, to speak up. Chief, can you inform the district attorney's office that the Aussie shouldn't be prosecuted because there is no evidence tying the man to the murder?

"Sam, I've already told the D.A.'s liaison deputy it probably isn't a good idea. So I don't know what else I can do."

"Chief, the way I would frame it," said the judge, "is call the D.A. himself. Tell him you read in the paper he was thinking about filing murder charges against the rapist. Advise the D.A. your department believes there isn't sufficient evidence for you to request murder charges against the rapist. Be firm. Tell him your detectives have no physical evidence or credible circumstantial evidence linking the Aussie to the murder of Claire Rewake. You only have evidence that ties him to her rape. As a consequence, you will only be submitting a request that the district attorney prosecute the Aussie for forcible rapes. Remember, you've got to be unshakeable in your opinion. Pointedly say the police department will not support a charge of murder against the Aussie, Jacob Wellington. Tell him the evidence just isn't there."

"I understand."

"And chief, don't forget, you've got a lot at stake. We don't want to lose you over this mess," added the mayor.

"Then we have a plan," concluded the judge.

As the group rose to leave, Morgan Mayfield cleared his throat and coughed, catching the attention of the mayor and the judge. Mayfield gestured with his head for the two to stay. The mayor grabbed Brodsly's arm.

"William, I want to talk with Morgan for a few minutes. I'll meet you back at the office."

"Yes, mayor," Brodsly replied and headed to the door.

"Oh, Chief Shaughnessy, please shut the door behind you."

"Yes, mayor."

"Well, Morgan, what is it?" asked Judge O'Shea.

"We've talked before about my Alta Rancho rural housing development in the back country near Pauma Valley. A group of troublemakers have raised a stink. My informant within the group told me these obstructionists have hired an environmental attorney to oppose the project. This is after I paid my usual expert for an environmental impact report; paid architects to layout the community and all planned roads connecting the community to the I-15 freeway and Route 79. The informant says the group is going to attack the environmental report because it did not properly disclose nor analyze the impact a 2,150-home community with a shopping center, business park, and golf course would have on highways connecting the community to the west and south. This is after the board of supervisors had already approved the project. The group will claim my access roads are inadequate to allow evacuations of residents in an emergency, and that the community will create congestion on the I-15 freeway and route 79. Not to mention the usual tree-hugger objections about endangered species and plants."

"Morgan, you're talking about the project we're running through our Cayman Islands corporation, right?"

"Yes, judge.

"I thought everything got approved after Sam and I talked to our friends on the board of supervisors."

"Yeah, the supervisors approved the plans alright. But now this group is trying to do an end around and undo everything."

"Morgan, I don't know what I can do further. I'm only the mayor of San Diego. This appears to be a legal matter."

"No, Sam. Morgan is talking to me," said Judge O'Shea.

"You want me to direct any lawsuit the group files to a judge who will find their claims insufficient."

"That's right, judge, just like you did for the resort hotel and condominium project in North County. And Sam, you are one of the most influential members of the San Diego County Planning Board, which regulates long-term county development and services. If you can get them to support the general development of the eastern areas of our county, particularly the northeast, then my project will have regional support as well as the support of the county supervisors. I estimate my project will generate a twenty-eight to forty million dollars profit for the three of us, if these troublemakers can be beaten down."

"OK, Morgan, send your environmental impact report and the latest plans over to my office, and I will analyze them and see if they fit into the planning board's current countywide development plans," responded Sam.

"You better do the same for me," said O'Shea. "I'll specifically review the environmental report to see where it is weak and how the group could screw up the project. If I find anything, I'll recommend some solutions and what arguments will be well received by the judge I appoint to handle the case.

"Morgan," asked the mayor, "how much longer until construction begin?"

"If there are no obstructions, ten months before we break ground on Phase One. Phase Two could start construction once Phase One is fifty percent sold out. I estimate total construction done within five years."

"Sam, this is a big project which could turn us a handsome profit, padding our retirement," said the judge.

"More than that, judge. The way I structured the community, we will maintain ownership of the business park, shopping center, and golf course, giving us a continuing source of yearly income."

"Morgan, I think you've planned this out well. Do you have any new financial projections showing all costs and profits?" asked the mayor.

"Sure do. You've already seen the financials I gave to the banks. But given the county's housing shortage, I think our eight hundred thousand unit sale price is too low. I believe, since the fact that we are planning a self-sustaining community, that our homes will sell between eight seventy-five and one point three mill each. I will have it hand delivered to both of you tomorrow. Destroy it after reading it, or put it in a safe place. I don't want those interloping do-gooders to get their hands on it."

Both men nodded in agreement.

"Thank you, guys. This is a gold mine waiting to be tapped. We can't let it fail," added Morgan.

CHAPTER 3

Law Office

THE AROMA OF fresh brewing coffee filled the room. A stout woman dressed in a dark burgundy business suit stood in front of the coffee machine savoring the smell of the rich Arabian blend. Small white ruffles of her blouse showed slightly below the sleeves of her jacket. A white silk scarf with streaks of faint red and blue stripes completed her very professional look. Her aromatic pleasure was interrupted by the ringing of the office phone. She turned and walked to her desk, cleared her throat, and answered,

"Good morning. Law Offices of A. J. Hawke."

"Debbie, it's me. I'm on the way to the downtown jail to meet a prospective client."

"Drew, you sound anxious. What's wrong?"

"Nothing! Well, possibly everything. Forget it. I'll be in the office in about an hour or so. I will explain everything then. Oh, have Matt and Liz there when I get in. It's very important."

The phone clicked as her employer hung up before she could say another word.

ooooo

Hawke's black BMW convertible slowed as he approached the arrestee receiving port of the county jail at 1173 Front Street. He pulled forward, past the fortress-like metal gates barring entrance, to a vacant parking spot. Drew pushed the button on the driver's door to power close the car's windows. Rummaging through the compartment in the console between the front seats, he retrieved a laminated four-by-six-inch parking authorization signed by Sheriff Commander Devon Mancini. Drew placed it on the dashboard next to the front windshield. As he walked to the entrance door for visitors, he set the Beamer's alarm with his key fob. Once inside, he was greeted by a deputy standing behind a sturdy glass window.

"Morning, I'm attorney Andrew J. Hawke here to see inmate Joshua Wellington. He may be held under the name Jacob Wellington."

"Do you have any weapons," the deputy asked, pointing to a sign that listed all prohibited items.

"No. Just me and my body," quipped Drew.

"No knives or other sharp objects?"

"No."

"Good. Place your driver's license, attorney bar card, and any metal objects including your car keys in the draw sliding out from under the window."

Drew signed the visitor log sheet, placed his identifications and car keys into the drawer, and waited as it slid back to the deputy. The deputy pulled up on his computer the inmate list.

"You said Wellington, Jacob, correct?"

"Yes."

He picked up the phone and dialed a cell block, and asked the sergeant to send inmate Jacob Wellington to the attorney interview rooms.

"Mr. Hawke, please walk through the metal detector and the opening door to my left. A deputy will greet you and take you to the attorney interview rooms.

Hawke rode the elevator up to the fourth floor of the jail with a young but strong looking deputy sheriff. The elevator door opened, and the two stepped out and walked down a corridor to a series of rooms. The deputy opened a door and Drew stepped into a small eight-by-ten-foot room, furnished with a single chair. The chair faced a narrow countertop and small window in the opposite wall; a telephone handset hung on the wall next to the window.

"Mr. Hawke, when you are done meeting with your client, push the buzzer on the right side of the counter. I will open the door and escort you back down to the visitor's entrance. Your client will be brought into the room on the other side of the glass any moment. You may use the phone to the right to speak to him. I'll be just outside."

"Thank you, deputy."

Drew sat the chair, and in a few moments the door on the other side of the glass opened and in stepped a young, blonde, twenty-something man about six-foot-two and a hundred eighty-five pounds. He sat down in a chair and faced Hawke through the glass. Surprised by the man's appearance, Drew just stared at the man, closely inspecting each of his seemingly familiar features. He looked very much like the man he had fought in the alley next to Sullivan's Irish Pub. But something was not right. The perplexed attorney picked up his phone and pointed at the phone next to the man.

"I'm attorney Andrew J. Hawke; you may call me Drew. I specialize in defending people charged with serious crimes. Your name?"

The man leaned forward and spoke in a decidedly Austra- lian accent. "I'm Josh Wellington from Port Hedland, Austra- lia. Why are you here? Did my father hire you?"

"No. I've been asked to represent you, but I haven't agreed to take your case yet. First, I have a few questions, if you don't mind."

"Go ahead."

"Do you have a brother?"

"Yes."

"What's his name?"

"Jacob. Jacob Wellington."

"What does he look like?"

"Well, like me, I guess. We're twins."

"Are you trained in the martial arts?"

"A little bit when I was in high school, but really, no. But Jacob is. He's actually very good."

"Are you close to your brother?"

"Yes. We are the best of friends. Why do you ask so many questions about my brother?"

"I do because you are charged with his crimes."

"I know. They think I am him."

"Do you know what Jacob has allegedly done?"

"Not really. The deputies say I'm charged with murder and rape."

"Did you rape anyone?"

"No. I would never do such a thing."

"Did you kill anyone?"

"No. I've never killed anything except a wild dingo attacking our sheep back in Port Hedland. Sir, who got killed?"

"One of the women raped by your brother."

"Oh, that's terrible." The young man looked directly at Hawke, his eyes riveted on Hawke's eyes. "My brother would never kill anyone."

"Would he rape anyone?"

The young man looked down.

"If your brother wouldn't kill someone, would he rape a woman?" Drew asked, this time more assertively.

Joshua wouldn't answer.

"OK, look. In America, when you talk to an attorney, what is said is confidential. The authorities can't listen in. They can't force me to say what you tell me. They can't even use in court what we talk about if for any reason they learn what we say. It's called attorney-client privilege. Do you understand?"

"I'm not a lawyer. But we have something similar back home. But, I prefer not to answer any more questions about my brother."

"You prefer to rot in prison for his crimes, is that it?"

"I didn't do anything they say I did Mr. . . . what's your name again?"

"Hawke, Drew Hawke."

Hawke paused and gathered himself. *Obviously I will get nowhere by being aggressive with this guy.* Hawke raised his right hand in a gesture of understanding to the young man. I see now that you truly love your brother. But, it will be difficult to keep out questions about your brother and what he is accused of doing. Do you understand?"

"Yes. But I have nothing further to say."

"All right, I get your drift. Jacob is lucky to have a brother like you. It is Jacob who asked me to represent you. He will pay my fee."

"How is my brother? Is he safe?"

"I am told Jacob is in Mexico, and I assume he is safe. Is there anything I can tell him for you?"

"Yes. Tell him I love him."

"Let's talk about something else. Why did you come to the United States?"

"I came here for a mining and mineral convention. My

father and I own a mining and shipping company in Port Hedland. It's been in our family for several generations."

"Is Jacob part of the company?"

"No. He refuses to have anything to do with my father."

"Where is your mother?"

"She left us when we were just little boys. I have no idea where she is or if she is even alive."

"How does Jacob afford to live? What's his occupation?"

"My dad set up a trust for him. It is now quite large. I don't know if he works or not. I

haven't seen Jacob for nearly three years."

"When and where did you last see Jacob?"

"I told you I didn't want to talk about Jacob."

"I need no specific details. Just answer the question generally. Please, I need to know more, especially about how you and Jacob live and the last time you two were together. It all goes to the murder and rape charges and my ability to defend you."

"So, you are going to defend me?"

"Yes. So please answer my questions. I am now your attorney, unless you disagree?"

"No, I need an attorney. Thank you."

"So when did you last see your brother?"

"OK, generally. I saw him last in Thailand at a monastery where he was living."

"It seems your brother and I trained under the same sensei at that monastery."

"You know my brother then."

"Not really, but he knows me. Let's just say we met in an alley next to a bar and had a beer together. That's when he told me he knew me from my stays with the monks every summer while in high school and college."

"I see. Jacob never said much to me about his time with the monks."

"Ah, Joshua, on another matter, do you know if Jacob has a girlfriend?"

"Yes. We talked by phone about two months ago when I told him about the convention.

He said he really likes her. I was very happy for him."

"I need to know who can testify to your whereabouts for the last couple of years. That is especially true if you were in the United States. Say your father, family friends, a girlfriend, or co-workers. Someone you may have met in the U.S.—like a business acquaintance."

"This is my first trip to the United States, except when I was a teenager. My father brought Jacob and I here when we were thinking of attending college at MIT in Massachusetts. I came this time because my father is ill, and it was an important conference, which I am now going to miss."

"If I may ask, what is wrong with your father?"

"His heart is not good."

"Is he well enough for me to talk to him and tell him what's going on?"

"I'd prefer you not. But since I'm stuck here, he will wonder what has happened to me, so, yes, do call him. Tell him I am all right and not to worry. I will be home soon."

"Joshua, you have been very helpful. I just have a few more questions. Did you know that Jacob was studying here at San Diego State University?"

"Yes, that's why I stopped here on my way to Chicago."

"Did Jacob ever tell you about the type of classes he was taking?"

The young man answered slowly, "Y-e-s."

"OK. I can see you still don't want to talk about Jacob much more than we have. I do have one more question. It will sound a little strange but it is very important to the defense of the rape charges. Do you shave your pubic hairs?

"My what?"

"Your body hairs. Do you shave any of your body hair—your chest, armpits, and groin?"

"No."

"To your knowledge does Jacob shave any of his body hair?"

"As I said earlier, I haven't seen Jacob since about three years ago, and I never saw him without clothes at that time."

"Good. Thank you for answering my questions."

Drew paused, in thought. *Until I talk to Jacob I see no reason to proceed further. Besides, I will need Jacob to somehow tell Joshua to open up to me since he obviously doesn't trust me.*

"Joshua, how are you doing in here? Any problems with the inmates or guards?"

"I'm all right. There is one tall, lanky guy, about six-five, who thinks he runs our cell block, but I just ignore him whenever I can."

"Is he an inmate?"

"Yes."

"Has he threatened you or made sexual advances to you?"

"No. Well . . . I don't think he . . . things appear OK in that respect. He just thinks anything we do, even to talk to the guards, will have to go through him."

"Do you want me to move you to another cell block?"

"Nah, the other guys say it's the same way in the other blocks. I'm all right. I just go along and keep a low profile."

"OK. I guess I had better give you my standard jailhouse legal advice."

The young man leaned forward and held his phone close.

"Joshua, do not talk to anyone if you can avoid doing so—especially to other inmates. If

they ask you what you are charged with, tell them you are not sure. Better yet, tell them the cops think you are somebody else and have arrested you because you are an Australian with a similar name to the guy they are after. If the authorities want to talk to you, refuse to answer any questions. Tell them to talk to your attorney. I will leave my card with one of the deputies, who will give it to you. You understand what I am saying?"

"Yes."

"This is really important, since any of the inmates in here will say you confessed to them

just so they could strike a deal with the district attorney in order to get a reduced sentence. People in here are desperate. So the less they know about you, the less they can put on that you confided in them. Agreed?"

"Yes. I shouldn't admit to nothing and don't talk to any of the inmates. Right?"

"Yes. Close enough for now, Joshua. Remember, say nothing to the cops or the district

attorney. Just give them my card and ask them to call me.

"I guess I am in a pretty bad situation?"

"Yes and no. But depending upon what you do in here, it can get worse. If you need to

call me, don't hesitate. I receive collect calls from clients all the time."

"Thank you, I will."

"I will be back to see you after I talk to your brother and his girlfriend. That should be

tomorrow or the next day at the latest."

Drew pushed the button. Almost immediately a deputy opened the door on the other side of the glass and ordered Joshua to stand and step out of the room.

Back at the car, Drew sat as he mulled over his thoughts about the interview. Several things kept bothering him. *Yes, Joshua looks a lot like the guy I fought in the alley. Almost a spitting image, as I remember him. But, this guy's speech has a thicker accent, and he talks much slower. Nor was he as demanding or take charge in the way he spoke. And the rapist's hair was black. Ah, but that doesn't matter, since all of Jacob Wellington's passports and photos show him blonde.*

"But, but..." Drew mumbled out loud. "His eyes! Yes, those eyes are decidedly different. The Aussie at the bar had dark-blue eyes. Joshua's eyes are not the same."

Drew continued to think about those eyes. *One was dark-blue but the left was a much lighter blue. The two eyes were very different in color. Surely, I would have noticed them when I fought him. I was inches away from his face.*

"Yeah, yeah, it was a fight and everything happens quickly, and who is admiring a son-of-a-bitch's eyes when he is trying to choke you to death?" Drew said, again recalling the brutal encounter.

Then again, I would have seen it if he had two different-colored eyes at the bar. The rapist sat only six feet away and made full eye contact with me several times, all within the bright lights of the bar.

Hawke shook his head and started his engine.

CHAPTER 4

Later Monday Morning

As the footsteps approached, the gait got more and more familiar. With anticipation, she stared at the door as it opened. Once again she was right. It was her employer, Andrew Jackson Hawke, the son of her best friend, who had died of cancer.

"Good morning, Debbie."

"Good morning, Drew. Here are your phone calls," Debbie said as she squeezed out of her office chair and stood ready with a fistful of messages.

"Hey, boss," added Matt, the nineteen-year-old college student Drew hired as a file clerk. The want-to-be lawyer and surfing fanatic sat at his desk in the corner, smiling from ear to ear. "Something special happening?" he asked.

"Yes, guys, we have a very interesting case. Debbie, where is Liz?"

"She's on her way," answered Debbie.

"When she arrives, the four of us will gather in the conference room so I can explain who we will represent. And Debbie, please call Assistant District Attorney Jack Farrat. I need to talk to him about a Jacob Wellington. I'll be in my office going through my messages, but don't hesitate to interrupt me."

Drew went to his office, pulled his desk chair back, and sat down while thumbing through his phone messages. He paused at a stapled group of five messages from Judy—Judge Judith Hudson. *Shit, she won't give up.* Drew picked up the phone and dialed her private cell phone. It rang just once.

"There you are, my gorgeous man. Why do I have to wait so long for you to call?"

Drew, determined more than ever to break off their relationship, mustered as strong a voice as possible. "We can't see each other anymore, Judy. Presiding Judge Brian O'Shea knows about us."

"Of course he does, darling. Who do you think told me where I could meet you?"

"What!"

"You sound so surprised. Brian said I wouldn't be a bit disappointed in you. And that was an understatement."

"O'Shea knows about our having sex?"

"Sometimes you are such a sweet, naive young man. So, Drew, I'm free tonight for a late-night cocktail at the Metl Bar Restaurant. It's down the block from your office. I could use a Pink Squirrel Cone. I can just taste that Merlet Cognac, Ruby Chocolate Raspberry Swirl with Dark Chocolate Truffles. Um-umm, exactly what I need to put me in the mood for tonight. Say nine o'clock?"

Drew took the phone away from his ear and stared at it. All he could say was, "Ah, ah, sorry, Judy, I've got other arrangements."

"With who? That woman you saw this weekend? Come on, she can't be as enticing as I. Nor even as satisfying. No one knows your body like I do. Admit it."

Drew was sweating profusely. His face was red from embarrassment, more like anger, his rage growing every second.

"Judy, I don't know what to say."

"Then it's a date."

Drew was numbed by the revelation that the presiding judge set him up with Judy. He did not know what to do. He just hung up. Shaken to the core, the young lawyer sat motionless, sweat oozing from his armpits. He stood but couldn't walk. He instinctively scratched his groin. His whole body was in a nervous sweat as he alternated between rage, fear, and bewilderment over what he had gotten himself into. He had done everything possible to prevent being ensnarled in Judge O'Shea's web of influence. And yet, here he was thoroughly trapped, having sex with a sitting judge, all arranged by O'Shea. Pat DeLuca's warning words to stay away from O'Shea reverberated in his mind.

The office intercom buzzed. Then came a knock at the door. Debbie stepped in, saying, "Liz and Matt are in the conference room. We're ready to begin." Her voice trailed off as she saw the rattled condition of her young employer.

"Are you all right?" Her query elicited no response. "Drew Hawke, has something happened?"

He looked up and muttered, "I'll be right there. Got to go to the bathroom." He stood, pushed his chair aside, and walked toward the door. Debbie stared at her boss as he walked past her and out the door.

The three sat in the conference room for what seemed an eternity. Finally, Drew walked through the law office door and joined them. All three stared at his wet, brushed-back hair and dampened face but dared not to ask what was going on. Drew walked to the head of the table and sat down.

"We have a new case."

A long pause followed. They stared at Drew as if wondering why their boss was not his usual self.

Finally, he added, "Remember the Sphynx rapist? Well, as you know, he has been arrested. It's been all over the news. I went to see him this morning in jail. I think the cops have arrested the wrong man."

"Boss, why did you go and see him?" Matt asked.

"Good question. I guess the best way to explain what we are about to do is to start at the beginning." Drew paused as he took a deep breath. "This morning, Silvia Estrada . . . ah . . . this morning I awoke to find Ms. Estrada watching me sleep. She apparently had been in my loft for several hours."

Liz and Matt looked at each other in disbelief. Debbie's mouth fell open as she shook her head back and forth. "The nerve of that woman. What have you been up to, Andrew Hawke?"

Ignoring Debbie's innuendo, he continued. "Ms. Estrada told me she had been living with Jacob Wellington, the Sphynx rapist, for several months. Jacob wants us to represent his twin brother, who has been arrested for Jacob's rapes and in all likelihood the murder of Claire Rewake. That is the person I saw this morning in the county jail . . . his twin brother, Joshua Wellington."

"How come Estrada has a key to your loft?" demanded Liz?

"Liz, she doesn't. Somehow she broke in."

"How could Silvia break in," Matt asked. "The place is a fortress. Tami controls elevator access to the third floor. The door to your loft is biometric and requires fingerprint identification."

"She said the Sphynx let her in. I asked over and over how he did it, but she didn't know or wouldn't say. I might have left the computer off."

"Dude, that doesn't matter. The loft door requires your fingerprint or it won't open," Matt said, shaking his head in bewilderment.

"Oh, come on, Drew. Can't you tell us the truth about you

and Silvia? Or is everything a big lie about you and your women?" snapped Liz.

Debbie interrupted. "We don't want anything to do with that crazy rapist. He's nothing but bad blood. He'll bring us only bad luck," she said, scowling with her eyes open wide.

"That's what I thought. But then again, I might be able to help the police capture the Sphynx and in doing so help our client David Caine in his recovery over the death of his girlfriend, Claire Rewake."

Getting right to the point Liz asked, "Why do you think they have the wrong guy? They have the rapist's DNA, thanks to us. And, the cops always take a DNA cheek swap when they book somebody. In fact, the San Diego Herald says the Feds matched the guy's DNA to the rapist. So what's the problem?"

"Joshua looks a lot like the rapist, but he just isn't the same guy. For one, his eyes are different. One's dark blue, the other is a much lighter blue. Both eyes of the rapist were the same dark blue. Even his hair is different."

"The guy has two different colored eyes?" Matt asked.

"Yeah. Not really a drastic difference in color, but really noticeable. And, he just speaks and acts totally different."

"DNA doesn't lie, Drew," Liz insisted.

"I know, Liz. That's what has been bothering me. But I swear he isn't the guy I fought in the alley or the guy I sat across from in the bar."

"Hey, boss. You were pretty . . . well . . . injured. Frankly, you had your ass kicked and had to go to the hospital because of the fight."

"Thanks, Matt. You are always such a nice guy—to the point, if not mockingly. You know, you never saw the other guy."

"Boss, I didn't mean . . ."

But Drew interrupted. "You're right, Matt. In the midst of a fight, one isn't exactly admiring his opponent's eyes or carrying on an astute conversation when injured. But, guys, deep down I just don't think he is the rapist. Here's what we're going to do. I've told Joshua Wellington we will represent him."

"Drew, I don't understand why you'd take this case," challenged Liz. "First of all, you've got this reporter woman who appears totally familiar with you, your body, and your loft. Next, you want us to represent what DNA says is one of the most despicable criminals San Diego has known. And yet you say, 'I have this feeling that he isn't the rapist.' Are you sure your compassion for this guy has more to do with his selfishness and total lack of respect for the feelings of women?"

Matt's eyes widened as he turned his gaze from Liz to Drew.

"I don't know what you are talking about, Liz."

"Your lothario conduct toward women certainly would have you sympathetic toward any man whose sexual behavior is centered solely on his own needs."

"Lothario? What the hell does that mean?"

Not a word was spoken as Drew looked at Liz, then Debbie, and finally at Matt for an answer.

"Ah, boss, I think lothario means selfish and irresponsible in one's sexual life. But I am sure that is not what Liz meant."

"That is bullshit. I am talking about a man's freedom not his sex life. Even the worst amongst us deserves to be considered innocent until proven guilty. Enough of this. If anyone doesn't want to work on this case, say so now."

A few seconds passed with not a word. Drew knew he was dodging Liz's accusation, but didn't know what to say. Finally, he spoke. "If everyone has had their say on this, let's move on. I will call Estrada and have her arrange a phone call with the rapist. He is supposedly hiding in Mexico. I will know if he is the one I fought by the way he talks and what he tells me we discussed when at Sullivan's bar after the fight. If I am convinced he is the rapist, then I will formally agree to represent his brother. I will try not to let any innate feelings I may have toward women, or the hurtful comments you have expressed today, affect my decision." Drew looked down, trying to collect his thoughts and determine how to diplomatically move on.

After a moment, he continued. "Debbie, in the meantime call Dr. Lawrence Rougtbeck at the California Forensic Laboratory in Berkeley and arrange for me to talk to him tomorrow. If the guy in jail isn't the rapist, I need to make sure the rapist's DNA reconstructed by the lab was accurate. Tell him I need about thirty minutes of his time.

"Liz, I want you to make a special appearance and arraign Wellington Tuesday afternoon. Please engage in a conversation with him so you can give me your thoughtful opinion about the man we might represent. If you think he is the rapist, tell me, and tell me why. It's not too late for us to withdraw right after the arraignment."

Drew paused to see if Liz would object. She just nodded, so he continued.

"If Joshua Wellington asks why you are there instead of me, tell him I have a phone call scheduled with his brother and I will see him afterward. I expect he will be charged with multiple counts of rape and torture. Please do not let your personal feelings toward this man interfere with you carrying out your duties. I am counting on you—the professional lawyer I know you are. At the arraignment, you should be given a copy of the complaint and arrest reports. If either is missing, demand a continuance of the arraignment as the defendant has a right to be apprised of what he is charged with and a minimal statement of the evidence against him before he enters a plea. If the judge will not agree for a brief continuance, enter a plea of not guilty on all counts. If the judge asks why we are making a special appearance for the arraignment, tell him we have just been asked to represent the defendant and need more time to evaluate the case. Oh, yeah . . . they arrested him as and have him booked under the name of Jacob Wellington, his twin brother, the rapist. OK, guys?"

Both Debbie and Liz nodded. Though Drew appeared calm on the outside, Liz's comments had his stomach churning and his mind questioning his every word.

"What do you want me to do boss?" asked Matt?

"Pull the David Caine file. I need to review it and all the evidence produced on the rapist and against our previous client."

"Done, boss."

Debbie slowly lifted herself up, and as she walked off said, "There's got to be a better way to make a livin'."

"You're right, Debbie, but not as much fun," Drew replied, trying to humor the moment as Matt and Liz followed her out of the conference room.

As Debbie and Liz exited, Debbie touched Liz's hand and in a low voice said, "Let's go to the ladies' room." Once in the bathroom, Debbie shut the door and softly advised, "Elizabeth, you may be right about Drew's womanizing, but I've got to tell you, attacking him directly about it and so publicly in front of us folks will not get him to want you. I've know this young man since he was born, and criticizing him so harshly will only drive him away."

"I'm sorry, Debbie, it just came out. I am so frustrated with him not noticing me. He has no idea how I feel."

"Remember, we want that inner animal which has young men on the prowl—otherwise they wouldn't chase us. Us women just have to learn how to get their attention and then keep 'em chasin' us 'round the house."

"But how do I do that, Debbie?"

You'll figure it out. But don't wait too long. There are a lotta o' sharks out there to choose from."

ooooo

Thirty minutes later the intercom on Drew's phone buzzed.

"Yes, Debbie."

"That weasel fella from the D.A.'s office is on the line."

Drew laughed and said, "Put him through, Debbie." His phone rang and he punched the button next to the blinking light. "Jack, thanks for returning my call. I hear you caught the rapist."

"Not us, the Feds."

"How so?"

"Customs detained him when he landed in San Diego on our warrant and turned him over to the F.B.I. who verified his ID through DNA and called us. He's now in the Central Jail."

"I know. I saw him this morning. How sure are you that he *is* the rapist?"

"Why do you ask?"

"Just making sure you got the right son-of-a-bitch."

"That doesn't sound like you. What are you up to, Hawke?"

"I don't know, Jack. But when I talked to him, he seemed as though he wasn't the guy I fought in the alley."

"Isn't that the same man that put you in the hospital?"

"Yep, but is he the rapist? What proof do you have that he is the same man that raped all those women?

"DNA. We swabbed his mouth and it matched the Berkeley lab's reconstructed DNA we had on the rapist." Farrat paused and then asked, "Are you representing the asshole?"

"Possibly. After talking to him, I just don't feel he is the same guy I fought and then talked to in the bar. But, if the

DNA checks out, go for it. Nobody wants to see him put away more than me."

"Hawke, you are one pain in the ass. How in the world can you defend the guy who killed your client's girlfriend?. For that matter, how are you going to explain that to David Caine, much less to the Rewake family what you are doing? You're just unbelievable."

"I said ,Jack, that I was *contemplating* being his attorney. OK?"

"Bullshit. You are fishing around for another news head-line: Attorney Hawke proves authorities wrong again. You enjoy making a fool of me, don't you?"

"Oh, come on, Jack. Is that any way to think of me? By the way, would you mind sending the new arrestee's swabbed DNA sample up to the Berkeley Lab for testing?"

"Hell, no! Get a court order." With that Assistant D.A. Jack Farrat hung up.

"Hmm, that didn't go so well."

ooooo

Drew's watch showed 8:55 p.m. as he entered the Metl Bar Restaurant. There she was, seated in her normal poised position, her back erect and one leg wrapped over the other, forcing her favorite black leather mini-skirt high up on her thigh as she flirted with the bartender, Pierre Lafon. Her blue, silk, long-sleeved blouse was unbuttoned one too many buttons. Judy immediately greeted Drew with her famous smile and gripped both of Pierre's hand, squeezing them tightly, ending their conversation.

"Right on time, Drew Hawke. I like a man that doesn't keep a lady waiting."

"You look ravishing tonight, Judy. Your eyes . . . they beckon from a distance. How do you do it? You are indeed quite the woman."

"Hawke, darling, you always were so good with words. Don't stop. After all, I did work extra hard on looking pretty just for you."

The two embraced, with Judy digging her nails into Drew's back in a loving but forceful indication she was ready for that night. Drew pulled a stool up to the bar and wrapped his arm around her petite waist.

"Are you ready for that Pink Squirrel Cone Metl is famous for?"

"Oh, yes, Drew."

"Pierre, one Pink Squirrel Cone for the lady. What do you think I should order ,Judy?"

Looking at the menu, she smiled. "How about the 'Dead Inside Cone' or the 'Tygrr King'?"

Drew laughed at the choices. "I feel adventurous tonight, Judy. Let's go with the Dead Inside Cone and its blend of Black Velvet Canadian Whisky, Don Fulano Tequila, Red Velvet Cake and cream cheese."

They both laughed at the decadence of it all. Their whispered conversation ended when Pierre brought the two ice cream confections. Drew paid and suggested that the two take a table near the back. They talked until the creamy cocktails were almost done.

Drew looked at Judy, his smile gone. "Judy, this whole thing about Judge Brian O'Shea is a problem. I really have to take a pause in our relationship."

The judge's flirtatious banter went silent. Her enticing lips pursed as she realized Drew's earlier comments over the phone were not just an effort to put off that night.

"But why, darling?"

"It has nothing to do with you, Judy. It's O'Shea. He continually interferes in my life and work. I've got to find out why."

"I see, even though it takes you away from me?"

"Yes. O'Shea for some reason wants to control my life—even my sex life. I am a man, Judy. I control my own life. I'm not a sex toy which O'Shea can hook up with any woman . . ." Drew paused, looking intently into her eyes. "No matter how vivacious, sexy, and enjoyable that woman may be."

"Oh, dear, this is really serious. I didn't know Judge O'Shea was so involved."

"Manipulative is the better word, Judy."

"Is there anything I can do?"

"No! Stay out of it. Let me handle this in my own way."

"I'm speechless, Drew. I do enjoy you. I . . . I think the better word is I want you. I am just crushed, Drew." Tears began to run down her cheeks. "Oh, dear, my makeup!"

Drew dabbed her cheeks with a paper napkin and hugged her as she fought back her tears. "I'm so, so sorry, Judy, but I have to do this."

"But why now after being together for so long. I just don't understand. Why can't you . . . oh, dear, I'm sorry to go on like this. But men always put the stupidest things before love."

"I don't know what to say, Judy."

"Don't try, Drew. I learned a long time ago never to force a man's affections . . . so I guess I will just have to wait . . . wait and see." Her voice trailed off as she quietly sobbed in Drew's arms.

"I'm sorry Judy. This is really hard but necessary."

CHAPTER 5

Tuesday Morning

"GOOD MORNING. The Law Offices of Andrew Jackson Hawke. This is Debbie, may I help you?" Debbie listened intently and nodded.

"Yes, Dr. Rougtbeck. Drew Hawke is in. Please hold." Debbie pushed the intercom button. "Drew, Dr. Lawrence Rougtbeck is on the line. Should I put him through?"

"Yes, please, Debbie."

She pushed the transfer button and sent the call to Drew's phone. But her curiosity got the better of her, and she pushed the button for the incoming call so she could listen in.

"Good morning, Dr. Rougtbeck."

"Drew, how did you know I was going to call you?"

"You were?"

"Yes. Assistant D.A. Jack Farrat called late yesterday and wanted to retain my services regarding that rape case you had nearly two years ago—the one in San Diego where one of the victims died."

"That slimy snake. I told him yesterday I was interested in representing a defendant in that DNA case. He turns around and calls you trying to keep me from using you."

"Don't worry. I told him I was still employed as an expert by you. He seemed somewhat distressed by that. You never did release me, correct?"

"Correct. In fact, I will need you to do some more work on that rape case."

What's up? Has the rapist struck again?"

"Not the way you would think. They have arrested a suspect. But I've been contacted by a news reporter who says the person in jail isn't the rapist, but his twin brother."

"Biological or fraternal twin brother?"

Not sure what you're asking."

"Biological twins are genetically the same."

"You mean they have the same DNA?"

"Yes. That's why their appearances are so strikingly the same. But fraternal twins, though conceived within their mother and born at the same time, are not biologically the same. They have different DNA and will appear similar but not the same."

"Then that explains everything. The rapist and my man in jail are biological twins. Remember that condom we sent you, which you used new PCR technology to reconstruct?"

"Yes, I do."

"The DNA you reconstructed matched a DNA cheek swab taken by immigration years ago. The matching of the immigration DNA sample and your reconstructed DNA gave the authorities the rapist's name. That information eventually led the cops to the rapist. Unfortunately, the rapist has eluded capture for the last several years. When the jailed twin was arrested a few weeks ago his cheek swab matched the prior DNA cheek swab taken by immigration."

"Drew, that's a distinct possibility. But before we can claim they are biological twins we will need to do some testing of the twin in jail."

"What do you need?"

"If you want me to testify, I will need some information

about both twins. Their names, date of birth, including birth certificates, if possible, and any medical records you may have on each twin. I would be especially interested in any laboratory work, such as blood tests or blood typing."

"I probably won't be able to get any medical records. They are both Australians. But I will check."

"Whatever you can find will help support my opinion when I testify. I will also need a cheek swab and blood draw of your client, if you can get that for me."

"I'm sure I can."

"Have you seen the twins yourself?"

"Yes."

"Have you noticed any physical differences?"

"Yes. Their eyes are different. The victims said their attacker had dark, steely-blue eyes. That's what I remember about the rapist from the time I confronted him. But the twin in jail has eyes of two different colors. One dark blue, the other light blue, and the twin in jail has fine, wavy, blonde hair, cut short in a business-style haircut. Photographs of the rapist show him with long, straight, blonde hair. Other than that they pretty much look like each other. Their features appear to be exactly the same. About the same height, weight, and skin color. Well, the one in jail seems a little taller and weighs a bit more. And, he doesn't appear as muscular as the rapist."

"You said the twin in jail had two different colored eyes?"

"Yes, one dark blue, similar to his rapist brother, and the other eye is a light blue."

"Interesting. I will have to do some research and get back to you on the type of testing we will have to do on the twin in jail."

"Did I say something wrong doctor?"

"Oh, no, I'm just being a scientist. Twins are always an interesting biological subject. But the different-colored eyes could help prove your client isn't the rapist. Today is Tuesday. Why don't we talk tomorrow in the afternoon, say around one p.m.?"

"That works for me Dr. Rougtbeck. I will call you at one.

ooooo

9:55 p.m.
The ground floor intercom of Drew's Loft buzzed. "Who is it, please?" asked Tami in a sexy Georgia drawl.

"It's me, Silvia."

Drew walked over to his computer and brought up his four outside cameras. Two cameras showed the ground floor parking area from two different angles. The third camera showed the building's rear entrance where Silvia was standing in front of the elevator gate, and the other camera inside the elevator showed its interior. Estrada looked up at the entrance camera's red sensor light and smiled.

"Just a second, Silvia." Drew buzzed the elevator door open. Once at the third floor, Drew opened the loft door. Estrada anxiously entered, asking, "Are you going to represent Joshua? Are you his attorney?"

"Hang on, Silvia. I asked you here so I could talk to your boyfriend. Did you bring a cell phone?"

"Yes, I'll call him now. He's waiting." There was a long pause, then, "Hello.

It's me, honey. Hawke is here. Let me give him the phone."

He took the phone and put it to his ear. "Drew Hawke. Who is this?"

"You know who it is. Nice to talk to you again, counselor. Did you see my brother?"

"Yes, but I have a few questions. Where did we see each other last?"

"Ah, a lawyer cross-examination, huh? Always the sharp one."

"Answer the question, please."

"It was when we fought. That was the last time we met."

"We went into a bar after we fought. Who was there, Jacob?"

"Your buddy the bartender, the big brut who tried to hide the club he had under the bar, and that dimwitted girl and her boyfriend."

"Oh, you saw the bat."

"No, but I'm not a fool. Bartenders always keep a club close, and he kept both hands under the bar."

"What did we talk about?"

"More questions?"

"Yes. I've got to make sure who you are. Your brother looks a lot like you."

"Yea, we are two handsome mates.

"Answer my question."

"Are we on the speaker phone?"

"No," replied Drew.

"You asked me why I rape. And, if you are still unsure about who I am, do you remember what you said to me just before we fought?"

"I sure do Jacob. Do you?"

"You said, 'Hey, punk, you afraid of me?' "

"Answer my question, not your own questions."

"I did."

"What did you say was the reason you raped."

"Damn, you are persistent. I said, respect. Yeah, I do it for respect and acceptance."

"Are you still raping women?"

"You shithead. What's that have to do with you representing my brother?"

"Answer my question, Jacob, or I won't represent Joshua."

"No. I haven't done that since I left San Diego. I found someone who loves me. Anything else, Hawke?"

"No. Thank you for being yourself and answering my questions. Here's where we are. They're going to charge Joshua with all your rapes. You know that. But the D.A. is also talking about charging him for the murder of that girl. Combine them all together and Joshua is looking at life."

"I told you at the bar I didn't kill her. How many times do I have to tell you that?"

"It's not me you have to convince, Jacob. Because you raped the girl and she ended up dead the logical conclusion is that you killed her. That's just one of the hurdles I face or shall I say Joshua faces, especially since Joshua looks a lot like you."

"You telling me, Hawke, you can't do anything for my brother?"

"Hold on. Everything looks bleakest before the sun rises."

"What the hell does that mean?"

"It means I have identical twins, with the same DNA, charged with raping women. The only possible defense is that Joshua has two different-colored eyes and you don't. Do you know why Joshua has two different colored eyes?"

"I don't know. He's been that way since birth, according to my father. That's why other people were so mean to him. They picked on him all the time, simply because he looked different."

"The reason I asked is I've hired a scientist to try to explain why your DNA cheek swab matches Joshua's cheek swab. The other thing I'm trying to do is find an explanation why Joshua's eyes are different from yours. It could help prove Joshua is not you—a case of misidentification."

"I don't know about you, Hawke. You seem to talk in riddles."

"Put simply, I've got to have my expert study Joshua's DNA to see if there is a scientific reason why his eyes are of two different colors, which might help support my argument he is not you. So I need to take DNA samples from Joshua and have them tested. I expect this will cost about eight thousand dollars, if the lab or an expert I hire has to testify about the DNA results."

"OK. Do it. Now, put the phone on speaker so Silvia can hear." Drew tapped the speaker icon, turned the volume up, and gestured for Silvia to listen. "Hawke, do whatever you think is necessary. There's a lot more at stake than you think. My worthless father is up in age, and Josh is needed back in Port Hedland to run the company. So the family fortune is on the line."

"So it's money you're worried about?"

"Fuck you, Hawke. There's a lot more involved than that. So don't go poking your nose into Josh's and my personal affairs. You got it?"

Drew did not respond. After a brief silence, Jacob continued. "I will transfer to Silvia's account two hundred thousand U.S. dollars. Use that money any way you want. I don't care how much it costs to get Josh free, you hear?"

"Jacob . . ." Drew paused, understanding the emotions coming from the other end of the phone. "I can't guarantee Joshua will walk free. But I can promise you this: I will not stop. I will use all my powers to get him free—free from your crimes and the punishment society wants to impose upon him instead of you."

"You had better, Hawke, or we're not finished."

"Jacob, grow up. Threatening me will not get me to work any harder or get your brother free. I am a man of my word. More than you are."

"Damn you, Hawke. Even though I still want to kick your ass for the way you talk to me, you are the right man to protect my brother. This is the only time I have never been able to protect Josh and it hurts—it hurts really bad."

"One more thing. Joshua doesn't trust me. When I told him you hired me, he still wouldn't open up to me. I need you to tell me something, a password or secret you two have, so he will know I've talked to you."

There was a long pause and then Jacob spoke. "Tell Josh I said he had to do whatever you ask. Tell him I was right when we were fourteen, and I said the two of us had to go see Dr. Greenfield the week after Fordham's son brought that woman to our barn, the one from the redlight district in Hedland. Tell Josh to follow my instructions because I was right then, and I am right now. If he hesitates, remind him that was the night we learned everything there was to know about a woman and the pinky swear still stands."

"OK. I will tell him that. But Jacob, I have to ask, why me? There are other more experienced lawyers in town who could adequately defend your brother."

"You're the one because I know you and what type a man you are."

"What do you mean?"

"When I was fifteen and arrived at the monastery, you were held out as an example for us to follow. The karate students, our sensei, even the monks all talked about you."

"About me!"

"Yeah. Not just about your martial arts skills, although our master said you were the best he had trained in decades. But sensei continually praised you for how you used your self-dis-cipline to control life-long conflicts. Conflicts which confront us all as we go through life. He told me to use such discipline to control my feelings about my runaway mother as you had done with never knowing your father and the subsequent death of your mom."

"You know about me being raised by friends of the family?"

"I've made it a point to know as much as I can about you. Why do you think I chose to study at San Diego State?"

"Jacob, the monks taught us to 'purge ourselves of selfish and evil thoughts for only a clear mind and conscience can un-derstand the teaching of Buddha.' When violence is necessary, they counseled, use our art to defend ourselves and others."

"I remember. So what?"

"If you lived with these monks since fifteen, how can you use your physical skills to rape women?"

"I am what life has made me, Hawke. You needn't concern yourself with who I am. Just defend Joshua."

Before Drew could say anything more, the phone went dead. Drew handed the phone to Silvia, who opened the phone's case and pulled out the sim card.

"Where's your bathroom?"

Drew gestured and she walked in, threw the sim card into the toilet, and flushed. Silvia took a towel, wrapped the phone in it, put the towel on the floor, and stomped on it with all her might—several times. She walked out and put half of the piec-es in her purse and threw the rest on the floor with the towel.

"You know, Silvia, the FBI and even some police depart-ments have programs that track phone calls real time?"

"Jacob knows that. But he said our call would be routed to several off-shore servers, which complicates tracing, if not prevents it."

"Does he know about Pegasus software by NGO?"

"Jacob said he hacked the program a couple of years ago on a challenge."

That's got to be a lie. This woman is really gullible. "I see that the two of you have it all

figured out."

"I sincerely hope so. A lot is at stake. Drew, thank you. You are doing the right thing. Joshua doesn't deserve what is happening to him." Silve moved toward the loft's door, then stopped and turned toward Drew. "I'll call Debbie when the money comes in and arrange for you to get paid—in full. If you require more, take that up with Jacob."

She departed, Drew shut the door, and walked over to the computer. "Tami, turn on the four security cameras."

"Turning on cameras—quad screen."

Drew watched Silvia as the elevator came to a stop on the ground floor. She pulled open the gate and stepped out. Drew's attention was drawn to camera four. "Tami, enlarge camera four." As the view filled the full screen and zoomed out, Drew saw a figure emerge from an alcove of the building across the street. It was a tall figure in a black hoodie walking parallel to Silvia as she stepped onto the sidewalk and headed south on Seventh Avenue.

That's got to be him. In Mexico, my ass. "I'll bet my life on that," he said out loud.

"Bet as in betting, Drew?" asked Tami. "Sports or Indian casinos?"

"Tami, save all security camera film for the last two weeks."

"Yes, Drew. Downloading security footage now."

"Save film under 'Sphynx video.'"

"Downloaded film saved under 'Sphynx video.'"

CHAPTER 6

Wednesday, 1:00 p.m.

Drew, Liz, Matt, and Debbie were all gathered around the conference room table, with a telephone at the table's center. Debbie dialed a number, then pushed the speaker button on phone so all could hear and talk. The phone rang three times before being picked up.

"Good afternoon, California Forensic Laboratory."

"Hi, this is Drew Hawke. I have a one p.m. call with Dr. Lawrence Rougtbeck."

"Yes. Just a second, please."

After a short pause, Dr. Rougtbeck came on the line. "Hello, Drew. Right on time."

"Doctor, I have my staff here. What's the next step?"

"Well, like I said, twins are very interesting. We need you to examine the twin in jail."

"We can do that."

"The problem is there will be extensive and intrusive testing. I think it would be best if a professional laboratory is involved."

"Doctor, my case is one of misidentification between twins. Do we really need a lot of testing?"

"Yes. You see, those different-colored eyes might mean the twin in jail is most likely a chimera."

"What's a chimera?"

"A chimera, Drew, is a person who has not one but two complete genomes or sets of

DNA in their body. The thing is, one complete genome can be found in one region or organ of the body, while the other genome can predominate in other organs, tissues, or parts of the body. Thus, a DNA test will produce an entirely different result depending upon where the sample is taken from."

Drew looked at Liz and Matt and said, "Really."

"So I need to conduct a thorough examination of your twin. Since your client is in custody, you must hire a San Diego genetic lab to do the inspection and testing. That technician will take an inner cheek swab, hair samples, draw blood, and extract skin samples, especially samples of any colored skin that is different from the rest of his body. Oh, yes. I also need a sperm sample and a prostate fluid sample."

"That's a lot of personal testing. I don't know if the client will cooperate."

"Trust me, it is all needed."

"Where are we going with this?"

Normally, a woman becomes pregnant when one of her eggs is fertilized by a sperm.

Identical twins, or biological twins, as they are called, occur if early in the pregnancy that fertilized egg divides into two separate eggs, each egg carrying the same exact DNA of the father and mother. This produces two babies that are identical.

"Now, fraternal twins occur when the woman releases simultaneously several eggs that become fertilized individually by different sperm but from the same man. Normally, the babies' features are similar. That's because the sperm comes from the same father. Things like the color of eyes are generally the same, as is the color and texture of their hair.

"Then there are heteropaternal superfecundation twins. If a woman . . ."

"Whoa, hold it right there," Drew said. He looked at the others and they shook their heads in unison. "Heteropa . . . you lost us, doctor. Please repeat the term and spell it so we can write it down."

Dr. Rougtbeck complied. Drew shot a questioning glance at Liz, who was scribbling notes as quickly as possible. She nodded.

"Got it, doctor," Drew said. "Please continue."

"As I was saying, if a woman releases multiple eggs within say a week of one another, and during that time has sex with two different men, and each man's sperm fertilizes different eggs, the result is fraternal twins but by different fathers. Thus, you can end up with two or more babies born at the same time with slight or in some cases strikingly different features."

"Interesting."

"Now, there are other but rare possibilities."

"What are those, doc?"

"Interestingly enough, it involves a set of identical twins just born in Australia. The twins who were supposed to be genetically identical were found to be only semi-identical or what are called sesquizygotic twins." He paused, then repeated the term and spelled it out before continuing. "In this case, we have a situation where one egg from a woman was fertilized by two separate sperms, but this time from the same father. Later, that fertilized egg divided into two separate cells. The results at birth were two twins supposedly identical, but with different DNA. Sesquizygotic twins carry 100 percent of the mother's DNA, but different percentages of the father's DNA, since each sperm is genetically different, which means they each carry a different mix of the father's DNA."

Drew shot a perplexed look at the others, who all shrugged and again shook their heads.

Drew leaned closer to the phone. "I'm sorry ,Dr. Rougtbeck, but I . . . we . . . don't understand what you're saying."

"Understandable, Drew. Think of it this way—each of a father's sperm has its own DNA. If two different sperms of the father impregnate one of the mother's eggs, there results three sets of chromosomes, each with its own unique DNA, within the one impregnated egg. One set of DNA coming from the mother and two different types of DNA coming from each of the two sperms of the father. Mother Nature usually doesn't accept such a situation and the embryo doesn't survive."

Drew wiggled his hand at Matt, signaling him to draw a picture. Matt nodded and began to draw circles and squiggly figures as the research scientist continued.

"However, in the case of the documented Australian pregnancy, the twice-fertilized egg did survive. It later developed into three such sets of chromosomes, which then split into two separate cells that grew into two separate fetuses, all within the same placenta. The thing is, each of the two fetuses contained 100 percent of the mother's chromosomes but different percentages of the father's DNA, since each sperm is constructed differently. Thus, at birth each twin had similar but different sets of DNA. So they were semi-identical twins. In the case of the Australian twins, their DNA was only about eighty percent identical."

"Now, a possible variation of sesquizygotic genetics is that two men have sex with the mother within a few hours, or the same day, and both men's sperm impregnate the same egg, which later divides, producing two semi-identical twins. Why is all this important to your case? You say the twin in jail is not the rapist, but his cheek swab matches the twin rapist's cheek swab, correct?"

"Yes."

"A possible explanation is that both twins' cheek DNA are the same but not the DNA of each twin's eyes—thus the different-colored eyes for the jailed twin. If this is true, then, one, they are not identical twins, but only semi-identical twins at best, and, two, you have a scientific basis for proving your twin is not the rapist."

"That just might work, doctor. It supports my argument of misidentification. Then all I have to prove is that my client wasn't in the country when the rapes occurred. But I have to ask, how come we don't hear about these different twin phenomena?"

"The Australian doctors discovered the sesquizygotic twins because they were of

different sexes. All identical twins are always of the same sex since they are formed from a single egg that splits. Further, doctors seldom test the DNA of twin girls or twin boys to see if they are exactly the same genetically. It is just assumed the twins are identical because they developed within the same placenta. The same applies to the possibility of two men impregnating a single egg of the mother. We just don't test identical twins for such possibilities."

"So, again, this is why you need me to do all the testing you described," Drew said.

"Yes. There are several other possibilities as well," Dr. Rougtbeck responded. "That's the reason I need the medical records of the twins. I need to rule out bone marrow transplants, in vitro fertilization, prior miscarriages by the mother, and any blood transfusion that could introduce someone else's DNA during pregnancy."

"But I don't know how I will be able to do similar testing on the out-of-jail rapist twin. His whereabouts are unknown. I only talk to him through his girlfriend."

"Let's worry about that later. Right now we need to do the testing on the one in jail. Then I will know what we are dealing with and what the next steps will involve. I will send your office an email listing the samples and tests I need done, and where you can hire a local lab technician to collect the samples."

"Sounds good, doctor. I look forward to receiving the email."

"Drew, remember, if your twins are biologically identical, then their DNA will be the same. That would explain why the jailed twin matches our reconstructed DNA of the rapist twin. So you can say I am on a fishing expedition, trying to find you another possible defense other than the misidentification of an identical twin."

"That's fine, doctor. I like to fish."

Drew hung up the phone and turned to Liz. "I need you to review Dr. Rougtbeck's email when it comes in and contact the local lab he refers us to so we can set up a date to examine, photograph, and take samples from the twin in jail. I will talk to Joshua sometime today and tell him what we're doing." He turned toward Matt. "You will observe and also photograph the twin and the taking of samples. Remember, anything that looks unusual, a mole, skin discoloration, scar . . . I don't care what it is . . . photograph it, and up close."

"Yes, sir. But, boss, how will they get a sample of the guy's prostate fluid and his
sperm?"

"I don't know, Matt. Maybe the old fashion way."

"Old fashion way?" Matt exclaimed, wide-eyed.

Liz looked at Debbie and smiled.

"Does that mean what I think it means? You're not asking me to watch him providing it—ah the old fashion way, are you?"

"Matt, if that is how the samples are to be gotten, then yes."

"Oh, Jesus, Drew. Are you getting back at me for my comment about you having to go to the hospital?"

"No, Matt, I wouldn't do that. Look, we represent a man who faces the possibility of life

in prison. It's our job to do anything and everything to exonerate him and set him free. That includes seeing him naked and everything else. Your job is to observe everything the lab technician asks the client to do, record how the samples are obtained, ensure the samples are turned over to the tech and properly recorded. And photograph it all. It's called chain of custody."

"Why can't you do it, boss?"

"Because I then become a witness. I can't be a witness because I am the client's

attorney. What am I going to do, ask myself questions?"

"Well, you could."

"Matthew van Dryden the Third, are you in or not?"

"Yes . . . sir, I'm in. Sorry."

CHAPTER 7

Wednesday Evening

A. J. HAWKE ARRIVED at the downtown county jail and, luckily, the same parking spot was open. As he entered the visitor's reception area, the same deputy greeted him.

"Back again, Mr. Hawke?"

"Yes. Here to see Jacob Wellington. Has he escaped yet?" Drew said with a wide smile.

The deputy played along and pulled up the inmate list on his computer. "Nope. He hasn't gotten away."

Drew produced his bar card, driver's license, and keys and placed them in the drawer under the bullet-proof window. He signed the visitor log sheet and added that to the drawer.

"Mr. Hawke, it's six-thirty p.m. It's a little late for visitors."

"I will keep that in mind. I shouldn't take too long."

"Great. We have Wellington scheduled for a suspect lineup at 10:00 a.m. We have to
transport him early in the morning. So he will need his sleep, given his busy morning."

"Oh, that's right. I almost forgot. Thanks for reminding me. Who's doing the lineup?"

"The district attorney's office."

"That's right, Assistant District Attorney Jack Farrat. Thanks for jogging my mind."

The deputy looked at Hawke questioningly, then slowly nodded while pointing for Hawke to walk through the metal detector. On the elevator ride up, Hawke kept his thoughts to himself. *That S.O.B. Jack Farrat, doing a lineup without telling me so I can't witness efforts to bias the victim's viewing. I guess Jack really does hate losing to me. His attitude on the phone was just a sample of how he's going to deal with me from now on.*

The door of the elevator opened and the deputy sheriff escorted Hawke down the hall to an attorney visitation room. Joshua was already seated on the other side of the glass. He picked up the phone before Drew was even seated.

"Mr. Hawke, I was worried you wouldn't come back. Did you talk to my brother?"

"Yes, and he is very worried about you. Is everything going well in here?"

"I'm getting used to how things work."

"Good. That's half of it."

Drew paused, making sure he phrased Jacob's words as accurately as possible.

"Jacob said I was to tell you this: Do exactly what I ask of you. Also, do you remember when Fordham's son brought that woman over?"

Joshua nodded.

"He wants you to remember the week after when Jacob said the two of you had to go to the doctor. The exact words I am to say to you are, 'I was right then, and I am right now. Do what Mr. Hawke asks you to do.' Then Jacob added, 'We were only fourteen at time. That's when we learned everything there was to learn about a woman.' Your brother added, 'We pinky swore then, and I will never break my promise.' Something to that effect. Sorry if I misstated anything."

"No, you didn't, Mr. Hawke. That's the time we swore to

take care of each other no matter what. Thank you for taking my case, Mr. Hawke. Jacob must really trust you."

"Joshua, I need you to trust me. I can't be successful without your trust and help."

"Mr. Hawke, please call me Josh."

"OK. And I go by Drew, not Mr. Hawke."

"I will call you Drew from now on."

"When we met last, I asked if Jacob raped. You wouldn't answer that question."

Joshua started to speak, but Drew held up his hand. "I always knew the answer—yes

Jacob rapes. But what you have to tell me is why he rapes."

Joshua remained silent for a moment, then asked, What does this have to do with my case?"

"Actually a lot. I need to know all sorts stuff about you and Jacob. The worst thing that can happen is for something about you two to come out during trial that I didn't know about. So now is the time to tell me all the bad things."

"Everything we talk about stays between us, right?"

"Yes."

"OK. It started the year after Fordham's son brought the lady over. We went to a new private boarding school in Hong Kong. It was a high school but academically advanced. I and Jacob didn't fit in well. Everybody picked on me because of my eyes, and Jacob always stood up for me. One night, two seniors sneaked into our dorm, pulled me out of bed, and tore off my underwear. I fought back, but somehow I ended up face down on the floor with a naked guy on top of me. Jacob, who was one bed away, jumped the guy on top of me. He really hurt him bad—slammed his head on the floor, and punched the other guy, who ran off. Jacob then ripped his own underwear off, got himself hard and . . . and . . ."

Drew interrupted, "Did to the guy what they had planned to do to you?"

"Yes. It was terrible. The guy screamed and cried and begged. The whole sleeping floor watched in horror as Jacob yelled over and over, 'How's it feel, shithead? You touch my brother again, I will kill you.' When he was done, he grabbed me and told me to fuck him. But I couldn't get hard. Jacob pushed me on top of the kid, but I just laid there on him. The floor monitor rushed in and pushed me off. Jacob hit the man and had to be subdued as other teachers rushed in. Long story short, we were expelled and Dad had to take us home. Once we got home, I told Dad Jacob was only trying to defend me. But he whipped Jacob with his big four-inch-wide work belt until Jacob's butt and back bled raw. Jacob never cried or yelled, even though the pain was intense. After that, Jacob asked Dad if he could go to a monastery in Thailand. Dad agreed, and so we've been apart ever since, except when I visit him. Jacob never comes home."

"What's that got to do with Jacob raping women?"

"When I would visit Jacob in Thailand, he would take me into town, and we'd pick up women. They always wanted to be paid. Sometimes Jacob would say yes, but would end up not paying after sex. Later, he just raped at will. Didn't even ask how much or pretend he would pay."

"Did you participate?"

"Yes. When he was done, he would tell me it was my turn. I know I shouldn't have, but I did. I guess my being arrested here is God's punishment for what I did with Jacob."

"Did you ever rape on your own?"

"No!"

"Did Jacob tell you about his rapes here in San Diego?"

"No. He didn't have to. I know how he is."

"Why is he that way?"

"Until Jacob met Ms. Estrada, I was the only person he ever loved or loved him."

"What about your dad or mother?"

"Dad was never affectionate. He called us his bastard children. And mother, well, he said she was a tramp. Others called her the town whore. I don't know why they did. We weren't poor. She never needed money. So it was only the two of us— me and Jacob after our mother ran off with that guy when we were six. Since then we protected each other. We were . . . we are . . . our only family."

"You still work for your dad."

"Yes, but that's business, and Jacob is not involved. He wants nothing to do with our father."

"Except his money."

Joshusa shrugged.

"I am sorry to hear this. But it doesn't affect how I represent you. And, I don't think you are an evil person. We do things to please those we love. We shouldn't sometimes, but love is a powerful force."

"If not now, then someday I will have to pay for what I did in Thailand. Those women didn't deserve what I helped do to them."

"Joshua let's talk about something else. Tomorrow you will be put into a lineup, if the information I just learned is true."

"What's a lineup? Like what they show on crime TV?"

"Yes. You will be placed in a room with several men. You may be asked to say things and stand certain ways. While in the lineup, I want you to be yourself. Try to relax. Above all, don't show fear or act agitated. That will only draw attention to you."

"I can do that."

"I don't know who will be observing the lineup. I have a strong suspicion it will be some of the rape victims. I will be in the other room, behind the two-way mirror, observing what happens. So don't be afraid. I will make sure the lineup is not rigged."

"Thank you."

"Moving on—did you think about who can testify to your whereabouts for the last two to three years?"

"Yes. It would be my dad and people I work with at home. I don't think it wise to let any

of our customers know about this mess. Besides, I haven't been to the States or Canada on business until now."

"Does that include Mexico or any part of South America?"

"Right. I have never been there."

"One more thing . . . I will send Matt from my office, along with a lab technician, who will photograph you and do some tests on you."

"OK. What tests?"

"They really won't be that painful, but they will be personal. They will swab your mouth, draw blood, examine you nude, and take skin scrapings from you. All this goes to prove you didn't rape any of the women the police say you did."

"That's fine. I've had worst done to me."

"Good. The worst part of all this is you will have to provide a sample of your sperm and prostate fluid."

"How do I do that?"

"They will tell you. Frankly, I think you will have to masturbate."

"O . . . kay . . . Do you know of any other way?"

"No. But you may have to perform with someone watching you."

"That's not good. I'm not shy, but I have never done that in front of someone. I may not

be able to."

"I know what you are thinking. But try to cooperate. All this is really necessary and will

be kept private."

CHAPTER 8

Thursday, 8:30 a.m.

HAWKE ENTERED THE SAN DIEGO downtown police station, accompanied by a court reporter. "Good morning, I'm Drew Hawke. I represent Jacob Wellington. I'm here to observe the lineup."

A female officer picked up the phone and called. A few minutes later, Assistant D.A. Jack Farrat emerged from a door to Hawke's right, followed by Sergeant Anthony MacNeal.

"What the hell are you doing here, Hawke," Jack Farrat demanded, obviously not pleased to see his nemesis.

"I'm here for the lineup."

"You represent Jacob Wellington?"

"Yup. Where's my client?"

"Fuck you, Hawke. Get the hell out of here."

"Jack, that is not going to happen. Right now my associate Liz Bernquist is sitting outside Judge Richard Brown's department with an appointment at nine a.m. to get an order telling you how the lineup will be conducted. Either we resolve our differences on our own, or the judge will. If the judge gets involved, the lineup procedure you have planned will be reviewed, and I get to ask for certain protections so the process doesn't bias my client. Play ball my way, or the umpire will call the balls and strikes, Jack."

A.D.A. Farrat paused in an apparent reflection on his choices. "Sergeant, please show our distinguished guest to his client and explain how we will conduct the lineup."

"Not so fast, Farrat. I want to observe how you prep the victims or any other potential witnesses who will view the lineup. And, I have brought a court reporter who will take down what the victims say during their viewing of the lineup. By the way, she has worked in Judge Brown's department in the past. I'm sure you will have no objection."

"Don't try my patience, Hawke." Farrat growled at the not-so-subtle jab.

"Don't try mine, Farrat. You want to play hardball, let's do it," Drew challenged as he took out his cell phone.

"Sergeant, escort the victims one by one into a room where suspects are interviewed and give them the normal briefing on how the viewing will be conducted. Hawke and the reporter can watch how they are briefed through a two-way mirror. Satisfied counselor?"

"Thank you, Jack, I appreciate the professional cooperation."

Farrat turned and stomped off. Sergeant MacNeal smiled and said, "This way, Drew. I'll take you to the interview room. How's everything been?"

"Getting better, Tony. Ask me that again after the lineup?"

"What do you want to do first, talk to your client or watch the prepping of the victims?" asked MacNeal.

"Who's doing the prepping?"

"Detective Clayton."

"What's he going to tell them?"

"He's going to go over their statements to the police following their rapes. You know—what the guy looked like, what he said, things like that."

"Tony, tell A.D.A. Farrat I want to see him."

"OK. Be right back."

A few minutes later Jack Farrat came in, "Now what?"

"Jack, I don't think the witnesses should be prepped on what they told the police right after their rapes. For some, it's been over two years since they were attacked. How about a compromise—let them view the lineup and make their choice, if they can. After that, why don't you ask them what they remember about the rapist. Then you can give them their statements and ask them to view the lineup again. It's not that I am against you refreshing their memory, but it is when you do it I would like changed."

"Now why would I do that? It's standard procedure to let them see their original statements before the lineup."

"Well, Jack, I can call the judge and let him decide. I'm not trying to stop you from showing them their statements. I just want to see what the victims currently remember when they view the lineup. I would like your cooperation on this."

Farrat thought a moment, then said, "Sure, why not. It will draw things out, but we got the right guy so why not."

"Thank you, Jack. You were always a fair prosecutor."

ooooo

Drew observed Detective Clayton explaining to each of the women how the lineup would proceed, including the two viewings each victim would observe of the lineup, the latter being after they read their victim statements.

Drew next viewed the lineup of five men. As he walked into the witness viewing room and stood behind the two-way mirror, officers escorted in the men into the brightly lit lineup room. There were five. Each was positioned against a white wall which had height markings on either ends of the wall connected by horizontal lines that allowed a witness to determine each man's height.

Drew shook his head in disgust. *That's a ridiculous choice for the lineup.* Once again he asked Sergeant MacNeal to bring in Farrat. After a minute or two, the A.D.A. came in.

"Now what's wrong? I have someone in a Santa Claus suit?"

"Very funny, Jack. Whoever chose the guys hasn't read the police reports or he is stacking the lineup. I know you wouldn't do such a thing."

"All right, what's wrong?"

"Look at that short guy. He's five-nine. The rapist by his own admission says he is six-two. Then you've got an older Hispanic guy with dyed blonde hair when the victims said the rapist was lily white and young. Your lineup has only three men who come close to the Sphynx's description—one of which is my client. Don't you have some fair-skinned cops that you can throw in that are over six foot and young? And Jack, I don't even mind if you have the men take off their shirts and flex as the rapist did. But let's make this thing real and fair."

Farrat walked off shaking his head. Forty-five minutes later, two new men joined the lineup.

"Is this better, Hawke?"

"Sure, fine. Thank you, Jack."

"Can we now proceed?"

"Absolutely. Would you please ask my court reporter to come in? She went outside for a smoke."

A.D.A. Farrat picked up the phone and asked the front desk to escort the court reporter back to the viewing room. He then spoke through the intercom to Detective Clayton, who was standing with the lineup of five facing the two-way mirror. "Clayton, have the officers take the men out and join me and Hawke.

As soon as the court reporter came in and set up her machine, Farrat addressed Hawke.

"You are not to say a thing. You are here to observe only. I've played fair, now you play fair. If you don't, I will throw you and your court reporter out."

Drew sat down on the chair to the left of the court reporter and nodded. Clayton joined them.

"Proceed, detective," Farrat said.

Clayton pushed the mic button and ordered the men to come in. They all wore black ski masks. Joshua Wellington was number three in the lineup. The first witness then joined the four in the viewing room.

"Ma'am, I'm Detective Clayton, whom you've met before." Clayton gestured toward the others. "This is Assistant District Attorney Jack Farrat and attorney Drew Hawke. The young lady next to Mr. Hawke is a court reporter who will take down everything we say here. Will you please state your name for the record?"

"Yes. Kristen Stark."

"Please feel safe and comfortable in here Ms. Stark. This window is actually a two-way mirror. We can see them, but they can't see us. When I switch the shade open for you to view the lineup, I need you to inspect the men and tell us if you see the rapist."

The young lady focused her eyes on each of the five men. After a moment, she turned to the detective and said, "I don't see him."

Clayton then sent the five men out. He gave Ms. Stark her statement to read. When she was done, Clayton ordered the five masked men back, this time all five were without a shirt.

"What do you see now?" Clayton asked.

Again the woman looked intently. She said numbers two,

three, and four could be the man because they were tall like the Sphynx. She pointed to the fourth man and said he was muscular like her attacker but not as big in the arms and chest.

Clayton then asked, "Was there anything distinctive about the rapist's speech?"

"No. He really didn't talk that much."

"Would you like the men to say something?"

"I don't think they are the rapist, so no."

Detective Clayton thanked the young woman and asked for the next victim, Margret Lane. He again explained about the two-way mirror and how the men couldn't see her. The victim took her time looking at each man. then said, "I'm sorry they don't look familiar."

The men were then ordered out. She read her statement and handed it back to Clayton. Again, the five masked men were brought back in but shirtless. She asked each man to step forward and turn around so she could look at them closer. She said they all were about the right height. But she wasn't sure.

"I'm sorry it has been nearly three years, and I've tried to blank the whole thing out of my mind. If I had to choose, it would be number four because he is muscular." She also said the Sphynx had bigger muscles. She did ask each man to say "pretty one," "you will die," and "let's play." After each man spoke, Clayton asked, "Now what do you think?"

"I don't know. When the rapist spoke he had an accent, but it was closer to how a surfer would sound. Number three has an accent, but it isn't the same. I just don't know."

And so it went. All five victims failed to choose Hawke's client. Instead, four of the victims said number four, one of the police officers Hawke talked Farrat into adding. He was the only one with a similar muscular body, but was "just not the one."

CHAPTER 9

Friday Afternoon

THE CALL BUTTON ON BRIAN O'SHEA's private phone lit up and started blinking, followed by a low buzz. The judge looked at the scrolling message indicating who was calling.

"Sam, what's up?"

"You heard the latest about who's representing the Sphynx rapist?"

"No. Why?"

"It's our favorite pain-in-the-ass attorney, A. J. Hawke."

"Drew Hawke?"

"Yes, judge, the one and only. Why would he get involved? Does he know something we don't? Did his investigator, that ex-cop . . . ah, DeLuca . . . find something?"

"Sam, I have no idea."

"Brian, we can't have this Sphynx thing blowing up in our face in the middle of the rapist's trial. The public will think we haven't been protecting the beaches after all. I have an election coming in ten months."

"Let's not make a big deal out this, Sam."

"It is a big deal. Chief Shaughnessy thinks so, too. He thinks Hawke has something up his sleeve and is going to turn this new trial into a media circus, which can hurt the police department's reputation and eventually me, since I hired the Irishman."

The judge was silent while the mayor rattled on. He finally interrupted the mayor.

"Sam, I'm baffled. I don't know why he would take such a case. I thought it was a loser."

"Judge, doesn't Hawke have a conflict of interest since he represented the man who pled guilty to the death of his client's girlfriend, Claire Rewake.?" There was a long pause. "Brian, you there?"

"Sorry, I'm thinking."

Not waiting, the nervous mayor asked, "Can't you talk to him? You know, lawyer to lawyer, or a mentoring judge to a young attorney. Show him the error of his way; point out how his new client could hurt his career. You know the law. Maybe you can find some ethical rule which prevents him from getting involved."

"OK, Sam. Calm down. I'll feel him out and try to learn why he's getting involved. Have Shaughnessy send me a copy of all the arrest reports on rapist."

"Judge, we've done everything you wanted. Shaughnessy talked the D.A. out of charging the new guy for the Rewake murder. I personally talked to the D.A., and he assured me there would be a quick conviction and no more embarrassing questions about the safety of our beaches."

The judge interrupted. "Sam, enough worries. Let me handle this."

"Even Morgan called and yelled at me about this, and how the Sphynx thing could hurt us all. To calm him down, I told him I didn't see how. But you know how he worries. If he gets excited, he could say something to the wrong people."

"Good point. I'll bring him into my chambers and calm him down. But first I need those arrest reports on the rapist so I can figure out why Hawke is involved."

"OK, Brian. I'll call Shaughnessy now. But there is one other thing. Hawke is now the plaintiff attorney in that suit against our company C. T. I., LLP. He's poking around, trying to find out who owns the company. If he does, that will lead him directly to us and our financial investments. We can't allow that."

"Hawke again, eh," the judge murmured. "Sam, let's handle one thing at a time. Our immediate problem is the Sphynx case."

"Brian, you've got to rein in that asshole attorney and now."

ooooo

Drew took two steps at a time up the stairs as he was running late for a settlement conference in the civil case Buckner v. Haines scheduled for Department 40. As he rounded the corner to the third floor, he saw Presiding Judge Brian O'Shea and a deputy sheriff standing in front of Department 40, talking.

Great, there he is again.

"Ah, here you are," said O'Shea as he sent the deputy away.

"Judge, I'm late for a settlement—"

The judge cut him off. "Yes, I know. But we didn't have time to call your office. Judge Thomas isn't holding settlement conferences this afternoon. We had an emergency. I had to assign him to a trial. The statute of limitations runs out today," the judge bemoaned as he walked to Drew. He put his arm around the young man, turning him around and walking him toward an alcove past the stairs.

Once there, the judge turned to face Drew. "You know, for a young attorney in his first few years of private practice, you've done spectacularly. I don't know if it's the year you spent in the district attorney's office or just natural talent, but everybody is talking about your wins."

"Thanks, judge, but if the conference is off, I really have to run."

"Nonsense. We need to talk. What's this about you representing the Sphynx rapist? That case is a career killer."

"Yes, I am his attorney."

"Get out of it. It will only bring you pain and sorrow. Career wise it will set you back a couple of years. I'll send you another big case."

"In all due respect, sir, I don't think you should be giving me any advice, especially about a case I am currently handling in court."

"None sense. You work with me and I will make your life not only glorious but extremely profitable."

"You see, judge, that's it. I don't want your help. Why can't you just butt out of my life, especially my personal life?"

"What's this?"

"You know exactly what I am saying. Judge Judy Hudson. You sicked her on me in yet another attempt to control my life."

"Well . . . I don't know what to say. I just thought you'd like a good fuck. She is one of the best I've ever had."

"Shit. You stand there and admit you have played with my feelings. Who are you?"

"The man who controls this building and runs San Diego."

"Well, you don't control my life."

"Bullshit, boy. Who do you think sends you all your cases? Clients come to me all the time for help and you get them. Do you really think a young attorney just starting out on his own could have the practice you have? No way. Look at that pathetic group of attorney friends you meet with every Friday. See how they struggle. No. You will do what I tell you or suffer like they do."

"Get out of my life, asshole!"

The judge laughed as Drew stepped back, his fists clenched.

"Andrew, I know you, and knowledge is power. When you can't think of an answer, you fight. You've been that way since you were a little boy. That's why you had so many fights in high school, and that's why you fight even now as an attorney. Did you enjoy your last stay in the hospital after getting your ass kicked by that rapist? Wake up, son. It's people like me you should come to when you don't know what to do."

"Fuck you," Drew shouted, stepping back even further. His fists clenched so tight the nails dug into the palms of his hands. He began to shake as he fought the urge to punch the man. *Don't give him the satisfaction. No, no. Don't let him control you.*

The judge laughed again, seemingly knowing the torment churning within. Drew turned and walked away as quickly as he could.

"Get out of that case, Hawke. It's your last warning."

Drew descended the steps, first one step at a time, then he grabbed the railing and did what he used to do in high school— propel himself down the steps, bouncing his two feet off each step as if skiing down a steep mountain. Once on the ground floor, he stood panting, still ready to fight. He wiped the sweat from his forehead and walked slowly out the courthouse.

CHAPTER 10

Saturday Afternoon

IT WAS A BEAUTIFUL DAY on San Diego Bay. Drew was at the helm of the 34-foot Artful Dodger, with Pat De Luca seated next to him. The mainsail was sheeted tight to port, with the jib slightly looser. The sloop was running fast, with the water high up to the gunnel of the leeward side of the hull. Mrs. De Luca, Lauren, was busy chatting with Drew's date, Kat, the waitress from the Tipsy Crow. Both women stiffened themselves as the thirty-four-foot sailboat lunged up and over the wake of a fast-moving forty-five-foot motor yacht racing through the Point Loma channel on its way out to the open sea. The Artful Dodger plunged down the backside of the wake and then up again, producing an engulfing spray of water over the bow.

"Those diesel smudge pots are always in a hurry," Drew noted in a derogatory manner.

"Motor yachts do love making waves," sympathized Pat.

"The bigger the smudge pot, the bigger the wake," Drew added in agreement.

"Admit it. You like the wave action," Pat teased with a smile to his grouchy captain. "So

Drew, what about this new Sphynx case, I'm surprised you have agreed to represent the guy."

"Me, too. I never thought I would represent a member of the rapist's family."

"So what's your defense?"

"Misidentification. They have the wrong guy. In fact, I'm glad you asked. I need you to fly to Australia and talk to my client's father."

"What a politician you have become. You ask us out on your yacht to get me to fly to Aussie land."

"Politician! Taking you sailing on this old floating bedroom in order to get you to fly? Come on, Pat, you know you will go if I ask. Nope, I just needed company to clear my mind about this case and sailing is the best remedy." They both laughed.

"So is it the rapist case that's bothering you?"

"Yup. I'm getting all sorts of shit over taking it. Even O'Shea cornered me in the courthouse and told me to get out of it."

"O'Shea? What's he got to do with it?"

"I don't know. Boy, do I really hate that guy. He continually plays with my head. Pat, was I a problem in high school?"

"What do you mean?"

"Did I get into fights?"

"No more than most kids. Why do you ask?"

"Never mind."

"Remember what I said. He is nothing but trouble. Stay away from the man."

"That's exactly what I told him and he laughed."

"Forget about O'Shea. He'll poison your mind. He tries to control everybody. Why don't we talk about O'Shea in a day or two. Put some time between your talk with him. How about that defense? What is it again?"

"Here's the thing. Dr. Rougtbeck thinks my client is a chimera—a person with two types of DNA. This would explain why his DNA mouth swab matches the DNA mouth swab of the rapist while other parts of Joshua's DNA, hopefully, are not the same as the Sphynx rapist. Rougtbeck thinks the two are biological twins but only semi-identical, so their DNA won't match one hundred percent. To support his theory, Rougtbeck needs the medical records in Australia of the two twins and any genetic or blood tests of the twins—whatever you can find. Also, I need the father and anyone you can find in Port Hedland that are willing to come to San Diego and testify. Joshua was in Australia at the time the rapes occurred. It would be great if you found some physical evidence to support the fact Joshua was there and not here. I have a two hundred thousand retainer, so we can fly you there and everybody back and forth for the trial. All expenses paid."

"Sounds like quite a fishing expedition to me, Drew."

"You're right. But you are my best fishing compadre. Besides, you do know how I like going out on a limb chasing wild defense theories."

"You keep doing this and eventually the D.A. will saw off one of those limbs."

"Pat, this case may well be the one. They have solid DNA evidence saying Joshua Wellington is Jacob Wellington—the Sphynx rapist. Frankly, I think a jury will take the prosecutor's DNA evidence over my client's family and friends' testimony. But I need something, maybe medical records or something you may uncover, to support my claim that they have the wrong twin. Especially since that selfish rapist brother won't step forward."

"When do I go?"

"As soon as you can fit it into your schedule."

"Let me clear everything with Lauren. Drew, I haven't said anything before, but what if you do lose?" DeLuca paused, checking his words. "Aren't you being set up for all sorts of malpractice claims given the fact you fought the Sphynx and are now representing a member of his family, a twin who can, if convicted, be sent to prison?"

"Pat, you're right. That thought has crossed my mind. So I have drawn up a retainer agreement where I reveal all my past problems with the Sphynx, including what I think of Jacob raping women. I've even arranged for another attorney to legally advise Joshua about my theory of defense, the risks of him being convicted, and my possible conflicts if I were to continue representing him. I hope that's enough to protect me."

"Drew, you do like walking a tightrope, not just in the courtroom but with your license to practice."

"Pat, that's not very reassuring. Talk about a cold shiver up the back of my spine. You certainly know how to plant doubt."

"Well, young man, on those cheerful notes, how about a nice cold beer on a beautiful day of sailing?"

"And, Pat, how about checking on our lovely women?"

As Pat checked on drink refills for everyone, Kat joined Drew at the helm. With Kat steering the boat and Drew standing behind her giving helpful touches on her handling of the helm. Suddenly, Lauren and Pat waved to a passing boat. Drew looked over. "Is that who I think it is," he asked, his voice rising.

"Oh, hi, Liz," shouted Kat, letting go of the helm as she waved both hands vigorously at

the couple on the passing yacht. Drew grabbed the helm as the Artful Dodger pulled hard to windward, causing Lauren and Pat to hold on, and Drew to hug Kat with his free left arm to keep her from falling.

"Who's the guy holding Liz around her waist," Drew queried.

Pat and Lauren looked at each other as Kat answered, "Oh, that's Denny. Liz has been dating him lately."

Drew replied with a surprised look. "I didn't know she was dating anyone."

Nobody commented further about Liz and her new boyfriend.

The sun was dipping low in the western horizon as the Artful Dodger slowed in preparation to executing a stern-first docking into its Marina Cortez boat slip. Pat grabbed a stern line and readied to step off the starboard side onto the marina dock as Drew slowly maneuvered the sailboat into the slip. At the last moment, Drew threw the engine shifter into forward and then neutral. The Artful Dodger vibrated slightly as though Drew had stomped on the brakes. The 34-foot Columbia sloop slowly glided to a stop, its stern inches away from the back of the dock and the walkway leading to the marina offices. Pat stepped on the dock and tied the mooring line to a deck cleat. Drew grabbed the port stern line and jumped on the dock, then tied the line tightly to a deck cleat, securing the boat to the dock. Kat threw the port bow line to Drew and then the starboard bow line to Pat. The men secured the lines to the dock. The Artful Dodger was safely at home.

The two men helped the women alight from the sailboat, first taking their beach bags and then helping them step onto the dock.

"Drew, I think you are getting to be a master at docking your 'floating bedroom' as you've called this nice old boat," Pat said with a smile.

"Yeah, a beautiful landing, if I do say so myself," Drew replied. "Now, guys, how about us having a light dinner as a way of celebrating a great afternoon of sailing on the bay, my treat. Frankly, I'm famished."

Pat looked at Lauren, who nodded. "The missus says yes, so it's a deal. Where do you want to go?"

"How about the Searsucker Restaurant on Fifth Avenue in

the Gas Lamp. They've got great steaks, burgers, and a good vegetarian menu for Kat."

"Sounds good to me," answered Lauren.

"We'll take separate cars, if that's OK," stated Pat. "We have to head home afterwards."

"Sure, meet you there."

ooooo

The waitress Shawna approached the party of four seated in the outdoor sidewalk café of the Searsucker Restaurant.

"Good evening. Isn't the sky a beautiful crimson orange tonight?" asked Shawna.

"Just a fantastic sunset," answered Lauren as she looked up at the red-orange streaks glowing against the growing evening night.

"Would you like to start with a cocktail or a glass of wine?" Shawna asked.

Drew looked at Pat, who shook his head no. "I think we'll pass this time," replied Drew.

The server handed them menus and said, "The specials of the day are a Caesar salad with baby gem lettuce and your choice of either shrimp or chicken. We also have a delicious baked salmon with asparagus, and baby red potatoes lightly dusted with garlic butter and olive oil. I'll give you a moment," she said and went to another table.

The each looked over the menus, then Drew spoke first.

"Guys, do you need time to choose?" he asked.

Lauren replied, "I don't, how about everyone else?"

Everyone was ready to order. Lauren ordered the Caesar salad with shrimp. Kat ordered vegan tacos with Beyond Meat, shredded cabbage, avocado cream, and salsa. Pat and Drew ordered Searsucker's famous eight-ounce blended burger, substituting fruit for the French fries. At the last minute, Drew asked for a carafe of red wine for the table, which got a laugh from everyone.

"Why stop drinking now?" responded Drew jokingly.

As Shawna turned to go back into the restaurant, Liz and Denny walked by.

"Hey, Liz," greeted Drew. "I think you know everyone." He pointing to the other three seated at the table.

"Hi, Lauren and Pat, and Kat, isn't it? I remember seeing you at the Tipsy Crow."

"Yes. Still serving drinks and taking orders from demanding customers," Kat said with a broad smile.

"Great day for sailing wasn't it, Liz, and I don't think we've met," said Drew as he rose to shake hands with Liz's date.

"Denny," replied the man. "And, yes, fantastic time sailing, especially with this nautical mate," he joked with a smile while hugging Liz.

Drew stood expressionless until Pat, recognizing the awkwardness of the situation, asked, "What type of boat did you go out on?"

"It's my new forty-two-foot Jeanneau. I plan on sailing it to Hawaii. How about it, Liz? Do you think you could get away for a month and see the Hawaiian Islands with me?"

Before Liz could answer, Drew interrupted, "I hope not, Liz. I need you on the upcoming Wellington trial." Drew looked directly at his associate lawyer, waiting for her reply. To his chagrin, she simply looked to Denny. "Let me think about it."

"Well, let's talk about it later then," Denny replied. "Besides, we have dinner reservations. I hope you will excuse us, we are running late. It was nice meeting you, Lauren and Kat," Denny said. "And you, too," he added, as he shook Pat's hand, then Drew's.

"I look forward to seeing you guys next weekend on the bay," added Denny. "Maybe we can have drinks together sometime."

Drew just stood there as the two walked off.

Kat had to speak up to get Drew to sit down. "Nice couple, aren't they," she stated. Pat and Lauren agreed. Drew said nothing, just staring at the two as they walked away. *What has just happened?* he asked himself. Fortunately, Drew's gaucherie was saved by Shawna returning with four wine glasses and a large carafe of the house red wine.

CHAPTER 11

Monday Morning

BRIAN O'SHEA'S CELL PHONE VIBRATED. He noted the time, 8:00 a.m., and shook his head.

"Hello."

"Why are you fucking with Drew?"

"Who is this?"

"Pat."

"De Luca, how'd you get this number?"

"I'm a detective, remember? Now what are you up to? I told you to stay away from the

man."

"Stay out of this, De Luca."

"I will not. You interfere one more time and I will publish a few things you don't want public."

"You slime ball. This is city business. It has nothing to do with Hawke. I could give a shit about him."

"I've known that since he was born. But you are playing with fire. I am serious about exposing your past."

"You are playing with fire. The Sphynx trial is bigger than the kid."

"Play your cards well, Brian. You have a lot to lose."

"So do you. I've recorded this call." O'Shea hit the off button and unplugged the cell phone from his taping unit, then played back the call.

ooooo

Drew was on the phone with a client when all of a sudden he heard a loud bang that shook his private office door. He quickly finished his call and opened the door.

"Debbie, what was that noise?"

"It was the front door," Debbie said nodding toward the corner desk, where Matt sat glaring at Drew.

"Matt, what's wrong," asked his boss.

"You want the size of his wanker?"

"What?"

Matt just stared at his lawyer.

"Oh," stated Drew, realizing what was happening. "You met the lab technician Sunday at the jail, didn't you?"

"Like I said, how detailed do you want the report I'm writing?"

Drew was taken back by the forcefulness of his normally easy-going file clerk. "I take it you observed the samplings. When you write your report, how about you just describe what type of procedures Joshua was asked to do. You don't have to describe the actual acts. We can talk later, after I review your report. Plus, I need to see the photos you took. And, Matt, thank you for going to the jail. I know it was a difficult task for you."

"Difficult? You didn't tell me the lab tech guy would hit on me, much less what he said I had to watch."

"Oops. That was unexpected. You OK?"

"I'll survive."

"Debbie, call the San Diego lab and verify the tech followed chain-of-custody protocols, and ask if they have sent the samples up to the California Forensic Laboratory. Have

Dr. Rougtbeck notify us as soon as the samples get tested. No, Debbie. I will call Dr. Rougtbeck myself."

Drew turned to go into his office but paused to look at Matt, who was nervously tapping a pencil on the desk while staring at his computer, apparently having trouble deciding what to write about his jail visit. Drew made eye contact and gave the young man a look of reassurance.

ooooo

One and half hours later, Drew sat at his two, thirty-inch computer screens, reading Matt's report. As he got to the page with the heading "Procedures" he intently stared at each of the procedures described by Matt. The young lawyer sat back in his chair.

I didn't know Matt would have to go through all this. The nineteen-year-old didn't deserve such an experience. Nor did my client. I'm surprised Joshua was so compliant.

Drew went to the second screen and pulled up the photographs and videos of the procedures. *My God, these are graphic,* Drew thought as he viewed a video of Joshua spreading his cheeks and the technician inserting a gloved finger for a milking of the prostate. And so it went on one exam after another, faithfully videoed by Matt.

I didn't know these exams were the ones needed in order to get the samples Rougtbeck wanted.

Drew turned off the computer, saying out loud, "These tests had better be worth it." He picked up the phone and dialed the Berkeley lab.

"Hi, this is Drew Hawke for Doctor Lawrence Rougtbeck."

"One moment, please."

"Good morning, Drew."

"Doctor, have you received the samples?"

"Yes, just after nine a.m. I've already reviewed the attached report from the lab documenting what tests were performed and how the samples were handled."

"I'm surprised, doctor, about the number and types of tests performed."

"I understand. I explained to Dr. Eddington of the San Diego laboratory the type of case I was dealing with, and he agreed his technician had do the list of tests I suggested, and, frankly, he recommended a few more. Dr. Eddington is very experienced in genetic testing. So I think we got a good examination and samples. Tell your client we appreciate his cooperation."

"When do you think I can get a call from you about your analysis?"

"Next Monday at the latest, maybe this Friday. The discovery of a patch of skin darker than the rest of Joshua's body is very interesting. We will run tests on the different-colored skin samples today."

"OK, doctor, I think I should let you go then."

Drew pushed the intercom button for Debbie.

"Yes, Drew."

"Please let me know when Liz comes in."

"She's here now. Should I send her in?"

"Yes, please."

As Liz walked in, Drew asked her to shut his office door and sit down.

"Elizabeth, I need to talk to you about this weekend.

"Oh, 'Elizabeth' is it," she quipped, making air quotes with her fingers. "And a closed door. Must be serious." As she sat down, she added, "I thought my personal life wasn't your business."

Drew blinked at the harshness of her answer. "Well . . . your boyfriend asked you to sail to Hawaii, and we have the Wellington trial coming up. Are you . . .?"

"Who said he's my boyfriend? Do I ask you about your girlfriend Kat?"

"Ah, I just assumed . . . look, Liz, Kat is not my girlfriend."

"Oh, another one-night fling."

"Kat was no such thing. And I am not trying to pry into your dating life. I Just need to know if you will be here for the trial."

"I haven't decided."

"I really need you. Is there any way you can let me know quickly so I can get a replacement if I need to?"

"So, I'm that replaceable?"

"No, you are not. But I can't have you leaving with some guy."

"Why not? You seem to have enough female company."

"Liz, I don't understand"

"I know. What else is new? I will get back to you in a couple of days," Liz said as she stood and walked out.

Drew didn't know what had just happened. He sat there, stunned at Liz's hostile response. All of a sudden his office door opened and in walked a disgruntled Debbie.

"What'd you say to that young lady?"

"Stay out of this, Debbie."

"Like hell! You treat her right. She loves you, and you're too stupid to know it."

"Debbie, please go back to work."

"Humph," grunted Debbie as she turned and walked out, pulling the door shut behind her.

Drew was slumped down in his chair, thinking about what Debbie said when the intercom buzzed. "Yes, Debbie, what now?"

"Randy Wright is holding. Do I put him through?"

"Ah . . . have him call . . . no, put him through."

"Randy what's up?"

"You dog. You're holding out on the four of us. We demand a gathering of the Gang of Five this afternoon at the Tipsy Crow."

"What are you talking about?"

"The Sphynx rapist, you sneak."

"Oh, that."

"Oh, that? The biggest case in San Diego history and you say, 'Oh, that.' Andrew Jackson

Hawke, penalty drinks and hors d'oeuvres are in order, and a full explanation on how you got such a case. No getting out of it."

"Come on Randy this is not the time to talk about such things."

"What do you mean? You sound upset."

"Ah . . . no, I'm just swamped. Can't we wait till Friday for our normal gathering?"

"You tell that to Kent, Greg, and Chad. Besides, you skipped last Friday. Had a hot date, huh? You're lucky we aren't over at your office now pimping you for hiding such big news from us. We will not take no for an answer. And it's Monday. Nobody has a date Monday nights, not even the great Drew Hawke."

"OK, OK. I give up. Tonight at five p.m."

"That a boy. Be on time and bring plenty of money. No putting our drinks on your tab.

Last time you did that, Bartender Jack kept asking us to pay up because he had to balance his cash register."

"Randy, since when have I not paid my bar tab?"

"Yeah, yeah. Be on time and with cash."

CHAPTER 12

Monday, Late

FIVE O'CLOCK CAME SOONER than anticipated. Drew looked about his desk. He had four more things to do, but if he didn't show up, he would never hear the end of their complaints. Drew walked around his desk and opened the door. Debbie was turning off her computer and getting ready to go home. Matt was still at his computer.

"Hey, guys, I need to get a few things done by noon tomorrow. Matt, please make a list of all the potential exhibits we will need in our civil lawsuit SMA Construct Fab v. C.T.I., LLP. Debbie, where is Liz?"

"She went home."

"Yeah, boss. She didn't look good at all," Matt added.

"Debbie, please call Liz and have her do up a list of issues and questions to

be covered in the SMA deposition. Have her work with Matt on the list of exhibits the defendant was supposed to provide us and didn't."

"Frist thing in the morning," replied Debbie.

Matt stood and advised, "Boss, I've summarized the three pervious

depositions in SMA Construct Fab. I will put them on your desk before I leave."

"Make sure Matt you attach the summaries to the original depositions."

"Yes ,sir. Ah, boss, there is one more thing."

"Yes, Matt."

"In preparing some of the documents for the forth coming deposition of Douglas Chandler, the CFO of C.T.I., there is a letter from Mr. Chandler to Morgan Mayfield of M&M City Built informing him how C.T.I. would be incorporated. At the bottom of the letter is a c.c. . . . ah . . . a notation of a courtesy copy to Judge Brian O'Shea. But I couldn't find the attached document describing how C.T.I. was to be structured."

"What?" interrupted Drew.

"Ah . . . yes, sir. And there's more. In doing a computer search, I saw that C.T.I. is a wholly owned subsidiary of a Cayman Islands corporation called Cayman Tri-Holding, LDC. The Cayman government lists one person as the president, treasurer, and secretary of Cayman Tri-Holding. That person belongs to the same accountancy firm as Mr. Douglas Chandler, the CFO of C.T.I.—the one and same Mr. Chandler we are going to depose."

"Really! Tell me more."

"Yes, sir. C.T.I. doesn't seem to own any assets. Large amounts of money come in, but Mr. Chandler sends it right out to a New Jersey bank account owned by C.T.I.'s parent company, Cayman Tri-Holding."

"Yes, yes, I got the players," interrupted Drew, captivated by Matt's discovery.

"I went on the Web to see what info I could find about Mr. Chandler and his accountancy firm . . . ah . . .," Matt paused looking at his paper work. "The firm of Heller, Frank & Chandler. Their website lists many of the world's largest international companies, most of whom are incorporated in tax havens, like the Cayman Islands, Isle of Man, Luxembourg, and Mauritius. Even one of San Diego's largest companies is a client of Mr. Chandler's accountancy firm."

"Which company is that?"

"M&M City Built, Inc., boss. That's the company owned by Mr. Morgan Mayfield, the wealthiest man in San Diego."

"Matt, you may have stumbled onto something important. I want to know who owns that Cayman Islands corporation. Also, I want you to put on a spreadsheet how much money comes into C.T.I. and how much of it goes out to the Cayman corporation."

"Yes, sir. "

"Hmm. Debbie, when you call Liz, tell her she will do the deposition of C.T.I.'s financial officer, Mr. Chandler. But I want to talk with her first, after she reviews all of the documents Matt has discovered. Including the letter to Mayfield. Tell her I will be there with her, but it's her show."

"Well, it is about time you let Liz do a deposition in a big case. She will be excited," exclaimed Debbie.

"Yes, I know. When I get in tomorrow, please set aside time for us to go over three other pressing matters," Drew added as he walked toward the office door.

"Where you going, Drew Hawke" Off to that cow place? If so, it's a little early in the week to be carousing."

"It's the Tipsy Crow, Debbie, and have you been listening in on my calls again?"

"Haven't you learned that all your carousing is just getting you in trouble?"

Drew thought for a moment about the earlier comments made by Liz and Debbie but decided not to say anything. Instead he replied, "Thank you, Debbie, but I'm meeting the gang to discuss the new Sphynx case. They may be first-year attorneys, but I value their opinions. I'm sure they will have a few pearls of wisdom about what I've gotten myself into."

"Gotten yourself into? How about what you've gotten us all into! I told you that case is no good. That rapist, that news reporter. They're all up to no good. Trust my words. No good."

"As usual, you're right. But the case is an interesting one. Have a good night you guys."

ooooo

As Drew stepped out onto the sidewalk and headed across F Street, Mario Rodriguez, the parking lot attendant, yelled, "Mr. Hawke, you need the Beamer?"

Drew paused and pointed toward the Tipsy Crow. "Got to see the gang. Be out later."

Mario smiled and gave a thumbs up in recognition. A few steps further Drew paused and turned. "Mario, you still taking classes at Mesa Community College?"

"Sure am. Jus' one class this time. Thinking full-time this January."

"Good for you."

Drew pulled open the door to the Tipsy Crow and was immediately greeted by Jack Thorn, the bartender.

"Evening, Drew. Something special happening? The guys are already upstairs and seem anxious to see you tonight."

"They're just thirsty because I am buying."

"But it's a Monday. What's happening?"

"You're right, a special night. I've got a new criminal case. You'll probably see it in the news pretty soon," Drew added as he headed up the stairs to the second-floor lounge.

At the landing, a cheer went up, followed by, "There he is."

"Hi, guys," Drew said as he pulled up a chair at the table where his four best friends were seated.

Right off Greg Turner asked, "So what's this rumor you're defending that Sphynx rapist?"

"Not sure if I'm taking the case yet, but I met the guy this morning and he's not the rapist I fought in the alley or the one I talked to in Sullivan's bar."

"So, Drew, fill us in on the whole deal," said Greg. "What led you to go see the S.O.B.?"

"That's a story you won't believe. Remember that news reporter for Channel Twelve, Silvia Estrada, the one that took a leave of absence a couple of months back?" His companions all nodded. "Well, last Sunday I woke up in my bed with her staring at me. Can you imagine that? I am stark naked asleep and by her own admission she had been watching me for hours."

There were several giggles from the boys, but Drew retorted, "Its' not funny, guys."

To which Kent Fields replied, "You dog. Sleeping with a news reporter. No wonder you've been getting good press."

"Not the case, Kent. Get this, She left the station because she's fallen in love with the Sphynx rapist. Been living with him for several months."

"How in the hell do you know that?" asked Chad Musante.

"She told me that Sunday morning. But, it gets better."

Drew had the full attention of all four as they leaned forward, following
his every word.

"The Sphynx rapist, who is Jacob Wellington, as you know, sent her to get me to represent the guy the police have in custody. The Sphynx says the one in jail is his twin brother, who would never rape anyone."

"Wait a minute," exclaimed Randy Wright. The rapist wants you to represent his brother?"

"Yup."

"The rapist who you fought and who put you in the hospital?"

"Yup."

"Are you crazy? You shouldn't touch that case with a ten-foot pole. Don't you see the conflict of interest you would be putting yourself in?"

"Wait a second, Randy. The cops think he is the rapist because his DNA is the same as the rapist's twin. But twins always have the same DNA."

"You mean biological twins?" offered Chad.

"Correct. So I hired Dr. Lawrence Rougtbeck, and he advised I should do some tests on the twin in jail, which I did. I'm waiting for the results now."

"You're missing my point, Drew. You can't represent the guy in jail."

"What do you mean, Randy?"

"If the twin gets convicted, he will say you intentionally did a poor job just to get even for the fight you had with his twin brother. On top of everything else, you represented David Caine, the boyfriend of the girl who died at the hands of the rapist. You even ended up pleading the boyfriend to manslaughter for her death. My God, anybody and everybody could sue you for what you've done. You just can't take the case, even if the guy is innocent."

"Does that mean, Randy, you want the case?"

"Oh, no, don't say that. I would never take a case you wanted. Back off, friend. That is actually mean."

"Well, Randy, what am I to do?"

"Will the rapist twin come forward and exonerate his brother?" asked Randy in a calmer voice.

"No. I already asked him to."

Kent spoke up. "Randy is right. You will probably lose the

case if the rapist will not come forward to save his brother. Biological twins have the same DNA, so as far as anyone is concerned there is only one conclusion—the one in jail is the rapist—unless you can prove the guy was somewhere else when all the rapes occurred."

"I've got a problem there. The only witnesses who can say the guy in jail wasn't in San Diego are his father and the employees of his father's company in Australia."

"That's right," added Chad. "I remember now the father lives down under. And the district attorney will claim such witnesses are biased because they work for the father."

Drew sat back in his chair, fully understanding what his friends were saying. "Your counsel is right, guys. I think I will have to wait for Dr. Rougtbeck's

test results. He has a unique theory that the twin in jail is a chimera. If so, I may be able to get around the twins having the same or similar DNA."

"What's a chimera?" asked Greg.

"It is where a person has two separate chains of DNA. So, I could argue that the DNA found on the condom doesn't belong to the twin in jail."

Randy spoke up again. "You still have a problem. Remember our talks about the DNA on the condom when you represented David Caine? You and Rougtbeck couldn't say for sure where the partially destroyed DNA sample came from. Was it from the sperm of the rapist, was it from flaked off skin from the rapist, was it from another man? It was, after all, found in a dumpster."

Greg added to the onslaught of criticism. "Yeah. The only thing directly tying the rapist to Claire Rewake's death was the DNA-destroying chemicals found on the dumpster condom and the syringe in her bedroom."

"I get what you are saying guys. The theory of two types of DNA doesn't help unless I can say where the reconstructed DNA came from—was it sperm or a finger print. Then, I have to prove it doesn't match the jailed twin's DNA ."

"Worse yet," spoke up Kent, "If both twins' DNAs match, you will end up having to attack your own expert's new advanced DNA reconstruction technique which led the cops to the rapist. The D.A. will have a field day, calling you a desperate fraud in front of the jury."

"It seems, guys, I don't owe you any drinks since you have convinced me not to take the case. And in the process, I will have to turn down the rapist's two hundred thousand dollar retainer to represent his brother."

Greg yelled, "Two hundred thousand dollar retainer? Shit, I will take the case."

Everyone but Greg laughed, and her persisted. "Are you shitting me? Did the rapist really offer that much?"

"Yes, he did. So I will wait and see what my award-winning scientist comes up with after he reviews the sample tests taken from my client in jail."

"You are a sly fellow, Andrew Hawke," Randy spoke softly. "Since you've enjoyed playing with us, I do think you owe us a round of drinks and hors d'oeuvres."

"Oh, all right. But remember, when this case blows up in my face, 'Audentis fortuna iuvat.' "

"What does that mean," asked Kent.

"It's Hawke showing off again," said Randy. "It's a Latin saying some attribute to Romans: 'Fortune favors the bold.' "

A chorus of boos followed, along demands for more beer.

Drew called the waitress to the table. "You're looking beautiful tonight, Kat.

I'm afraid once again I have to open up my tab and let these four thirsty hounds drink and eat at my expense."

Kat laughed and looked to the group, asking, "The usual drinks guys?"

"Yes," answered everyone, except Randy, who added, "Kat, no tab tonight. Drew is paying with cash. He seems to have hit an oil well and is filthy rich."

CHAPTER 13

Friday Morning, Later That Week

THE OFFICE STAFF GATHERED in the conference room, circled around the telephone centered on the conference table. Drew drummed the table top, unable to contain his nervous energy as they waited for the call from Dr. Rougtbeck.

"Hey, boss, we got this," Matt said. "Don't worry, if the guy is truly innocent you will find a way, even if the DNA says he's the rapist."

Liz sat there, not saying anything.

"Matt, I like your enthusiasm," Drew said to his young charge. But deep down the young attorney knew his options were greatly limited.

The phone rang, and Debbie answered the call. "Good morning. Law offices, this is Debbie. Yes, Dr. Rougtbeck, he's here. Let me put us on the speaker phone."

"Good morning, doctor, " Drew said.

"Good morning, Drew. I see you are all anxiously waiting my call."

"I didn't know we were on a Zoom call, doctor."

Everyone laughed at Drew's attempt at levity.

"Let me tell you what I've discovered," Dr. Rougtbeck said. "Joshua does indeed demonstrate chimera. He has two distinctly different types of DNA. They have a split of approximately eighty percent one DNA and twenty percent the other

DNA. This is why Joshua has two different-colored eyes, and why he has two different skin colors, as shown in photographs of his body."

"Astonishing, Dr. Rougtbeck," Drew responded. "But what parts of his body are the two types."

"The majority DNA we will call Type One. This DNA was found in the following areas we tested: the cheek swab, the nasal swab, and his light-colored skin. The smaller group of DNA, or Type Two, included the head hair sample, pubic hair sample, the darker skin samples, and the sperm and prostate samples. The percentages of the two types of DNA are just estimates. They could vary by five to eight percentage points either way. One of our geneticists did a genome comparison of the DNAs and found, interestingly, about ten percent of the Type Two genome matched a previously known Australian aborigine DNA, specifically the Yidinji people. The rest of the genome for the Type One and Type Two DNA were of Anglo-Saxon, Germanic, and Scandinavian heritages.

"Doctor Rougtbeck, what does all this mean?"

"It means our testing proves why Joshua has two different-colored eyes and a patch of darker skin, which are due to his chimera genome. For your defense, it means if all the witnesses say the rapist had dark-blue eyes and all-white skin, you now have a scientific reason to support your argument Joshua is not the rapist. This gives you a defense against the argument that his DNA swab of the mouth is the same as on the condom, which the police used to identify your twin as the rapist."

"That's great, doctor, but the problem is, I have two biologically identical twins who should have the same DNA."

"True. So now we need to test the other twin. If the he has only the Type One genome, and, most importantly, no aboriginal DNA, then we have solid evidence that we have two genetically different people, which allows you to argue the police have misidentified your client as the rapist. Frankly, from my experience in DNA cases, any favorable testing I may develop will only provide a minimal defense."

"Would that be because the victims are not studying a rapist's body features closely, such as the color of his eyes, when being attacked?"

"Yes, Drew. And because the prosecution has a cheek swab from immigration that matches Joshua's cheek swab. I'm sure the prosecutor will argue biological twins have the same DNA. So where is the other twin, if one really does exist? The prosecutor may even argue, if a twin does exist, how do we know they aren't fraternal twins rather than identical. So, can you get the other twin to provide DNA samples?"

"I already asked him to step forward and he said no way. But I can ask again. Doctor, is there any way the partial DNA you reconstructed came from the rapist's sperm?"

"Good question. You are thinking if Joshua's sperm DNA is different from the rapist twin's sperm DNA found on the condom, you would have a solid defense even if the two mouth swabs are the same. Unfortunately, the rapist sprayed or washed the condom's outside with the DNA inhibitor and flushed the inside with the same fluid in his effort to deconstruct all DNA. The only reason we got a partial was because the rolled end covered up what DNA was there. Is that partial DNA from sperm? Maybe. But I'm not sure. Let me do some more testing, since I have Joshua's semen and sperm sample. We've been tinkering with our advanced replicating program. Since I know what we're looking for, I may be able to come up with a match and rule out your client."

"How long will all this take," asked Drew.

"Two to three weeks, depending on how things go."

"That's cutting it close. For some reason the Presiding Judge is rushing the case to trial. We start in four weeks."

"I'll do my best, Drew."

"OK. So until you call, the mystery continues."

"I'll call as soon as I have something. And please try to convince the brother to come forward so I can test him."

"Will do." Drew turned to Liz and Matt as he disconnected the call. "Do you guys have any suggestions?

Liz shook her head.

"None here, boss," added Matt.

"Liz do you still think we shouldn't represent Joshua?"

"Ah . . . that question seems a bit unfair, Drew," she replied. "If I understand what the doctor said. the cheek swab still says Joshua Wellington is the rapist. The only possible way he might not be the rapist is if the lab finds sperm DNA on the condom that is not Joshua's. That's not going to happen if the other twin, Jacob Wellington, is a true biological twin who has the same two types of DNA. Frankly, I think you're reaching for the stars."

"Doesn't sound good for us, boss," Matt said. "I think we need either a strong alibi, like Joshua wasn't in the country, or testing of the rapist to know where we stand. I hope I'm not missing something."

"Nope, you two are absolutely correct. However, I believe Joshua is innocent, so for now we proceed. Liz, first let me say I appreciate you committing to stay for the trial. You are a valuable part of our team."

"Thank you, Drew."

Matt looked at Liz with a questioning look. "Liz, you are leaving?"

Before Liz could respond, Drew interrupted. "Liz, I need you to call James Wellington, the father, and ask him to fly here for the trial. We need him to testify. Also, explain how we need to have documents, business records, etc., showing Joshua was not in California or the United States during the time of the rapes. Have him call once he has something for us. Matt, thank you for your very constructive thinking."

"Thank you, boss," said Matt, smiling from ear to ear.

"And Liz," Drew continued. "After we know who will testify that Joshua wasn't in the U.S. at the time of the rapes, I want you to make sure we get all telephone records, charge-card statements, flight itineraries, anything that says where Josh was at the time. It's up to you to make sure we have documents to support every witness's testimony. If not, get on the phone with the father and tell him what more is needed. Remember, there is no stupid question. So ask, and ask until we have the proof we're after."

Drew turned to his office manager. "Debbie, please supervise and coordinate all of this. I'm counting on you to make all this work. Until trial is over, the Wellington matter takes precedence over everything. Postpone all other matters, including depositions, and even court appearances, if possible. Liz that includes your deposition of Douglas Chandler of C.T.I., Inc."

ooooo

Silvia Estrada pushed the button next to Drew's name and looked up at the loft security camera.

"Come on up ,Silvia," came the reply through the small speaker. Once the elevator came to a stop, Drew opened the loft door and pulled up the elevator gate for Silvia to enter.

"Silvia, did you call Jacob?"

"Yes. He's waiting for my call." She pulled out another burner phone and called. When Jacob answered, she said, "Hi, hon. Here's Drew," and handed the phone to the lawyer.

"Hello, counselor. How's my brother?"

"He's adjusted well to jail and always asks about you."

"Tell him I will protect him no matter what."

"He knows that Jacob. Can I move on to our defense?"

"Yeah."

"The DNA tests came back. They show that Joshua has two types of DNA in his genome, which explains why Joshua has eyes that are two different colors. It also explains why he has that dark-colored skin patch running from his right buttocks to his waistline and across to the center of his back."

"How can Josh have two types of DNA?"

"There are all sorts of ways that can happen. But the question is, since you are twins, do you also have two types of DNA? You see, in order for me to prove Joshua didn't do the rapes, I have to show you only have one DNA and that DNA matches the condom."

"What do you mean?"

"As I've said before, Jacob, the D.A. says Josh is you. That's why I've got to show scientifically you are not genetically the same as Joshua.

"But I don't have two different colored eyes nor do I have any birth marks. Can't you go with that?"

"Yes, but how do I prove you don't?"

"Ask the women. I was with them each for nearly two hours. They saw me buck naked and up close."

"None of the victims mentioned any birth marks or that you had two different-colored eyes."

"Isn't that sufficient? Why do you still tell me you need my DNA?"

"Because it explains why Joshua has two different-colored eyes even though he's an identical twin. It also explains why the swab of his mouth is the same DNA as yours while the rest of his DNA is, hopefully, different from yours. Without such evidence, Joshua is the only one that matches your immigration DNA sample—a cheek swab that's the same as the reconstructed condom DNA— the DNA evidence that led the authorities to your apartment and proof you are the rapist."

There was no answer. Drew intentionally remained silent, thinking, *This is it. Will Jacob finally understand he has to come forward?*

"How do we arrange that, counselor?"

"Arrange what?"

"My getting tested."

"I'm not sure. One possibility is for you to be tested by a laboratory in Mexico. That laboratory's scientists also have to be willing to come to San Diego and testify. Most importantly, their facility has to be a highly respected laboratory; an accredited facility that Dr. Lawrence Rougtbeck recognizes so he can say the Mexicans collected the samples the way he wanted."

Drew paused again. *This guy's gotta realize he has to come to San Diego.* When Jacob did not reply, Drew waited a little longer, then continued. "The other option . . ." Drew paused yet again, suspecting Jacob was the guy he'd seen in the dark hoodie outside the loft. ". . . is for you to be tested in the United States. I can give you any number of labs in Southern California where you can go."

"Yeah, very funny. And be arrested. I thought that was what you were angling for."

"The border patrol and FBI would definitely arrest you. That's a given, which is exactly how Joshua got arrested—coming to see you."

"Damn you, Hawke. Cut out the guilt trip. All right, what type of tests do you want?"

"They are extensive and personal. I need a blood sample, head hair and pubic hair samples. Especially the pubic hair samples, if you can provide them. Also skin samples, prostate sample, and a semen-sperm sample. And numerous color photographs of you, full length and close up, clothed and nude, to show you have no different-colored skin patches and your eyes are the same color."

"Did Josh have to do all this?"

"Yes. That's why I need to test the same exact areas of your body. You provide me the name of the Mexican lab, and I can have our lab send them what is required."

"No way, Hawke! If I do that, you will have the cops there to arrest me when I show up."

"Then how are we going to do this?"

"You give Silvia the name, address, and phone number of your California laboratory, as well as a list of the tests you need. After I find a laboratory in Latin America, I will tell them to call and arrange for the transfer of my body photos, fluids, and skin samples to whatever lab you want."

"Fine. But you've got to find a reputable laboratory or else we are wasting our time."

"Money, counselor, can buy anybody if it is the right amount. You ought to know that."

Drew tensed at the implied insinuation as Jacob hung up.

"I suppose, Silvia, you want to flush the memory card and destroy the phone," Drew said as he handed the phone to her.

Silvia smiled as she pulled out of her purse a small metal box and a small bottle of liquid. "Nope. I thought you would expect that."

She pulled the memory card from the phone, put it into the metal box, and poured a small amount of liquid over the card.

She shut the lid to the box as a faint odor and a few small puffs of smoke appeared.

"Did you get the money I transferred to your bank?" she asked.

"Yes, thank you."

"Then we are done today." Silvia turned and walked toward the loft door.

"Not quite, Silvia. I forgot to tell Jacob that I need all personal testing done and to my lab within two weeks. Trial starts in four weeks."

Silvia nodded as she walked to the loft door.

CHAPTER 14

Monday Morning, Two Weeks Later

DREW PUSHED THE INTERCOM BUTTON on the phone. "Debbie, when will Liz and Matt get here? It's eleven-thirty."

"Any minute. They got everything you asked for, so patience."

Drew pushed the button to disconnect and sat there, impatiently tapping his fingers on his desk. *It's nerve wracking to let others handle such important matters for trial. Any screw-up leads to last-minute rushes. That's how mistakes happen,* the young lawyer nervously contemplated. *But then again, I can't do everything, what with having to meet with clients and make court appearances.*

After five minutes Drew checked the clock in his office and started to push the intercom button, but stopped. Instead, he continued to methodically rotate tapping his four fingers one after another on his desk. Nervously he kept checking the time until Debbie knocked and entered.

"We're ready."

Drew immediately rose, grabbed his notes, and followed Debbie into the conference room.

"Good morning. Or should I say, good afternoon, guys. Let's start with our alibi and who is coming from Australia to testify and what they will say."

Matt took the lead. "Boss, Liz and I got a hold of the father and he's coming. He will bring his very trusted office manager. I've already amended our witness list, given it to the D.A., and arranged air flights and lodging."

"Good. Liz have you prepared a list of questions we will ask each witness?"

"Yes. Here's a binder with questions and all supporting evidence for the father, James Wellington, and Cadel Campbell, the business manager. Mr. Campbell is the one who maintains all company business records and knows where Joshua was at any given time. When Joshua travels, he is in constant contact by phone or video conferencing and authorizes all expenses for our client. Ah, I must add. The father is quite ill with a bad heart but insisted on coming and testifying. So you've got to take things easy with him and calm his fears about Joshua."

"I understand. Thank you, Liz."

She continued. "Here's a second binder with questions for all of the anticipated prosecution witnesses."

Before Liz could go on, Drew looked to his office manager. "Debbie, have you reviewed everything these two have done?"

"Yes. I've indexed everything. There's a table of contents and all chapters and headings have been tabbed in all the binders. Liz also has a brief summary of cross-examination and direct-questioning objectives for each witness. These precede each witness's sample questions. Everything double spaced for your editing. I must say, they've done a very professional job," she concluded, smiling at the two.

Matt responded to the compliment with a large smile and looked as though his chest was about to pop. But Drew ignored the praise and continued on point.

"Matt, how about the iPad Pro?"

"Everything is on the iPad, including what Debbie has done. The binders are just backup. Debbie and I also created three evidence binders, one for you and one each for the court and prosecution. We're good to go, boss."

"Now to our scientific defense. What has Dr. Rougtbeck said?"

Matt continued. "Boss, he has provided us with copies of all the scientific evidence he will testify to, including chimera and the test results of Joshua and Jacob's bodily samples. He's found sperm on the condom, but he doesn't seem too confident he will have enough of the sample to determine whose sperm it is. He is still working on the condom and trying to find enough snippets of DNA to compare to the DNA of Joshua and Jacob's body samples. He says as soon as he has more information he will let us know if the sperm is from Joshua or Jacob."

Liz handed a third binder to Drew. "This is everything Dr. Rougtbeck has given us to date, plus my suggested direct-examination questions. I've also included three pages on what I think Farrat will attempt to do during cross-examination. This binder is also on the iPad. Drew, all you need to do now is study our work, amend anything you don't like or would want to add. I'm available to discuss everything twenty-four hours a day, including strategy for the cross-examination of the victim witnesses."

"Liz, go ahead and continue working on cross-examination objectives for the victims. See how any of Dr. Rougtbeck's new testing results compares to any of the victim's prior testimony. After I finish reviewing everything, we will strategize further."

Drew inhaled deeply and smiled. "Well, guys, I am truly impressed. It looks like I have a lot of work to do." He turned to his office manager. Debbie, please set a meeting for us in one week to go over everything the team has done. Oh, and, Liz, one more thing," he said, facing his associate. "I need you to prepare a defense juror questionnaire for us to submit to the judge."

"Will do," she said with a nod.

Drew passed along his thoughts. "I think we want jurors who are nurturers and want to help others, like doctors, nurses, elderly grandmothers, and the like. Corporate decision makers might be good since we have the Aussie business witnesses. Most business executives can relate to how companies document and track employee activities. What we don't want are people with little or no education, people who think the police can do no wrong. Or anyone who has a grudge against medicine or is skeptical of new scientific theories. I look forward to your comments. Please review our other criminal defense juror questionnaires for ideas. In the meantime, I am counting on the three of you to handle everything, especially you, Liz. I need you to now make one hundred percent of all court appearances while I absorb your work. On that happy note, let's go to lunch. The office is buying."

"Outstanding, boss, I could eat a horse," Matt said.

Drew smiled. "That's exactly what I'm afraid of."

ooooo

Monday, One Week Later

Liz and Matt stood whispering near Matt's desk.

"What's you two mumbling about over there," snapped Debbie. "I can't get nothin' done. What is goin' on?"

"Nothing. Really, Debbie," replied Liz.

"Well . . ." spoke up Matt, pausing to look at Liz. "We're concerned we haven't heard from Drew. We'd like to know if our work is OK? Look at the time. It's eleven-twenty. He's an hour late."

"If that man was dissatisfied with your work, he'd a said so right off. Let sleepin' dogs lie, I say."

"But, Debbie, the trial is in less than two weeks. If we have to make changes or do more research, then we got to have time," Liz replied.

Just then Drew walked in, carrying his briefcase. "Sorry I'm late. Let's move into the conference room."

The three followed Drew into the conference room, where their boss opened the briefcase and spread out three piles of paperwork.

"First off, great job by you three. I've gone through all the binders and the Wellington case files. Made some changes but for the most part everything is right on." Pushing forward the first pile of papers, he continued. "Here are my comments on your suggested areas for cross-examination of the prosecutions' witnesses. This is the thumb drive for the same." He placed the USB flash memory stick on top of the pile of notes.

He pushed the second pile of papers forward, placing a second thumb drive on top. "These are my changes for questions to our own witnesses. The third pile . . ." he paused as he pushed it and a third thumb drive forward, "sets out who I want as jurors and the questions I will be asking during voir dire in order to reveal their relevant past experiences and possible juror biases.

"Remember, there is no such thing as a non-opiniated juror. Our individual experiences, family backgrounds, and our interaction with others determines how we see other people and to a great extent who we are. Case facts are case facts. Rarely can we change them. But, how each juror views those facts determines how they will vote for innocence or guilt. Choosing jurors who will view the facts most favorable to our defense is the key to victory. Some say the voir dire process, the time where attorneys can ask jurors questions, is the most important phase of a trial. Therefore, we will ask broad questions in an attempt to get jurors to talk. In the process, our follow-up questions must be tactfully worded so as to get jurors to reveal their inbred biases and expose the way they think. I also redid the proposed juror questionnaire we want the judge to submit to prospective jurors before trial begins. Thanks, Liz, for getting the draft questionnaire to me mid-week."

Liz nodded. "Just doing my job."

He smiled. "And you're doing your job well."

She smiled in return. "Thanks, Drew."

He looked back at his documents. "Now, here are some of the questions I added. They are designed to find jurors who will understand the relationship between Joshua and his brother, and how growing up without a mother drove the two boys close together." Drew opened the binder on jury selection and to the tab marked juror questionnaire. "By way of example, here is one set of questions I added to the jury questionnaire." He laid the paper on table where they could read it.

Do you have brothers, sisters, or half siblings you grew up with? Answer Yes or No.

How close are you to your siblings and they to you? Rate one to ten with ten being the closest.

Would you do anything to help your brother or sister? Answer Yes or No, with explanation if necessary.

How important was your brother or sister to you when growing up and dealing with the pressures of being a teenager? Rate closeness on scale of one to ten, with ten again the highest.

Who protected you from bullies or your brothers and sisters from bullies? Explain.

After the others had read the questions, Drew continued. "The objective of these questions is to find those jurors who can relate to Joshua and his relationship with his more dominating brother, Jacob. Everybody is going to wonder whether Josh knew his brother was a rapist and what the relationship is between the two twins."

The others nodded in acknowledgement and Drew went on.

"We need to ask jurors questions that will tell us about their family members when growing up and especially while they were in their teens and twenties. Remember, Josh is in his early twenties, unmarried, and therefore very much tied to his twin brother. We've got to play this up in our juror questioning as well as the twin's strict authoritarian father. Put simply, we want jurors to tell us about their past experiences and relationships with their siblings and close family members."

Liz spoke up. "Drew, won't Judge Gonzales-Black want to know why you are prying into the juror's family relationships?"

"I expect she would. My response will be that Joshua has family members who may testify. Therefore, I want to know if any juror will have difficulty believing a family member could testify truthfully about our client. I have a right to question any juror about the biases they may have. Besides, I will point out that the questionnaire is private and will not be made public."

Drew went to a tab marked Experts/Chimera. "Now, I have added other questions about science and experts. Here our objective is to identify and eliminate jurors who are skeptical of scientific theories or facts, and are hesitant to believe an expert who is paid to testify for the defense. We want jurors who will believe our expert and the theory of chimera. These questions and follow-up hypotheticals to possible juror responses should give us an insight into how jurors think and their hidden biases about scientific evidence. I have added specific questions about DNA and whether the jurors know how DNA is used in criminal cases. Pointedly, I ask if any of the jurors have watched TV programs where DNA is used to solve crimes. My follow-up questions ask whether the jurors have heard of DNA evidence convicting an innocent person."

Drew went on, explaining that his intent to layout their entire chimera theory in the voir dire and how DNA is not infallible. By way of example: a person having two sets of DNA can be arrested for a crime he didn't commit. All these DNA questions would be a setup for their defense that the police have the wrong twin. What he doesn't want to do is expose the fact that Josh has a biological twin; that Josh's two DNAs prove he didn't rape or that testing shows Jacob is the Sphynx rapist.

"But, boss," Matt pointed out, "Dr. Rougtbeck hasn't stated he can prove Josh isn't the rapist."

"I know, Matt," Drew replied. "He's still testing. But we have to put the chimera theory out there and raise the possibility the cops have the wrong twin. If Rougtbeck can say the DNA evidence proves Jacob is the Sphynx, and that Joshua is not the Sphynx, then we have science to back our defense of misidentification. Otherwise, we have to argue Joshua's two types of DNA raises reasonable doubt as to the accuracy of the DNA tests by the police. Hopefully, that will help the jurors believe our alibi witnesses who will say Josh wasn't in the United States when the rapes occurred. Not the best defense, but at least we have a rebuttal DNA argument."

"You want to raise all this in the voir dire?" asked Liz.

"Exactly. Remember, a defense lawyer strives to choose jurors who think in a way that they will be open to accepting the defense theory of the case. If they are, then they will most likely vote acquittal. We can't find that out without going into

DNA and chimera—the heart of our theory that DNA testing misidentified Joshua as the rapist."

Drew sighed as stared at the piles of documents on the table. "Well, those are just a few examples of what I want to ask. Please review the rest. They all relate to our theory of defense and why Joshua isn't the rapist. Liz, I want you to review everything I have done and get back to me with your comments. I am counting on your gut reaction to the additional questions I have added to the jury questionnaire and my oral questions to the jurors. Don't hesitate to recommend changes and additions."

Liz nodded while reaching for the pile of paper and thumb drive.

Drew continued. "I think it would be best for us to meet this Friday and have a final discussion on everything. But I do need your feedback on what I have handed you before we meet. I expect we will be having impromptu meetings as you go through everything before our final meeting Friday. Debbie, as usual I need you and Matt to put everything together in final form."

CHAPTER 15

Monday, Two Weeks Later

IT HAD BEEN A LONG MORNING of jury selection, but twelve jurors, five men and seven women, plus two male alternates, had been sworn in and were seated. The jury questionnaire had proved most helpful and actually shortened the attorney questioning of the prospective jurors.

Drew's voir dire had revealed that two of the twelve seated jurors had brothers and sisters to which they were very close. Another juror was a triplet who stayed close to her siblings even after the three married. Two of the three lived in the same neighborhood. A retired physician and a practicing nurse were also on the jury. Drew felt very comfortable with the selection and was buoyed by all the jurors' answers to his questions.

Now the battle begins, Drew thought as he faced the judge.

Judge Sonja Gonzales-Black, following her normal admonitions and instructions to the jury on how the trial would proceed, addressed the audience in the courtroom.

"I am glad to see all of you present, in particular the media. According to an agreement with the district attorney's office, Mr. Hawke, and the media, there will be live video coverage of these proceedings, given the wide public interest surrounding this case and the previous trial. Is that correct Assistant District Attorney Farrat?"

"Yes, Your Honor."

"Mr. Hawke, does your client agree to these proceedings being televised?"

Liz Bernquist, seated to the right of Joshua Wellington, prompted the young man to stand.

Drew rose with Joshua. "Yes, Your Honor. We have signed the court order regarding the televising of these proceedings."

"Thank you, counsel. According to our agreement, the live coverage of this case will be delayed sixty seconds unless ordered differently by this court. All of the media have signed my court order acknowledging same. Finally, it is the intent of this court to present a fair and orderly process of the law during this trial. Therefore, there will be no demonstrations or outbursts. Do I make myself clear?"

The audience responded in unison, "Yes, Your Honor."

"Our jury selection went longer than anticipated, and we are now close to the noon hour. Therefore, we will begin with opening statements and testimony after lunch."

"All rise, we are in recess until 1:30 p.m.," announced Deputy Sheriff Joseph Castro.

ooooo

The jury was in place, along with court staff. Seated at the prosecution table and closest to the jury box was A.D.A. Farrat, to his right the case's lead investigator, Detective Thomas Clayton. At the defense table were Drew Hawke, the defendant Joshua Wellington, and co-counsel Liz Bernquist. As was the practice of A. J. Hawke, a family bible rested on the left front corner of the defense table and behind it, Drew's iPad computer. Case files and trial binders were in boxes on the floor behind Drew and Liz. The gallery was full, with camera operators and reporters anxiously waiting for testimony to begin.

"Hear ye, hear ye, Department Twenty-Eight is now in session, the Honorable Sonja Gonzales-Black presiding."

"Good afternoon, everyone, I hope you had a good lunch and are ready to proceed."

The audience nodded yes. "Assistant District Attorney Jack Farrat, are you ready?"

"Yes, Your Honor."

"Then Mr. Farrat, you may proceed with your opening statement."

A.D.A. Farrat rose and walked toward the jury. "Ladies and gentlemen of the jury it has been nearly three years since the crimes you are being asked to sit in judgment on occurred. The five victims of these crimes have had to live with the horror and pain of being brutally beaten and raped. The evidence will show that after their attack, they were then tortured when the defendant bathed the five women's bodies in chemicals and injected those same chemicals into their vaginal and anal orifices. Tied and gagged, these poor women's screams were muffled as they thrashed about in agony."

The description of those women being tortured had an effect on the faces of the jurors as even the male jurors shifted about in their seats. Many of the female jurors looked down and away from A.D.A. Farrat, some shaking their heads in apparent disgust. Farrat paused so the full effect of his words could be imagined in the minds of all present. He then slowly spoke so his words could further enrage.

"You will hear from some of the rapist's victims how their torture went on for what seemed an eternity. They will tell you about how they suffered then, and how their lives have been forever changed by their ordeal. You will not hear from one of the women because she is dead."

Drew quickly wrote a note to Pat DeLuca. Pat opened it. It read: "It is going to be hard to get past the horror of these rapes." Pat looked at Drew and nodded as A.D.A. Farrat positioned himself in front of the jury box. In a rising voice, he said, "The people will present evidence, indeed DNA evidence, which shows the defendant, Jacob Wellington, that man there . . ." Farrat pointed directly at the defense table, "is the rapist and torturer. Our experts will explain what DNA is and how it is used to reliably identify perpetrators of crimes such as these charged against the defendant Wellington.

"At the conclusion of the presentation of the evidence, I will ask, in the name of the people of the State of California and the County of San Diego, that you find Jacob Wellington guilty of five counts of felony false imprisonment, five counts of felony battery, five counts of felony rape, five counts of mayhem, and five counts of felony torture all while committing a burglary with the intent to commit these felonies."

Farrat turned and walked toward his desk. Midway he stopped and faced the jury. "Ladies and gentlemen, after all the evidence is in, I will ask you for a swift and just verdict against Jacob Wellington . . ." He paused mid-sentence, then added, "so that this animal is taken off our streets forever."

Hawke sat speechless, but looked directly at the judge, turning his hands up and outward in a questioning manner.

"Yes, Mr. Hawke, you are correct. Mr. Farrat, you will refrain from calling the defendant an animal. Ladies and gentlemen of the jury, you will ignore such inflammatory comments by the assistant district attorney. As jurors, you are the final determiner as to what facts are to be believed in this courtroom, and as you discuss such facts as a jury of twelve during your deliberations. Mr. Farrat, you will not utter such inflammatory words again in my courtroom, do you understand?"

"Yes, Your Honor."

"Mr. Hawke, do you wish to make an opening statement or wait until you present your defense?"

"Your Honor, I wish to proceed now."

"Very well."

Drew rose and walked slowly toward the seated panel of jurors. In a soft and somber tone he spoke. "Good afternoon."

The jurors nodded in return to Hawke's greeting.

"I am Andrew J. Hawke. You will hear me from time to time referred to as Drew Hawke. I prefer to be called Drew because it is less formal. I represent Joshua Wellington, charged in this case as Jacob Wellington." Pointing to Joshua, he said, "He is the young man seated at the defense table.

Drew took a deep breath and began his opening statement. "My fellow citizens, the offenses you will hear about during this trial are indeed shocking and emotionally hard to bear. Because these terrible acts are so disturbing, I must ask you to set aside your emotions and answer the following question: Is Joshua Wellington the perpetrator of these crimes? Yes, I am asking you to decide not only who committed these crimes, but most importantly answer a second question: Why would the authorities believe my client is a person named Jacob Wellington, the real rapist? I know there are several among you who are saying the police in this day and age of biological science do not misidentify people, much less those they arrest when they have DNA evidence."

Drew moved closer to the citizen judges and walked slowly along the rail separating him from them as he looked each juror in the eye.

"The life of Joshua Wellington rests on your ability to

separate fear, anger, and your desire to give the young victims in this case retribution for the acts committed against them. In its place, I entreat you to listen carefully to the experts I present as they will explain why and how DNA testing has not accurately identified my client, whose name is not Jacob Wellington, but Joshua Wellington. Further the evidence, will show Joshua is an Australian who flew from down under to San Diego on his way to a mining and mineral convention in Chicago. His family owns a mining and ore shipping company in Port Hedland, Australia. Testimony will show he wasn't even in the United States when these poor women were attacked."

Drew Hawke turned and walked over to the defense table and stepped behind his client. Placing his hands on Joshua's shoulders, he continued. "This man's future, indeed his life, rests on your ability to place the logic of science before the emotional desire to give the five victims retribution for the crimes committed against them. I have faith in your ability to do this."

Hawke looked down at his client and gave a tender squeeze to his shoulder.

Drew looked back up at the jurors "Thank you for being such attentive listeners. We will talk again during closing argument. For now, Joshua and I appreciate your willingness to keep an open mind until you hear our defense."

The judge turned to the jurors and announced, "Ladies and gentlemen, we will now take a short break. Feel free to use our restrooms."

As the judge rose, Deputy Sheriff Joseph Castro announced, "This court stands in recess."

CHAPTER 16

After The Break

WITH THE COURT BACK IN SESSION, the judge ordered A.D.A. Jack Farrat to proceed.

"The People call to the stand Ms. Margret Lange."

A deputy sheriff opened the courtroom doors and in a loud voice said, "Ms. Margret Lange, please step forward."

Through the doors came a 23-year-old, five-foot-six woman dressed in a very chic, light-blue jacket, white blouse, and dark-blue slacks. Her long blonde hair was pulled back into a high bun with teasing wisps of blonde hair at the sides of her face. The woman's blue eyes looked straight ahead as if unaware of her surroundings. No matter how beautiful she appeared, there was an undeniable sadness about her. Her face was drawn, giving the impression of a person who had been drained of any emotion, one ruled by a lifeless, morbid hollowness. As all heads turned toward, her she showed not even a sociable glance of recognition. She stepped forward with a stoic determination as she strode between the two banks of gallery seating. A second deputy sheriff opened the gate of the nearly waist-high barrister's railing as she stepped into the well of the court.

The court clerk stood and asked her to raise her right hand. "Do you swear or affirm the evidence you will give today will be the truth, the whole truth, and nothing but the truth?"

"I do," she answered in a low voice.

"Please take the stand," instructed A.D.A. Farrat, pointing to the witness box to the right of the judge and not more than six feet from the twelve seated jurors.

Farrat walked up to the seated witness. "Thank you for coming." She acknowledged his greeting with a slight movement of her head. Farrat pointed to the court reporter and stated, "For the record would you please state your full name."

"Margret Louise Lange," she answered as she looked to the defense table and stared at the young man seated next to Drew Hawke.

"Ms. Lange, I wish to take you back to a May morning while you were a junior at San Diego State University. Where were you living?"

"I shared an apartment with a girlfriend at the Beachside Condominiums in Mission Beach." Once again she looked intently at the defendant as she answered. Drew, well aware of her piercing look at Joshua, stealthily glanced at the jurors. The twelve, following every word and every movement of the witness, turned and looked at the young man seated between Drew and Liz.

"In the early morning hours of a Saturday, did something terrible happen to you?"

"Yes. I was raped." She stared at Joshua again. Then she burst forth in a torrent of emotion. "I was beaten, gagged, bound, and raped, and raped, and raped . . . He then chemically burned me with some fluid."

She pointed directly at Joshua Wellington so forcibly, she appeared to almost stand in her anger. A murmur rose in the courtroom gallery as the jurors all took their pencils and wrote into the spiral note pads the court had provided.

"Ladies and gentlemen, please come to order. I must insist

that you remain quiet so the witness's testimony can be heard," ordered the judge, gaveling those present to order.

"Ms. Lange, are you pointing to the defendant seated next to attorney Hawke," asked Farrat?

"Yes, the man between those two," she answered, motioning at the defense table with her left hand.

Hawke stood in an effort to quell the drama and stated calmly, "For the record Your Honor, the witness has pointed to my client Joshua Wellington."

"Thank you, Mr. Hawke. It is so noted. Mr. Farrat you may continue."

"Ms. Lange, I know this is traumatic for you, but will you describe to the jury how you were first awakened the night you were attacked."

"I was a sleep when that man," again pointing to Joshua, "grabbed me from behind, pulled me up against his body. The next thing I knew he had a knife to my throat."

"Did he say anything?"

"Yes. 'You move, I cut your throat.' "

"Did you try to resist?"

"Yes. But he had his hand over my mouth, and he was very strong. I couldn't move."

"What happened next?"

"I tried again to get away, but he pulled the knife across my throat, cutting me."

Once again a murmur went up in the gallery. The judge again gaveled silence.

"What did you or your attacker do next?"

"I stopped moving. I was petrified. I thought he was killing me."

"Did the attacker do anything else?"

"He threw me onto the bed with him on top of me. I tried

to get away but he hit me two or three times in the jaw and on the side of my face."

"What happened after he struck you?"

"I don't remember. I lost consciousness."

"When your senses cleared, what was the first thing you remember?"

"He had my hands tied to the bed's metal headboard. He had taken off his clothes and stood next to me." Ms. Lange stopped. Tears swelled in her eyes. With her head hung low, she could no longer look at anyone.

"Margret," pleaded Farrat. "Margret Lange, please look at me." In an unusual expression of sympathy Farrat said, "I understand. It's all right. Take your time."

"Ms. Lange, would you like us to take a recess?" asked the judge.

After a pause, the witness shook her head no. "I want to get this over."

"Ms. Lange, look at me," Farrat again commanded. "Please, try to breathe—deep, slow breaths."

The woman took several deep breaths and cleared her voice.

"Yes. Thank you, Farrat said.

She began again, but with a stronger voice. "He stood right in front of my face. His penis just inches away. He had put on a condom. That's when I knew what he intended to do to me. He touched my face where he had struck me. His touch sent sharp, jabbing pains through my jaw. I cried and pulled away."

"Please bear with me, Ms. Lange, but did you give the defendant permission to have sex with you?"

"Of course not."

"I have to ask that question for legal reason, so thank you." Turning and looking toward the defense table, Farrat pointed to the defendant and asked, "How many times did the defendant have intercourse with you?"

"Twice. But after a while he would roll me over and . . . and." Her voice trailed off as she once again lost control of her emotions. Then through tears, she said, "It was horribly painful. I screamed and pleaded for him to stop. He wouldn't."

"You mean he penetrated you anally?"

The witness still in tears answered meekly, "Yes."

A.D.A. Farrat stepped back from the witness. "Now Ms. Lange, we are almost done. Please tell us what the defendant did once he had finished with you?"

"He poured a liquid all over me and began to rub me down with it. He used a very rough cloth. He hurt me."

"Go on. How did the fluid feel?"

"The liquid was at first chilling, but then it felt like a thousand pin pricks, almost burning, especially when he injected the fluid into me. He was relentless, rubbing all over my body, my hair, my face, even my private parts. He rolled me over. He poured the liquid all over me again, rubbing it in everywhere he had been."

"After he finished with the liquid, what did he do?"

"The man wrapped me in the sheets and left."

"How did that feel?

"I felt lost. I had trouble breathing because my mouth was gagged. I panicked as the wet sheets smothered my nose. I couldn't scream for help."

"Did you feel as though you were going to die?"

"Yes. It was like being entombed with no way to get help."

"Today how are you?"

"I still have nightmares. Every time I see a young man similar to the defendant I freak out."

"Did you have any physical problems following the attack?"

The witness stopped and looked at the jury and then at the people in the gallery. In a low voice, she said, "Yes. For the longest time my menstrual period was irregular. I don't date at all. It's been very difficult."

Farrat walked up to the witness stand and moved the microphone closer to the witness. "Are you currently being treated by any physician because of the attack?"

"Yes. I am in counseling, and I am being treated by my personal physician."

"A gynecologist?"

Again in a low voice, "Yes."

"Ms. Lange I want to thank you for having the courage to come here today." Farrat turned and walked back to his seat.

"Mr. Hawke, would you like a recess or do you wish to proceed with cross-examination?"

"Your Honor, I note that it is slightly after 2:30 p.m., and I do believe the court has another matter this afternoon. This might be a good time to end the court day. It would allow Ms. Lange time to relax and be fresh tomorrow morning."

"I agree. Ladies and gentlemen, this trial was assigned to me on short notice. As a consequence, I must attend to a short matter this afternoon so we will now recess for the day. In addition, tomorrow morning I have a civil matter which has been scheduled for a long time. Therefore, we will not start until one-thirty in the afternoon."

Turning directly to the jurors, "Ladies and gentlemen of the jury you are not to discuss this case with anyone. You may not even discuss this case amongst yourselves until all the testimony has been received. You have been instructed by me in the law, and you have retired to the jury deliberation room. This includes not discussing the case with any loved ones or any persons you may meet. Please avoid following the news on television and in the press. The opinions expressed by such entities are not evidence which you are to use in your deliberations. I thank you for your patience, and I assure you we will proceed expeditiously after tomorrow afternoon."

As the judge rose, Deputy Joseph Castro ordered, "All rise. This court stands recess until tomorrow afternoon at 1:30 p.m."

CHAPTER 17

Tuesday, 1:30 p.m.

ALL PARTIES WERE PRESENT and seated. Detective Pat De-Luca entered the court room and took a seat directly behind Drew Hawke and Liz Bernquist. The witness Margret Lange was seated in the witness box. Drew Hawke rose to address the witness. The young woman watched him intently. She straightened herself within the witness chair.

"Ms. Lange, I'd like you to clarify certain parts of your testimony you gave yesterday. Actually, I think I will be asking questions that the jury will find helpful."

"Objection, Your Honor," Farrat said, rising from his seat.

"Mr. Hawke, please proceed without any commentary," the judge instructed.

"Yes, Your Honor."

"Ms. Lange, you said my client Joshua Wellington raped you is that correct?"

"Yes."

"According to the police report, you told the police that the rapist bragged to you about his height, weight, and physical strength, is that correct?"

"Yes."

"How tall did you tell the police the rapists was?"

"I don't quite remember. Six something."

"Could he have said he was six-foot-two?"

"Yes, that sounds familiar."

"How much did the rapist say he weighed?"

"I don't remember."

Drew looked at her as though he expected her to say more.

Finally, she added, "I was traumatized. He had beaten me unconscious."

Drew nodded but had an expression that seemed to indicate she should go on.

"I was more afraid about what he would do to me next than listening to what he was saying."

"I see." Waiting a few seconds, Drew asked, "Did the rapist tell you anything about the young college men you had been dating?"

"No. He did say he had been stalking me and knew when I would be alone."

"Didn't the rapist call your male friends 'nerdy boys'?"

"I don't recall."

"Your Honor, may I approach the witness and let her read portions of her statement to the police?"

"You may."

"Ms. Lange, I give you a copy of the statement you gave to the police. For the record it is Exhibit 23. I've tabbed with a yellow sticky the appropriate page. Please read the highlighted portions and see if that refreshes your recollection." After reading the portions of the report that had been marked, Ms. Lange looked up and answered, "Yes, he did."

"In fact, didn't the rapist say, 'Well one thing is sure, pretty one. You ain't had a lover like me before. I'm nothing like the nerdy boys I've seen you with.' Were those the exact words you told the police?"

"Yes. I remember now."

"And didn't the rapist also say, 'I'm your big bang for the

night. I'm a healthy, six–foot-two, hundred-eighty-pound bloke, with an eight pack and not an ounce of fat. I'm just pure muscle. I can go all night!"

"Yes . . .yes," she cried out ". . . yes."

"Ms. Lange, I'm not here to make you relive your terrible nightmare. But, I do need you to have your memory as accurate as possible since you say my client is the rapist. So please forgive me for asking you to recollect such a horrible experience."

The young woman just stared at the attorney in front of her.

As Drew looked around, he saw that everyone's attention was fixed on the distraught woman. With her head turned toward the jury, as if pleading for understanding, she had sunk down in the witness chair, her shoulders slumped, her face ashen, and etched with a painful expression. *Too much sympathy. I've got to redirect everyone's attention to her desire for revenge—a revenge that has led her to misidentify Joshua.*

Hawke broke the silence. "Ms. Lange, when you saw my client recently, it was after he had been arrested, is that correct?"

"Yes," she answered with a slight sob.

"How tall did he appear to be?"

"I'm not sure."

"The same height as the rapist?"

"Yes."

"His weight?"

She looked at Hawke and then answered, "The same as the rapist."

"His build?"

"The same as the rapist."

"His color of hair?"

"The same as the rapist."

Farrat started to rise but Hawke continued as if he hadn't heard the last answer.

"Now when you saw my client, Joshua Wellington, did he say anything?"

"Your Honor, I object to this line of questioning," Farrat said.

"How so A.D.A. Farrat?" the judge responded.

Hawke immediately interjected. "Your Honor, I object to any speaking objection by Mr. Farrat and ask for an immediate sidebar."

"But, Your Honor, Mr. Hawke is eliciting—"

"Your Honor," interrupted Hawke, "sidebar, please, and without any attempt by the prosecutor to coach the witness."

"Very well. A.D.A. Farrat, please step to left side of my bench."

The two men walked to the bench where the judge directed them, and the court reporter joined the three in order to record the conference. Hawke spoke first.

"Your Honor, the reason Mr. Farrat is objecting is because Ms. Lange never saw the rapist with his ski mask off. Therefore, I ask you to tell Mr. Farrat to sit quietly as I explore why the witness feels my client is the rapist. Here is the core of our defense—the true rapist is my client's twin brother. It would be natural that the two twins would be of similar height and weight."

"Well, A.D.A. Farrat, your comment."

"Your Honor, Mr. Hawke is tricking Ms. Lange into agreeing to things that are not true.

The judge interrupted. "Isn't that what your redirect is all about, Mr. Farrat? You will have plenty of time to resurrect the credibility of Ms. Lange. Your objection is overruled. And, gentlemen, I don't want any further speaking objections from either of you. If I need an explanation to your objection, I will ask for it. You know the procedure I am talking about—state a formal objection. 'Objection, hearsay; objection, leading.' Any questions?"

"But, Your Honor . . ."

"Mr. Farrat, I have made my decision. I don't need anything further from you. I know exactly what is going on."

Jack Farrat dejectedly turned and walked back to the prosecution's table as Hawke approached the witness.

"Ms. Lange, did you have a chance to hear my client say anything when you observed him recently in a police lineup?"

"Yes."

"Did my client's voice sound the same as the rapist?"

"Yes."

"So you are convinced that Joshua Wellington is the rapist?"

"Yes, I am, and I hope he pays for what he did to me."

The jurors were feverously taking notes, looking at times at Joshua and absolutely riveted on the witness.

"Ms. Lange, isn't your presence here today an effort to seek revenge for the terrible acts the rapist did to you. You want your pound of flesh for his attack?"

Several of the female jurors put down their pencils and looked at Ms. Lange, waiting for her answer. Instead they heard, "Objection, Your Honor."

"Overruled, Mr. Farrat. Please answer, Ms. Lange."

"Yes. I want justice. He deserves to die."

"I ask you to think for a minute, Ms. Lange. Is there any chance your desire to get back at the man who raped you is so strong you would allow your anger to cloud your judgment and accuse any man as being your rapist?"

"No, absolutely not."

All jurors had stopped writing and were intently watching Hawke as he walked to the defense table, where Liz handed him copies of a transcript.

"Your Honor, I ask that the transcript of the police lineup, which included my client, be marked as an exhibit next in order. I believe that will be Exhibit number thirty-eight. I have a certified copy for the prosecutor and Your Honor. Drew turned and gave a copy to Deputy Sheriff Castro for Judge Sonja Gonzales-Black; he then gave a copy to Farrat.

"The exhibit is so marked," stated the judge.

"Ms. Lange, do you remember attending a police lineup several months ago?"

"Yes."

"Did you see my client in that lineup?"

"Ah . . . I am not sure."

Drew handed the witness a copy of the lineup transcript. "Ms. Lange, I attended that line up as you did. Do you remember me?"

"I think so."

"Please turn to the second page of the transcript. I refer you to the fourth paragraph from the top. Do you see that?"

"Yes."

"Do you see a list of the names of the men who were in the lineup you viewed?"

"Yes."

"Do you see my client's name? The police have him listed as Jacob Wellington."

"I see the name."

"Ms. Lange, the prosecution agreed that I could have a court reporter present during the lineup. That woman recorded everything that was said during the viewing of the men. Do you remember seeing her in the room with A.D.A. Farrat, Detective Clayton, and myself?"

"Yes, but I vaguely remember that lineup. It was very stressful. The police said they had just arrested the rapist and wanted me to identify him."

"Who told you the police had just arrested the Sphynx rapist?"

"Detective Clayton."

Drew looked over at Detective Clayton, who was seated next to Jack Farrat. He held his gaze so the jury could see Hawke's look of disdain. "Did anyone tell you the men you were to viewing might not include the rapist?"

"No."

"So you expected to see the rapist?"

"Yes."

"Did anyone tell you the rapist would be in court today?"

"Objection, Your Honor," shouted A.D.A. Farrat.

"Overruled. Answer the question, Ms. Lange."

"Detective Clayton told me they had the man who raped me. He asked me to testify today. I said no. But Mr. Clayton insisted."

"How did he insist?"

"He said he needed my testimony to convict the rapist. He also said I would be safe. Mr. Clayton reminded me how he had placed police officers outside my house right after I was raped. So I decided to do my part."

"Is that why you agreed to testify today?"

"Yes. I want to put the man who hurt me in jail."

"Let me ask some more questions about the police lineup you viewed. Did you in fact identify any of the men as the rapist?"

"It was very hard for me to look at the men. As I said, I was afraid about seeing the rapist again."

"Does that mean you didn't see the rapist in the lineup?"

"I saw somebody who had a body similar to the man who attacked me."

"You mean he was muscular, was of a similar height and weight as your attacker?"

"I am not good at estimating height and weight. But yes, he did appear to be the same."

"Did you ask the men in the lineup to speak?"

"No. Detective Clayton did."

"Do you remember what they said?"

"Yes. I was petrified when they spoke the words."

"Is that because they spoke words the rapist had said to you?"

"Yes."

"Please go to the second yellow tab and read lines ten through twenty-five and line one through fifteen on the following page. For the record that is pages eleven and twelve of the transcript, Exhibit Thirty-eight."

"Your Honor, the witness has not indicated that she has forgotten . . ."

"Sit down Mr. Farrat your objection is noted and overruled. Remember my admonition."

"Your Honor may we have a brief sidebar?"

"Very well approach. With all gathered including the court reporter, "Well Mr. Farrat?"

"Your Honor Ms. Lange has been on the stand since 1:30 p.m. shouldn't she be allowed a break. I'm sure the jurors would like one."

"Your Honor I have made significant progress with this witness," interrupted Hawke. "I would prefer we proceed without Mr. Farrat coaching the witness during a break and ruining my opportunity to get to the truth."

"How much longer do you have Mr. Hawke?"

"Another 20 to 30 minutes judge."

"A.D.A. Farrat I think we will continue on. If I see Mr.

Hawke going over the same area I will call a halt and take a recess. Unless, of course you need a break now Mr. Farrat in which case we can stop and wait in court while you use the restroom."

"That won't be necessary judge. Let us proceed."

A.D.A. Farrat sat back down and whispered with a smile of reassurance to Detective Clayton who appeared quite upset with how things were going.

When the witnessed finished reading Hawke asked, "Isn't it true after you initially viewed the five men in the lineup you said, 'I'm sorry they don't look familiar.' "

"Yes. But that's because they all had black ski masks on."

"The man who raped you, he wore a ski mask did he not?"

"Yes."

"Did your attacker ever take his ski mask off?"

"No."

"After you said the men in the lineup 'don't look familiar,' Detective Clayton ordered the men sent out, isn't that correct?"

"Yes."

"And shortly thereafter they were brought back in, this time without their shirts on?"

"Yes," she answered as she sat lower in her seat.

"Isn't it true Detective Clayton had each of the shirtless and still masked men say," Drew paused reading from the transcript, "He had them say, 'pretty one,' 'you will die,' and 'let's play'?' "

"Yes," the young woman answered looking defiantly at Drew.

"Isn't it true Detective Clayton asked if you thought any of the men who spoke those words was the rapist?"

"I think so. I am not sure."

"Let me read what your answer was and then tell me if that refreshes your memory. You said, and I quote, 'I don't know. When the rapist spoke he had an accent, but it was closer to how a surfer would sound like. Number three has an accent but it isn't the same. I just don't know.' "

Ms. Lange appeared upset and in an emotional outburst yelled pointing to Joshua, "But that man there is the rapist."

"Ms. Lange. Please look at page 12, lines 5-10 of the transcript." Drew paused as the woman once again read the section requested.

"Isn't true, when directed by Detective Clayton to look closely at the shirtless men you said, 'I'm sorry it has been nearly three years and I've tried to blank the whole thing . . . blank it,' "Drew looked at the jury and clarified "it" by saying, "the rape," and continued reading from the transcript, " 'blank it out of my mind. If I had to choose it would be number four because he is muscular. But the rapist had bigger muscles.' "

Looking up from the manuscript the woman answered, "Yes sir."

"Ms. Lange. Did any of the five shirtless men have chest hair?"

"Yes. They all did except for number four, the muscular one."

"Do you know why the man who raped you is called the Sphynx Rapist?"

"Yes, because he has no body hair."

"You mean similar to a sphynx cat, correct."

"Yes."

"Did your attacker have body hair?"

"No."

"Isn't true your rapist had no groin hair—pubic hair, armpit hair, chest hair or hair on his arms and legs."

"He was totally clean shaven Mr. Hawke."

Drew next asked the witness to look toward the back of the transcript she was holding. "Do you see Appendix One?"

"Yes," she answered as the witness opened Appendix One.

"Please turn the transcript sideways. Ms. Lange, look at the colored pictures of the men standing in a lineup. There are two long photographs of the lineup. The top one is of the masked men without shirts. The photograph below was taken after you left. The shirtless men in the second photograph are not wearing masks. You may hold the photographs close so you can get a good look. Have you had a chance to review them?

"Yes."

"Do you see the man third from your left?"

"Yes."

"That is my client, Joshua Wellington," pointing to the defense table. "Do you agree the third man from the left in the lineup photo is my client?"

The witness looked at Joshua and then the transcript photographs. With a sigh she answered, "I do."

The jurors once again picked up their pads and began writing. A low whisper could be heard in the audience followed by a stern look from the judge to those talking in the gallery. Deputy Castro turned and held his finger to his mouth for silence. Hawke continued,

"The man to my client's right as you view the photograph is number four in the lineup.

He would be the muscular one you spoke of—isn't that correct."

"I don't know," she said as she put the transcript down.

Drew walked over to the jury box so the witness had to

turn her head to look at him. Ms. Lange what color was the rapist's eyes. You do remember his eyes don't you?"

"They were blue."

"Light blue or dark blue? Please look at me Ms. Lange," Hawke insisted as she started to look to her left towards Joshua.

"Dark blue," she answered.

"Were both of the eyes you saw the same color?"

"I'm sorry what did you say."

"The eyes were they both dark blue."

"Of course."

"Now Ms. Lange, please pick-up the transcript again for me," the witness complied.

"Look at the colored picture of the lineup in Appendix One. Please look closely, does my client, gentleman number three, have a muscular body?"

"Yes."

"Ms. Lange, remembering your earlier testimony where you told Detective Clayton, 'if I had to choose it would be number four because he is muscular,' does my client look more muscular than the fourth man in the lineup?"

"No he does not."

"Your Honor may we have a sidebar?" asked Drew.

"Yes." The judge gestured for A.D.A. Farrat and Hawke to come to the side of the bench, the court reporter joining the conference.

"I have two requests judge. First, I ask that Exhibit 38 with the pictures of the lineup we have been talking about be moved into evidence. I also ask that the lineup be published to the jury. It is the only thing on this memory peg."

"Any objection, Mr. Farrat?"

"No, Your Honor."

"Exhibit Thirty-eight is received into evidence. Deputy Castro would you join us at sidebar," summoned the judge.

"Joseph, please turn on the court video system, and after we resume I want you to publish to the jury and audience the photos on Mr. Hawke's USB memory stick."

Drew handed the USB memory stick to the deputy and said, "I would also like my client to stand and come close to the witness and the jury so they can view the color of his eyes. If you think Ms. Lange would feel safer, my client can stay seated and the witness, escorted by Deputy Castro, can walk up to the defense table and view his eyes."

Mr. Farrat, do you object?"

"No."

"Then we shall have a showing of the defendant to the witness and the jury and view the lineup photograph."

Your Honor, I will have one more series of questions for Ms. Lange once she retakes her seat after the viewing. I would like to question her before the jury views my client's eyes. After that she can be excused until tomorrow."

"Very well."

"Mr. Farrat, since it is three forty-five, would you like to start your redirect of Ms. Lange tomorrow morning?"

"Yes, that would be helpful, judge."

"Ladies and gentlemen, the defense has requested that the photographs of the lineup in Appendix One of Exhibit Thirty-eight be published. I have so ordered. Thereafter, we will have a viewing of the defendant's eyes and recess for the day. Joseph, if you please?"

A 110-inch screen on the wall directly across from the jury motored down. As the media cameras in the court focused on the screen, the image of the five shirtless men in the lineup appeared. After about 25 seconds, the image changed to a closeup of each of the men in the lineup, focusing first on each of their faces and then moving out slowly, showing their entire bodies. The video repeated itself one more time and the scene went black.

The judge asked, "Is that sufficient, Mr. Hawke?"

"Yes, thank you. Your Honor, I ask the transcript of Exhibit Thirty-eight be moved into evidence, and the memory stick which contains the lineup photographs also be marked next in order and moved into evidence."

"So ordered. Joseph, you may turn off the video system."

"Ladies and gentlemen, we will now have a viewing of the defendant's eyes. Ms. Lange, at this time I would like you to walk with Deputy Castro over to the defense table and view Mr. Wellington's eyes."

As Margret Lange stepped down from the witness box and was escorted over to the defense table, another Deputy Sherriff stepped behind the defendant. After the viewing, she retook the stand.

Hawke rose from the defense table and walked toward the witness. "Ms. Lange, what are the colors of Mr. Wellington's eyes?"

"They are blue," she answered.

"Both eyes the same color?"

"No. One is dark blue. The other is light blue."

Drew then approached the witness within an arm's reach. "Do you still say my client is the man who raped you?"

There was a very long pause. "I feel he is."

"Feel or desire him to be the rapist?"

"Objection, Your Honor, Mr. Hawke is badgering the witness."

"No, I will allow the question. Please answer, Ms. Lange."

"I'm very confused, Your Honor, I don't know what to say."

Hawke moved even closer, resting his hands on the witness box railing. "Ms. Lange, do you remember your answer earlier when I asked if my client was the same height, weight, and build as the man who raped you?"

"Yes, I do."

"I also asked if the rapist had the same color hair as my client and you said yes. Before you answer my next question, please look at Appendix One. Isn't it true no one in the lineup ever took off their ski masks?"

"I never saw the men without their masks," she answered.

"Nor did you see the rapist without his mask, isn't that true?"

"No, he never removed his mask."

"Isn't it correct, Ms. Lange, you never told the police you had seen the color of the rapist's hair?"

"That is true."

"It is true because he had no body hair and his head was totally covered?"

"Yes, Mr. Hawke, I never saw his head."

"Then Ms. Lange, how can you say my client, who is strikingly blonde, has the same color of hair as the rapist."

A hush came over the courtroom. It was so quiet everyone in the courtroom could hear the witness's rapid breathing. All the jurors leaned forward, anticipating her answer. Drew intentionally did not ask another question, hoping the silence would magnify her inability to answer. The judge looked at the witness, who had her head down, then looked to Hawke, who intentionally ignored the judge's eyes.

After a moment, the judge broke the silence. "Ms. Lange, do you want the question read back?"

"No, Your Honor." Looking up, she answered, "I guess I was mistaken about the hair."

"Do you mean mistaken, Ms. Lange, about my client being the Sphynx rapist, the man who assaulted you?" asked Drew.

The witness looked at Hawke, then slowly turned her head and made eye contact with the jury.

"Ms. Lange, you are under oath and everyone is waiting. Would you please answer my question."

The witness looked directly at Hawke and said, "I don't know if he is the man that raped me."

There was a rush to the courtroom doors as several reporters and their camera crew made their way into the corridor to get the breaking news on air about the Sphynx trial's explosive first day. The judge gaveled for silence.

During the slight commotion, Drew was in deep thought. *Should I press her further or live with that answer? To go on risks her diluting her stunning admission.* Looking up to the judge, he said, "I have no further questions of this witness." He turned and walked back to the defense table.

"Mr. Farrat, I see you are standing. Do you wish to do your re-direct now?" the judge asked.

"Your Honor, may we have a sidebar?"

"Yes, of course."

Both attorneys and the court reporter took their normal places at sidebar.

"Judge, we talked about ending early today and putting Ms. Lange on tomorrow morning. That is still agreeable to the prosecution. However, I am having scheduling problems with my witnesses. I would like to put on after Ms. Lange one of my expert witnesses instead of another victim."

"Mr. Hawke?"

"I have no objection to us ending forty minutes early. But Mr. Farrat, do you have anything you wish to tell me about your expert witness so I can prepare?"

"After Ms. Lange, I will then call Dr. Ethan J. Brown, my DNA expert. After that I am not sure who I will call."

"Thank you, gentlemen. Then let's go ahead and finish up with the jury viewing the defendant and call it a day."

Everyone returned to their respective positions, with the court addressing the witness. "Ms. Lange, you may step down. But you are still a witness, and I expect you here tomorrow morning at nine a.m."

The witness nodded yes, and she walked through the gallery to exit the courtroom, all eyes followed—with the exception of Drew. He turned to Liz, who was seated next to Joshua, "Liz, follow Ms. Lange and tell me if those reporters outside corner her for an interview. I need to know what she says."

The judge resumed the proceeding. "Deputy Castro, would you please escort Mr. Wellington to the jury box so the jurors may examine his eyes."

"Yes, Your Honor." Another deputy joined Joseph and the two walked the defendant up to the seated jurors, allowing every juror to look closely at his eyes. Some leaned way forward and looked him straight in the eyes for the longest time. Afterward, the jurors took made notes in their spiral notepads.

Drew watched with satisfaction as the jurors appeared not to stand back or show fear of his young client. A feeling of satisfaction came over him. *I think I have neutralized a potentially damaging witness.*

Once Joshua retook his seat, the judge announced, "Ladies and gentlemen, this will conclude the testimony for the day. Ms. Lange will resume her testimony tomorrow at nine a.m."

The judge rose from the bench and Deputy Castro raised his voice above the increasing chatter of the gallery, "This court is adjourned until tomorrow at nine a.m. I will open the doors at eight forty-five a.m."

CHAPTER 18

That Night

IT HAD BEEN A LONG DAY IN COURT, yet Drew was having a hard time falling asleep. Things had gone too well in court that day. Yes, Farrat is a blunderbuss, but still he really didn't protest that much or that hard about the cross-examination of Margret Lange. That's just not how the man works.

Hawke lay there, looking up at the ceiling, when his cell phone started to vibrate. He looked at the caller I.D. It read "Caller Unknown."

"Hello."

"Great job today, counselor."

"Jacob. How did you get my cell number?"

"Silvia wrote it down after I let her in following your rumpus date with that woman."

`"You son-of-a-bitch."

"Yes, I am. But let's talk about why I called. Congratulations on your smashing performance today. You were actually quite the spellbinder. You had everybody on the edge of their seats as you undid that woman, Margret Lange. Sexually, she wasn't my type. She was too young and inexperienced. Cried every time I shoved it in."

"You are indeed a merciless animal."

"Merciless but cunning, Hawke. Merciless but cunning. A real Vader at heart, eh, mate."

"Don't crow too much, Jacob. This was just the first round. Frankly, things went not as well as they could have."

"Not by my book. You just keep it up and undo those other bitches the prosecutor brings in."

"You really don't understand do you?"

"What do you mean?"

"All I did today was discredit Lange's identification of Joshua as the rapist. In doing so, she crumbled on the stand, garnering sympathy from the jurors and adding to the jurors' hatred of you."

"Maybe so, but her identification of Josh is out."

"That's not the point. The prosecution already has Joshua identified through DNA as you. Therefore, he is the rapist. It's all about your DNA, Jacob. Since you will not step forward, I have the terrible task of proving Joshua isn't you."

"Look it, I did what you asked. I had that Mexican doctor play with my body, get me aroused, and watch me whack-off. I paid him a shit load of money. He will say whatever you want him to say."

"I know those tests are embarrassing. But they are needed to prove Joshua isn't you."

"So why all the worry?"

"I've told you a dozen times, we have a DNA theory for our defense. I just I don't know if it will work. You saw how those jurors were moved by the testimony of Lange about how you tormented her."

"So what?"

"It's emotion versus our chimera theory. The jurors will be looking for any reason to convict Joshua—chimerism be damned."

"Just do what you're born to do Hawke—attack, attack, attack. I know I chose the right attorney. Remember, there is a lot riding on you getting Josh out of this mess. My dad won't live forever. See you on telly tomorrow."

Before Drew could say anything, Jacob hung up. Drew tapped the phone icon and scrolled through recent calls. All that showed up was "unknown" for Jacob's phone number. Drew put the phone down and lay back in the bed. *What the hell does Jacob mean there is a lot riding on Joshua's defense? Forget it. Getting inside Jacob's head is a lost cause. But what is Farrat up to? Why put up a victim on the stand that he knows will lie?*

After a moment he yelled, "That's it. The shithead fooled me. Damn you, Farrat. Every time I underestimate you I get suckered in."

ooooo

Wednesday, 7:55 a.m.

The next morning Drew arrived early to court only to be surprised to see his investigator and Liz waiting.

"You guys are here early."

"Thought we would talk about what happened yesterday and the plan for today," offered Pat DeLuca.

Liz added, "That poor girl. She was just scared to death. She would have identified anyone looking similar to the rapist."

"And because of that Liz, Farrat knew she would lie. I fell right into his trap."

"What do you mean?" asked Liz.

"Farrat wanted me to rip Lange apart and expose how traumatized the rape was to her."

"I don't know, Drew. You had to discredit her identification."

"Pat, there's more than one way to discredit identification. I could have just listed all the different reasons Joshua wasn't the rapist, asked her if she still felt he was the man, and left it to the jurors to decide rather than forcing her to admit she was wrong."

"I think you're being too harsh on yourself, son. Anyway, where do we go from here?" asked Pat.

"One thing's for sure, I won't make the same mistake with the other victims."

"Do you think Farrat will put Lange back on the stand today?"

"I doubt it, Liz. He used me to get what he wanted out of Lange yesterday. That jury is now swimming in sympathy for the victims. No. I bet he will move on to stronger evidence identifying Joshua as the Sphynx."

Drew glanced at his watch, "Hey, I haven't eaten breakfast yet. Why don't we head to the cafeteria. It's not the best food, but I need to fuel up."

The three walked off, theorizing who would be the next witnesses and how Drew should respond.

ooooo

By nine o'clock, everyone was in court, the gallery filled, and cameras rolling, with commentators back at the studios analyzing the previous day's testimony and pontificating on what would happen next in court.

The bailiff called out, "All rise, Department Twenty-eight is now in session, the Honorable Sonja Gonzales-Black presiding."

"Good morning, ladies and gentlemen," the judge said as she took her seat.

"Good morning," answered the courtroom.

"I see you are standing, A.D.A. Farrat. Are you ready to proceed?"

"Yes, Your Honor. But if I may, I am having more scheduling

problems. Our bio-geneticist would like to testify now to accommodate his work schedule. May I proceed with him and have Ms. Lange on redirect at a later time?"

"Mr. Hawke, is that all right with you."

"Yes, Your Honor."

"Very well. Proceed, Mr. Farrat."

"I call to the stand Dr. Ethan J. Brown."

As Dr. Brown entered the courtroom and made his way to the witness stand, Drew turned around and motioned for Pat, who was in the first row of the gallery, to lean forward. Drew whispered, "I told you, Pat. He used Lange to whip the jurors into a hanging mob. Now he moves for the jugular—DNA identification."

After the witness was sworn in, Dr. Brown took the stand. A.D.A. Farrat approached.

"Would you please state your name for the record."

"I am Dr. Ethan J. Brown."

"What is your occupation?"

"I am a professor of biology and genetics at University of California at Berkeley."

"Doctor Brown, have you ever testified in court and been certified as an expert witness?"

"Yes, hundreds of times as an expert regarding victims, both living and deceased, and the identification of their attackers through DNA evidence. I have also testified as an expert in paternity lawsuits and ancestry genealogy."

"Dr. Brown, did I provide you with any evidence regarding the rape of five women, in particular the results of testing on a condom and syringe by the San Diego County Criminal Laboratory and the California Forensic Laboratory located in Berkeley, California?"

"Yes. I even went over to the Berkeley laboratory, which

is located about a mile from my office, and viewed their test reports and the equipment used to replicate through PCR the damaged specimen samples found on the condom. I also did the same regarding the chemicals used by the defendant to destroy his DNA. Those chemicals were found at the defendant's apartment here in San Diego."

"Objection. My client denies he is Jacob Wellington, and no physical evidence has been produced showing he is the man who rented the San Diego apartment."

"That is correct, Your Honor," responded Farrat, looking at Hawke with a smug expression. "At least not until now."

"All right, gentlemen, it is only fifteen minutes after nine. Do I have to admonish you both again about making extraneous comments? Dr. Brown, the identity of the accused has been challenged. That is one of the issues in this case. Please listen carefully to the questions of the prosecutor and frame your answers accordingly.

"Yes, Your Honor."

Proceed, Mr. Farrat."

"Dr. Brown, what did you think of the California Forensic Lab's new DNA replication program?"

"Impressive. Very advanced, and useable on many types of contaminated DNA samples."

"First, for the jury what is DNA?"

"DNA stands for deoxyribonucleic acid which is the fundamental building block of our bodies. DNA determines our entire genetic makeup. In simple lay terms, DNA is our individual hereditary blueprint given to us by our parents, our parents' parents, and so on back in time by all our ancestors."

"Doctor, where is the DNA found?"

"DNA is found in all our cells. Thus, each of us has our own unique DNA throughout our body. For example, each person's unique DNA is found in our saliva, skin tissue, organs, blood, sweat, bone, hair, urine, semen, vaginal and rectal cells, just to mention a small list."

How does our unique DNA affect us?"

"It determines our physical characteristics, such as eye and hair color, bone structure and height, et cetera. DNA is everything that says who we are individually."

"Does our DNA change over time?"

"No. DNA does not change during a person's lifetime."

"Has science found a way to use DNA in the criminal justice system?"

"Yes, it is the primary means by which we identify people. In almost every crime scene, DNA of the perpetrator is left behind. Match the crime scene DNA to the DNA of a man or woman and you have a primary suspect. It's the same way we use finger prints to identify suspects."

"Turning back to the five rape cases here in San Diego, did the California Forensic Laboratory in Berkeley successfully reconstruct the DNA found on a condom?"

"Yes. I reviewed all their work; even ran a duplicate test on the small sample they had, and I successfully reproduced DNA that matched their previous reconstruction. I wish to thank Dr. Lawrence Rougtbeck for allowing a fellow colleague like myself to conduct such an experiment. By my doing so, I can now say emphatically that the work done by Dr. Rougtbeck was accurate."

"Doctor, to your knowledge was the DNA found on the condom matched to any person?"

"Yes, it was."

"Who?"

"Dr. Brown looked over at Joshua and said, "To a Jacob Wellington."

Drew rose and the judge asked, "Yes, Mr. Hawke?"

"Your Honor, I stipulate the DNA replicated from the condom by Dr. Rougtbeck was matched to a person by the name of Jacob Wellington, the twin brother of my client."

"Mr. Farrat."

"Your Honor, I do not accept such a stipulation because it is our intent to prove that the defendant is Jacob Wellington."

"Very well. The stipulation is not accepted. Proceed, A.D.A. Farrat.

"Doctor Brown, how do you know the reconstructed DNA matched to a Jacob Wellington?"

"Immigration and Customs took a mouth swab of Jacob Wellington when he entered the United States on a student visa. That swab's DNA matched the condom's DNA reconstructed by myself and Dr. Rougtbeck."

Farrat turned toward the defense table and said, "Your witness, counselor."

Hawke, staying seated at the defense table, asked, "You said that we all have our own unique DNA, a finger print as it were of our individual genetics. A one-of-a-kind, is that true?"

"Yes."

"But there are exceptions to that rule is there not?" Hawke said as he rose and walked toward the witness.

"How do you mean, Mr. Hawke?"

"How about biological twins, otherwise known as identical twins? They have the same DNA is that true?"

"Why, yes. Identical twins do have the same DNA."

"Do you know if my client, Joshua Wellington, is an identical twin?"

"No, I don't know that."

"Thank you, Dr. Ethan Brown." Drew turned and walked toward the defense table as almost everyone in the courtroom was a buzz about how Hawke had neutralized nearly an hour of prosecution testimony with just three questions. The judge uncharacteristically did not immediately gavel the audience to order. Instead, she had an unusual look on her face as she, too, appeared to realize what Hawke had just done. Without asking whether the defense had any further questions of the witness, she instead turned to the prosecutor. "Mr. Farrat you, may redirect."

A.D.A. Farrat, seemingly unfazed by Hawke's swift attack, said, "No. The witness may be excused. But I wish him to be subject to recall."

"Very well. You may step down, Dr. Brown."

Judge Gonzales-Black looked at the clock. "Ladies and gentlemen, at this time we will take our morning break."

As the judge rose, Deputy Castro announced, "This court is in recess. We will reconvene at 10:30 a.m."

CHAPTER 19

Court Reconvened, 10:30 a.m.

"A.D.A. FARRAT, you may call your next witness," the judge said.

"The People call Dr. Anjou Okuda-Tyler to the stand."

As Dr. Okuda-Tyler walked to the witness stand, Liz leaned over to Drew and asked, "Who is she?"

"I haven't the foggiest Idea. Pat and I tried to find her, but Farrat had her listed as Anjou Tyler. We couldn't find such a person. Now I know why."

After the witness had been sworn in, Farrat confidently walked toward her. "Doctor, please state you name for the record."

"Dr. Anjou Okuda-Tyler, spelled A-n-j-o-u, O-k-u-d-a- T-y-l-e-r. You may address me as Dr. Okuda, my maiden and professional name."

"Please tell us about your academic background."

"I have a Bachelor of Science in Business, a second Bachelor of Science in Education, both from the University of Michigan at Ann Arbor, a Master's Degree in Educational Administration from the University of Pennsylvania, and a doctorate in Higher Education Administration from Baylor University in Texas."

"What is your current employment?"

"I am the new Admissions Administrator for San Diego State University."

Drew and Pat had looks of total surprise on their faces.

"Doctor Okuda, did I subpoena documents which you were supposed to bring to court today?"

"Yes, you did."

Drew rose. The court noticing, "Yes, Mr. Hawke?"

"May we have a sidebar regarding the prosecution's subpoena of new evidence—evidence not on the Exhibit list?"

"A.D.A. Farrat, please come and bring any documents you may have subpoenaed from the university."

Once again the two attorneys and the court reporter gathered at sidebar.

"Mr. Farrat, what have you subpoenaed?" asked the judge.

"The college records of Jacob Wellington."

"Anything I should be appraised of?" asked Hawke.

Farrat looked at the judge, who said, "Yes, Mr. Farrat, I would like to know, too."

"Judge, the documents are Jacob Wellington's admission application, date of admission, the courses he took, and his current status at the university."

"May I see them, Mr. Farrat?" asked Hawke.

The judge stuck her hand out. "Let's not keep me in suspense either, Mr. Farrat."

The prosecutor handed the file to the judge. She opened it, stopping to look at the backside of the front cover for several seconds, looked at Hawke, and then thumbed through the rest.

"Here you are, Mr. Hawke," she said, and handed it to him.

Drew opened the file and stared at a picture on the inside of the file. "What is this?"

Hawke asked, pointing to a picture in the file.

"It's a picture submitted by your client when he applied to

San Diego State for admission. It is your client, don't you agree? See the different-colored eyes? And, check out the name and signature on the application. It reads Jacob Wellington, Port Hedland, Australia."

"This is outrageous, Your Honor. A total blindside."

"Yes you are right, Hawke," Farrat said. "The People were totally blindsided by your claim there is an evil identical twin rapist. This kills your bullshit defense."

"Up yours, Farrat!"

"All right, gentlemen, enough, enough, I say," the judge ordered as Hawke and Farrat turned to face each other.

"Your Honor, Mr. Farrat has violated FERPA, the Family Educational Rights Privacy Act. He just can't go around subpoenaing college records willy-nilly."

"That is an interesting argument, judge," Farrat countered. "Is Mr. Hawke now claiming standing to object because his client is Jacob Wellington?"

"You try my patience, Farrat," responded Hawke.

"OK, let's not make this personal," the said. Please address all comments to me and not to each other, gentlemen, if that word is at all appropriate."

"Actually, defense counsel does have a point," answered Farrat smugly. "Educational records are private and not normally subject to a subpoena. That's why we got a court order from Judge Brown. Otherwise, the university would not have complied with our subpoena. Judge, here's a copy of the order," he said, with a smile to Hawke.

The judge reviewed the order and then handed it to Hawke.

"Your Honor, before we proceed I need to talk to my client," Hawke said.

"I think, counselor, that would be a good idea. We will recess for thirty minutes."

"Thank you, judge." Turning to A.D.A. Farrat, Drew added, " Mr. Farrat, I want a copy of that file and the court order."

"I have copies for you at my desk and a copy for the court."

"A.D.A. Farrat, give my copy to Deputy Castro," the judge ordered.

"Yes, ma'am."

Turning to the courtroom, the judge announced, "Ladies and gentlemen, we will now take a thirty-minute recess and reconvene thereafter."

Walking back to the defense table, Drew pointed to his client and told Deputy Castro, "I want to see him in the court holding cell. Now. Pat and Liz will join me. If there is a problem, please call your sergeant."

"What's up, Drew?" Liz asked.

"I'll tell you once we get to the holding cell."

At the holding cell, everyone was seated except Drew, who paced back and forth like a caged animal, snapping a rolled copy of the admission file against his palm. "What's this, Joshua?" he demanded and tossed the file onto the table in front of his client.

Joshua picked it up and looked inside, stopping to look at the picture and application form. "Oh, this?"

"Yes, that."

"Jacob asked me to fill out his admission form to the university."

"For God's sake, why?"

"He never got a regular high school education because he was in the monastery. They don't give diplomas. He was told he needed a high school transcript to qualify for the university."

"Why didn't you tell me about this?"

"I just forgot about, Mr. Hawke."

Liz interrupted. "Did you forge any part of the high school transcripts?"

"We just changed the first name from Joshua to Jacob. They never questioned it."

"But what about the different color of your eyes and Jacob's?" asked Pat.

"Jacob usually wore sun glasses or a colored contact lens in eye if he thought anyone would question it," answered Joshua.

"That is bullshit!" Drew said.

"But Mr. Hawke, Jacob and I always say we're each other when talking to strangers, especially girls. What's the big deal?"

"I'll tell you what the big deal is. You are now Jacob Wellington because you said so in the application. I have no defense for you. Without your brother saying he is Jacob, no one will believe you are Joshua."

Liz grabbed Drew's arm as he paced back and forth. "Can't we put Joshua on the stand and have him explain why he applied to the university for his brother?"

Drew jerked his arm away. "What? Say he lied on an application form? What do you think Farrat would say? 'You lied then, are you lying now?' Nobody is going to believe he is Joshua after seeing that picture and the application. Besides, where is Jacob? Produce Jacob, the jury will say."

Pat rose and in a calm voice said, "Drew, ask for a continuance until tomorrow. We need time to think, maybe even ask for a mistrial."

"Think? Shit, Pat, there's no way out. We are totally boxed in. If I ask for a mistrial and she grants it, what will our defense be the next time around?"

"We still have the Mexican doctor. Or how about convincing Jacob to testify by video from Mexico," offered Liz.

Drew stopped and looked at her, thinking over what she said. "Liz, go back to the office and research on how courts allow witnesses to testify by video. There's got to be some judge who has allowed a witness to testify by video due to the past pandemic. We arraign defendants all the time from jail by video. There are case management conferences through Microsoft Team. We even do civil depositions by video. I need your research done by six p.m. If you get a plausible argument, we will have to pull an overnighter to write the motion and request a trial continuance. If granted, I will need time to arrange Jacob's testimony via Microsoft Team."

"Pat looked at Drew. "Do you really believe the judge will grant such a motion?"

"What have we got to lose? Everything is already lost." Drew beckoned Joseph to open the holding cell. "Joseph, we are done here, but I need to talk to the judge. Please see if she is available for a chamber conference with me and Farrat."

A few minutes later, A.D.A. Farrat appeared in the hallway with a smile of total satisfaction, following Deputy Castro, who said, "This way, Mr. Hawke."

"Thank you, judge, for seeing us," Drew said.

"Absolutely, Mr. Hawke. Please be seated, gentlemen." Before Drew could say anything the judge addressed Farrat. "Mr. Farrat, I have a few questions regarding the student transcript."

"Yes, Your Honor."

"When did you first know you should seek the transcripts?"

"When Mr. Hawke started talking about the rapist not being the defendant and his not so subtle hints that there was an evil twin."

Let me phrase my question another way. When was the first time you even knew Jacob Wellington was going to San Diego State?"

"We learned from the Feds several years ago that Jacob Wellington entered the United States on a student visa and would be studying at San Diego State University."

"That was during the trial of David Caine for the rape and murder of Claire Rewake, is that right Mr. Farrat?"

"Yes, judge."

"Why didn't you then subpoena Mr. Wellington's college transcripts?"

"There was no need. The Feds had his DNA from a cheek swab when he applied for a student visa, and we had the matching reconstructed DNA from the condom. This all led us to raid Jacob Wellington's apartment in Pacific Beach, where we found all sorts of evidence tying the defendant to the rapes."

"So the earliest time you thought of getting the transcripts was after Mr. Hawke's opening statement?"

"That's correct. We just didn't buy Hawke's theory the defendant had an identical twin brother."

"Mr. Hawke, any comment?"

"Your Honor, the prosecution is supposed to disclose all evidence and witnesses it intends to present at trial to the defense. That includes potential evidence. It's the only way the defense can properly prepare to rebut the prosecution's case. It is not the defense's duty to prove my client's innocence. We only need to establish the prosecution has not proved its case beyond a reasonable doubt. I can't do that if I don't know in advance what evidence the prosecution's case includes. A.D.A. Farrat did not inform me about possible new evidence such as the admission file. Therefore, the proffered evidence should be denied."

"Judge, you can't deny the People evidence that proves who the defendant is. I have the right to impeach all theories presented by the defense, especially a theory the accused is not who we say he is."

"Jack," interrupted Hawke, "if that evidence comes in and the jurors convict my client you know the appellate court is going to overturn the conviction and send the case right back for a retrial."

"I doubt that, Hawke."

"So, gentlemen, you are suggesting I am damned if I do and damned if I don't, is that it?" surmised the judge.

"There is a third way, judge," offered Hawke.

"And what is that?"

"I can arrange for Jacob Wellington to testify by video from Mexico, where he is hiding."

"Oh, no you don'., I have the right to confront and cross-examine a witness in person. There is no way the jury can evaluate and accurately judge the demeanor and truthfulness of such an important witness over a television screen."

"Your Honor, we use Microsoft Team video all the time. It is used in arraignments, was used during the pandemic, and is now being used for depositions, especially for out-of-state witnesses in civil proceedings. We are right now researching this issue and are prepared to have a motion to allow video testimony in your hands by tomorrow morning."

"If the supposed twin wants to testify, let him come to court," responded Farrat.

"Sure, so you can arrest him. Is that it, Farrat? Judge, the issue is: Who is Jacob Wellington? I have an out-of-country witness, Jacob Wellington, who refuses my subpoena to come to court. I have no legal way to compel such a witness to appear. But he will testify by video—through Microsoft Team. Judge, you must allow this to happen."

"Gentlemen, please." The judge thought for the longest time and then spoke. "All right, we will suspend testimony for a day. I want written briefs on these matters. Mr. Hawke, your motion will be due tomorrow. I assume you will also ask for a mistrial?"

"Yes, judge."

"You must deliver your motions to my clerk and the district attorney's office by nine a.m. tomorrow."

"Mr. Farrat, you will file briefs in opposition to the defense motions by two p.m. tomorrow. Can you live with this schedule?"

"Yes, ma'am."

"We will reconvene with the jury the following day at nine a.m., at which time I will give you my decision. Mr. Farrat, you should be ready to resume your case after I make my ruling."

"Yes, Your Honor."

"Now, gentlemen, we have a jury waiting who I am sure is anxious to know what is going on."

CHAPTER 20

That Evening, 8:00 p.m.

IT WAS ONE OF THOSE TYPICAL EVENINGS where locals, tourists, young and old, were enjoying the magnificent short-sleeve weather of San Diego. The Gaslamp Quarter was abuzz with plenty of revelry, especially around the restaurants, bars, and dance clubs near Hawke's office in the George J. Keating Building. High up on the fourth floor it was all bright lights and the quiet noise of computer keyboards clicking away as Matt, Liz, Debbie, and Drew feverishly worked away. A knock came at the office door.

"Yes, come in," yelled Debbie.

In walked Randy Wright and Chad Musante. "Is Drew in, Debbie?"

Through Drew's open office door came a greeting. "Hey, you two, what are you doing here? I'm afraid we are in crisis mode. Got three briefs do by nine tomorrow morning."

"That's why we are here. The court clerk told us all about your client's identity problem," answered Randy as the two walked into Drew's office. Waving a USB memory stick, Randy added, "Here's a Hastings law review article on video testimony and two legal briefs on surprise evidence dealing with a defendant's identity. Thought you could use them."

"Is the Hastings article the one from 1974?" asked Drew.

"Yes," Randy said as the two sat down in front of Drew's desk.

"Got the Hastings Law School article, but what's this about two legal briefs? Who wrote them?"

"I wrote one about two years ago, and the other is the D.A.'s opposition," answered Randy.

"Yeah, and I found a really good 2020 U.S. federal case that says modern technology and video display offer the viewing jury the ability to observe the demeanor of witnesses adequately to judge credibility," added Chad. "We thought you might want these."

"Fantastic. Let me plug in the stick." As Drew perused Randy's legal brief, he looked up at his old friend. "This is really good, Randy. Liz, come in here."

"Yes, Drew."

"Randy and Chad brought us some additional research. The brief by Randy is right on our problem. Randy did you win?"

"Yes. Judge Haines was going to declare a mistrial, but we ended up settling the case. D.A. buckled."

"I'm afraid Farrat won't do the same," bemoaned Drew.

"Liz," spoke up Chad. "There is a U.S. district case on the memory stick that praises modern technology in support of allowing video testimony and cross-examination. It goes through the entire history of the constitutional right to confront and cross-examine a witness and how modern technology promotes rather than diminishes such rights. Good stuff you might be able to use."

"Liz, I've saved everything under 'research: Randy-Chad' in the Wellington file. Please review it and use whatever you can." Liz turned and headed back to her computer.

"Guys, thanks. How in the world did you get any info out of the Department Twenty-eight's clerk?"

"I have my ways," answered Randy with a big smile.

"It doesn't matter. You guys are angels. Thanks."

"If you win, Hawke, you know what that means?"

"Yeah, yeah, drinks at the Tipsy Crow. And trust me they will be well worth every penny."

"Penny?" Chad said, looking at Randy.

"You're right, Chad. I would say more like dollars, forty, fifty, don't you agree?"

"Before Chad could answer, Drew spoke up. "All right, you two, out of here. I've got an all-nighter ahead."

Randy, Chad, and Drew walked to the office door, and Drew opened it. "Again, guys, thanks."

Shutting the door, Drew turned and looked at his tired employees. "Debbie, why don't you and Matt go home. Liz and I will finish up the briefs."

"Thanks, boss." Matt saved everything he was working on, turned off his computer, and stood to leave. "Boss, Liz has all the exhibits you asked me to get. My part is done. Good luck. I'll be in tomorrow after three."

Debbie was much more resistant. "I can stay, Drew. You will need me to format and print out final drafts."

"Nah. You go home. The two of us can get it done. Thank you for staying this late."

ooooo

It was 1:00 a.m. when Drew's head finally hit the pillow back at the loft. No sooner had he started to doze off when his cell phone rang. In a cloud, he instinctively reached for the phone and answered.

"Counselor, what the hell happened in court today? Everything seemed to go bonkers."

Drew, still in a daze, tried to process what was being said.

"Why did everything stop, Hawke? We got a problem?"

"Who is this?"

"Me, who else?"

"Jacob?"

"You asleep? Yes, it's me."

"I just got in. And, yes, we have a problem."

"What problem?"

"The D.A. presented evidence that Josh is you."

"That's an impossibility."

"No, it isn't. You had Joshua forge your application forms to San Diego State. They have the application, including Joshua's picture and his signature on the form. As far as the judge is concerned, Joshua is you."

"How about Josh's different-colored eyes. That's not me."

"I have no idea how the jury will think at this point."

"Counselor, get your head out of your arse. You are not a defeatist."

Drew just sat on the edge of the bed, surprised by Jacob's assessment.

"How about the Mexican and my DNA samples? What are you going to do about that?"

"I've been up all night with my staff writing motions. My associate will file three motions tomorrow morning. One, to keep out the San Diego State college application and class records; two, to declare a mistrial because of the last-minute evidence about the college records, and three, the fact I already told the jury Joshua isn't you. The third is to allow you to testify by video from Mexico."

"Good thinking."

"If the judge won't allow you to testify remotely, then I will put on the Mexican, then my DNA expert and our theory on chimera to explain the eyes. Oh, yes . . . your father and his office manager are flying in this weekend. I will put them on the stand to testify you two are twins. That's all I can do."

"How about the other two motions?"

"If the judge won't let you testify remotely, I expect her to deny the other motions."

"Joshua . . . can't he testify?"

"If I thought he could stand up to cross-examination, I would put him on. But right now I don't know. I will have to see how things go. God knows what else you two have done where you switched identities. You have such a tendency to use him for your shortcomings."

There was silence on the other end of the phone and then a loud click.

"Hello? Hello?" The line was dead. Drew rolled over and went to sleep.

CHAPTER 21

Thursday, 9:00 a.m.

"MADAM COURT REPORTER, we are now on the record in my chambers. Gentlemen, please make your appearances."

"Assistant District Attorney Jack Farrat for the People."

"Andrew Hawke for the defendant Joshua Wellington, charged in this complaint as Jacob Wellington."

All right, I wish to compliment you both on your excellent briefs. Mr. Hawke, your three briefs were exceptionally helpful from the point of view you not only stated your positions for prohibiting the admittance of the college transcripts, your request for testimony by video and, if denied, a demand for a mistrial. I say your briefs were helpful in that you not only stated your argument for each motion, but then in anticipation of Mr. Farrat's opposition to your motions, you provided logical rebuttals."

"Your Honor . . ."

"Yes, Mr. Farrat."

"I didn't have much time to attack Mr. Hawke's rebuttal arguments."

"That's understandable given the short time you had to brief everything. But let me finish, please. Mr. Hawke, your arguments are compelling and the authority cited is persuasive except for the fact the issue in this trial is which twin is Jacob Wellington. Therefore, I believe the only way to evaluate the two men, and for the trier of fact to accurately decide this case, is if both twins are here in court. With both present, the jury can see, hear, and evaluate each twin, if they really are twins, and decide the truthfulness of their testimony."

Drew bowed his head, realizing the full implication of the court's statements.

"With that said, Mr. Hawke, I deny your motion to allow testimony by video. I believe you have other means of convincing the jury of your theory. In regards to the second motion, I admit the university transcripts as I find them probative to the issue of who is Jacob Wellington. Finally, regarding your motion for a mistrial . . ." The judge paused and thought for several seconds, then said, "I also deny that motion. I believe an appellate court should have before it as much evidence as possible in order for it to consider any appeal you may make after trial. Do you have any comment, Mr. Hawke?"

"No, Your Honor. I thank you for your thoughtful consideration of my motions."

"A.D.A. Farrat?"

"No comment, judge. But I appreciate the wisdom of your decisions," responded Farrat with a broad smile to Hawke.

"Wisdom!" Judge Gonzales-Black said in a loud echoing voice. "Mr. Farrat, this is not a time to gloat. I may yet declare a mistrial if you fail to emphatically prove the defendant is Jacob Wellington. Now let us proceed with your case A.D.A. Farrat."

ooooo

With the court back in session the witness Anjou Okuda was back on the stand.

"Dr. Okuda, I have marked during our recess Exhibit Forty

the San Diego State University records you brought to court. Please tell the jury how these records are created."

"These admissions records contain the college application form which is submitted by the student. The file also contains high school academic records, SAT results, or other scholastic assessment tests, which the student had sent directly to us."

"When is the photograph taken, if you know?"

"The photograph in the file is taken by us the first day of college."

"Any way the student can provide the photograph?"

"Oh, no. Like I said, it is taken during the admission process the first day. The student shows us their driver's license—in this case a passport—which we copy for our files. A copy of Mr. Wellington's passport is on page three. We then take their photograph, which we put on their student I.D. card, give them a welcoming packet that includes the student ethics booklet, regulations for campus living, and maps of the campus. The students then go through a series of stations where they get their dorm assignment, courtesy hygiene kits, purchase their cafeteria food booklet and parking permit, just to mention a few."

"Who is the custodian of these records?"

"Technically, I am since they are kept in my department. A student file can't leave the department without my permission."

"Your Honor, I ask that Exhibit Forty be admitted into evidence."

"Exhibit Forty is so accepted, Mr. Farrat."

"One last question, Ms. Okuda. Do you see Mr. Wellington in court today?"

"Objection Your Honor. Lack of foundation. This witness has not stated she personally remembers dealing with my client. And, she testified that she is new to San Diego State University."

"That's all right, Your Honor. I withdraw the question. I have no further questions for this witness."

"Mr. Hawke, do you wish to cross-examine Dr. Okuda?"

"No, Your Honor."

"Dr. Okuda, you may step down. A.D.A. Farrat you may call your next witness."

"The People call Ms. Eve Bloch."

A young, pretty brunette, about five feet, four inches tall, entered the courtroom. All eyes followed her, with some people whispering 'was she one of the victims?' After being sworn-in, A.D.A. Farrat approached.

"Please state your name."

"I am Eve Bloch."

"Ms. Bloch, were you enrolled at San Diego State University three years ago?"

"Yes."

"Where did you live at the time you were a junior?"

"I lived in Pacific Beach in a condo facing the ocean called the Breeze Apartments."

"Did something terrible happen to you while living at the Breeze Apartments?"

"Yes. I was attacked while sleeping alone in my condo."

"When you say attacked, do you mean raped?"

"I was raped and tortured," the witness said as tears welled up.

"Do you know who raped you?"

"No. But he was later called the Sphynx rapist because of his appearance and his method of torture."

"What did he look like?"

"He was tall, young, muscular like a bodybuilder, and spoke with a surfer accent or slang."

"Anything unusual about his appearance?"

"Yes, he was metro shaved."

"What do you mean by 'metro shaved'?"

"I mean he shaved his body hair like some young college men do."

"Did he have chest, arm, leg, or pubic hair?"

"No. Not even armpit hair. He was clean shaven. I mean not a bit of body hair anywhere."

"Could you see his face?"

"No. He wore a black ski mask."

"When you say he tortured you, what do you mean?"

"After he got what he wanted from me, he washed my body in a liquid. He even washed the hair on my head."

"Was there anything unusual about the liquid he washed you with?"

"The fluid burned like fiery pin pricks all over my body. It was horrible."

"Did you try to get away?"

"Yes, but I was gagged and my hands were tied to the bed."

"Did anything happen to the hair on your head afterward?"

"Yes. It fell out in small handfuls for several weeks."

"Did he wash your private parts, and if so, how?"

The witness looked at the jury and then at the people in the gallery. She asked, "Do I have to say?"

"Please, Ms. Bloch, you may generally describe the areas."

"After washing me head to toe, he took out a large syringe and injected a fluid into my private areas."

"Private areas—you mean front and back?"

" Yes," where he had put his thing—his penis."

Members of the jury who had been taking notes stopped and looked intently at the witness, who avoided all eye contact. One elderly female juror shook her head and then wrote a few words.

"Was the fluid from the syringe also painful?"

"Oh, my God, yes. It felt cold at first. Then it was like a thousand pin pricks. But it soon became unbearable. Everything inside of me was on fire. I tried to scream, but the cloth in my mouth muffled my cries. My body jerked with pain. I seemed to levitate off the bed at times. I just didn't know what I was doing—my body was totally controlled by the pain."

"What about the rapist?"

"He just watched. I begged for him to untie my hands."

"You were gagged. How do you know he could hear you?"

"He was right next to me. He just stared at me. He never tried to help, even though I screamed for help—for him to stop it."

"Ms. Bloch, had you ever seen this man before he attacked you?"

"No."

"Did you in any way invite this man into your condo or agree to have sex with him?"

"No, I did not!"

"I have no further questions for Ms. Bloch," Farrat said as he walked back to the prosecution table.

"Mr. Hawke, you may proceed," the judge said.

"Your Honor, I have no questions for this witness. She has been through enough. Thank you, Ms. Bloch."

Farrat looked surprised and appeared to fumble around with the papers on his desk.

"Ms. Bloch, you my step down. Thank you for your testimony," the judge said.

The young woman looked at the judge. "Thank you, Your Honor."

Again, all eyes were on her as she walked toward the courtroom door, some women with tears in their eyes.

The court turned to the audience. "Ladies and gentlemen, it is that time of day for us to take our morning recess."

Joseph Castro stood. "All rise. This court is in recess for ten minutes."

CHAPTER 22

10:45 a.m., After The Morning Recess

"A.D.A. FARRAT, you may call your next witness."

"The People call Anthony MacNeal to the stand."

A man not quite six feet tall entered the courtroom dressed in a blue uniform, his hat tucked under his left arm. Physically, he looked to be in his forties, but his thinning hair, furrowed forehead, crow's feet bordering his eyes, and soft lines of his jaw implied his true older age. The patches on the shoulder of his uniform, a blazon in a blue field, read San Diego Police in gold letters. On his left breast an oval gold shield signified the same. The five stripes on his upper arm connoted his high rank, and the six gold hash marks on his lower left sleeve conveyed the appearance of a man who had served a long and dignified career. The officer stopped in the well of the court. The court clerk administered the oath and the officer took the stand.

"Officer, please state your name for the record."

"Sergeant Tony MacNeal with the San Diego Police Department."

"Sergeant MacNeal, did you have an occasion to serve a search warrant on an apartment about two years ago—an apartment occupied by a Jacob Wellington?"

"Yes, sir."

"Briefly explain how that warrant was served and for what purpose."

"We were looking for a Jacob Wellington wanted for a series of rapes along the boardwalk in the Mission Beach and Pacific Beach area. He was called by the San Diego Herald newspaper and the media the Sphynx rapist. To effect the search and arrest warrant, we set up a three-tiered perimeter. We had plainclothes officers surveilling the apartment, backed up by sharp shooters one hundred yards back. Bicycle officers patrolled the adjoining streets near the apartment and beach as they normally would but in greater number. The final tier of officers controlled all roads leading north, east, and south into and out of the beach area. These officers were part of supposed sobriety checkpoints, which stopped all traffic and engaged all vehicle occupants."

"How long, sergeant, did you keep the apartment under surveillance?"

"Five hours."

"Did Mr. Wellington show up?"

"No. So I ordered uniform officers to serve the warrant and enter the residence."

"Did you find Jacob Wellington inside?"

"No, he was not there. So we tightened the perimeters and road blocks, and started our search of the apartment."

"What did you find?"

"May I read from my police report?"

"Yes, please."

"We found large bottles of chemicals which later matched the chemicals used by the rapist to destroy his DNA. We found a box of large syringes, several rolls of blue carpet tape and a roll of thin nylon rope. The tape and nylon rope were later tested and found to match those found at the rape scenes. We found driver's licenses of the rape victims, pictures of near-ly fifty women—some of them were of the rape victims. We found several passports, some in the name of Jacob Welling-ton, others in fictitious names. Two were issued by Australia, two were from Hong Kong, and one from Thailand. In total we took 96 items from the apartment, including a computer and iPad."

"Did you find any legal contracts?"

"Yes. We found a copy of the apartment rental agreement signed by Mr. Wellington."

"Sergeant MacNeal, did you do a search for other forms of identification issued to Jacob Wellington?"

"Yes. I ran an international and domestic search for all governmental-issued identifications in the name of Jacob Wellington."

"What did you find?"

"Nothing until this morning."

"Objection. Your Honor, sidebar please," requested Hawke.

"Yes, gentlemen, please approach."

Once the court reporter was in place, Hawke spoke, "Your Honor this is again a blindside maneuver by the prosecutor. I have not been presented with any new, last-minute evidence of documents in the name of Jacob Wellington. The A.D.A. didn't even inform me this morning Sergeant MacNeal would be testifying or that he had new evidence."

"Mr. Farrat?"

"What Sergeant MacNeal is referring to is a Hawaiian driv-er's license issued to Jacob Wellington." Farrat passed the li-cense up to the judge while Hawke objected again.

"Judge, Mr. Farrat doesn't even have the courtesy to show the license to me first," Hawke said.

"Calm down, Mr. Hawke. I agree A.D.A. Farrat should have

shown the license to you, even before the sergeant took the stand, but what is done is done."

After viewing a copy of the license, she handed it to Hawke. There, emblazoned on the certified copy, in color, was he picture of his client, Joshua. "This is outrageous, Your Honor."

But before Hawke could say another word, Judge Gonzales-Black interrupted. "What is your explanation, Mr. Farrat?"

"I was as surprised as Mr. Hawke, Your Honor, when this turned up. I frankly didn't expect to find anything other than the passports we had found in the apartment raid years ago."

"When did you first learn of the license, Mr. Farrat?"

"During the recess. That's when I had the sergeant send someone over immediately with this certified copy. As you can see there is a front and back view of the license and a declaration under oath by the custodian of records for the Hawaiian Department of Motor Vehicles."

"Mr. Hawke?"

"I move to keep out such last-minute evidence," he answered and handed the copy back to the judge.

After several seconds of thought, the court stated, "A.D.A. Farrat, I find such evidence very prejudicial but that does not mean it can't come in. You may mark it next in order. The defense motion is denied. Mr. Hawke, do you wish to make another motion?"

"Yes. I move for a mistrial."

"Understood, but I deny your motion. Yes, the license is very prejudicial against your client, and indeed your entire defense, but that does not mean it can't come in. You may proceed, Mr. Farrat."

Farrat took the documents back from the judge and walked up to the witness. "Sergeant, I show you this document." He handed the papers to the witness. "Please describe for the jury what it is."

"It is a certified copy of a driver's license issued five years ago to a Jacob Wellington, which we received through our secure interstate government computer system."

"If it please the court, I move the certified copy of the Hawaiian license be marked next in order, which I believe will be Exhibit Forty-one."

"So ordered."

"Do you see a picture on that driver's license, sergeant?"

"Yes."

"Do you see that person in court today?"

"Your Honor, I object."

"So noted Mr. Hawke. Overruled."

The judge looked to the witness. "You may answer, sergeant."

"Yes. The picture on the license is that of the defendant seated at the defense table."

"Sergeant, is there a handwritten signature on that license?"

"Yes."

"Do you recognize that signature?"

"Objection, Your Honor. Lack of foundation. The sergeant has not been qualified as an expert in handwriting."

"I withdraw my question, Your Honor. Let me ask it this way. Sergeant, have you seen a signature similar to that on the Hawaiian driver's license?"

"Yes."

"Where?"

"It was on a contract for the rental of the apartment we raided."

"Officer, I show you Exhibit Thirty-two. Is that the rental contract you just described?"

"Yes."

"So you are saying the signature on the apartment rental contract in the name of Jacob Wellington is in your opinion the same as the signature on the Hawaiian license, is that correct?"

"Objection, Your Honor. The officer has not been qualified as an expert."

"I agree, Mr. Hawke, but he can give his personal opinion, which the jury may disregard if they don't agree. Sir, please answer the question."

"Yes. Both signatures in the name of Jacob Wellington appear to be the same."

"Just to be clear, sergeant. In your opinion, the signature on the rental contract appears to be the same signature on the license, the Hawaiian license with the picture of the defendant?"

"Yes, sir."

"I have no further questions, sergeant. Your witness, Mr. Hawke," A.D.A. Farrat said as he strode confidently back to his desk.

Drew stood, but the court interrupted. "Ladies and gentlemen, I am afraid that my heavy case load once again raises its ugly head." Turning to the jury, she said, "I think this would be a good time to take our lunch recess."

"All rise. This court is in recess until one-thirty p.m.," echoed Deputy Castro.

CHAPTER 23

Court Resumed

DREW HAWKE WAS SITTING at the defense table with his client and his chief investigator Pat Deluca. Liz was seated in the first row of the gallery behind Drew with notepad and pen in hand. Sergeant MacNeal was just seating himself on the witness stand when Judge Gonzales-Black entered the court and sat down.

"Mr. Hawke, do you wish to cross-examine the witness?"

Drew rose. "No, Your Honor. He may be excused but subject to recall by the defense."

"Sergeant MacNeal, you may step down, but please be available by phone in case either party wishes to recall you."

"Yes, Your Honor."

"A.D.A. Farrat, you may call your next witness."

"At this time, I move into evidence all previously mar ked prosecution exhibits."

"Any objection, Mr. Hawke?"

"No, Your Honor, except I respectfully restate my objections to Exhibits Forty and Forty-one, and move to strike all testimony given regarding those exhibits."

"Your objections are so noted and your motion to strike is denied."

"Your honor, the prosecution rests," stated A.D.A. Farrat and he sat down.

"Mr. Hawke, do you wish to proceed at this time with the defense's case?"

"Yes, Your Honor."

"Then call your first witness."

"The defense calls James Wellington to the stand."

All heads turned as Deputy Sheriff Castro opened the courtroom door and summoned James Wellington. In walked a six-foot-tall elderly man with thinning gray hair dressed in a business suit. His gait was slow and noticeably hesitant as he leaned on a wooden walking cane. He paused to look at Joshua seated at the defense table, and then turned to face the court clerk.

"Your Honor, Mr. Wellington, as is the Australian tradition, asks that he use a bible when he takes the oath."

"Very well," replied the judge.

Drew picked up a bible from the defense table and held it as the man raised his right hand, placing the other on the book of scriptures.

"Do you swear or affirm the evidence you will give today will be the truth, the whole truth, and nothing but the truth?"

"I swear to almighty God that I will tell the truth." Mr. Wellington then turned and, with some difficulty, stepped up onto the elevated witness stand.

Drew approached. "Mr. Wellington, are you comfortable?"

Breathing with some difficulty, the witness answered, "Yes, Mr. Hawke, I am fine." Hawke walked closer the witness, stopping about 10 feet from Mr. Wellington so he could observe the jury during questioning.

"Please state your name for the court reporter seated to your left."

The witness leaned forward, looking at the court reporter. "My name is James Wellington."

"Where do you live, Mr. Wellington?"

"I live in Port Hedland, Australia."

"Where is Port Hedland located?"

"It is on the northwestern side of Australia in the state of Western Australia."

"What is your occupation, Mr. Wellington?"

"I own a mining, ore trucking and shipping company in Hedland."

"Mr. Wellington, do you have any children?"

"Yes. I was blessed with twin boys."

"What are their names?"

" Jacob and Joshua Wellington."

"Do you see either of your sons in court today?"

"Yes, Joshua. He is seated at the table to your right. Hello, son." Joshua nodded and smiled in response to his father. As Drew scanned the jury. They appeared to take in the warm greetings between father and son.

"Sir, do you know where your other son is—Jacob Wellington?"

"No. I haven't seen Jacob since he was fifteen-years-old."

"Why is that?"

"Jacob and Joshua had some difficulty at the private high school I sent them to in Hong Kong. Thereafter, Jacob asked to join a monastery in Thailand. He has never come home since."

"Have you tried to visit your son at the monastery?"

"Yes, numerous times. But on each visit he refused to see me."

"Why is that?"

"While the boys were at the high school, two seniors attacked Joshua late one night and, according to Joshua, Jacob came to his defense and beat the three boys up. The school kicked both of my sons out because of what Jacob did to the seniors."

"Isn't it true the school told you that Jacob not only beat the boys up but he also raped one of them?" As he finished his question, Drew observed the jury once again put down their pencils and pads, and appeared attentive to each question and the answers that followed.

With hesitancy the father answered, "Yes."

"Did you discipline any of your sons for what happened?"

"Yes. I punished Jacob for his despicable act."

"You mean you beat him with a four-inch-wide work belt."

"Yes," Mr. Wellington answered more assertively.

"Until his back and butt bled raw. Is that correct, sir?"

"Yes. I did not want him to ever do that again."

"Is this why Jacob has not seen you ever again?"

"Yes. At least that is what Joshua told me."

"Do you employ either of your sons in your business?"

"Yes. Joshua is president of my company."

"When did he become president?"

"My heart is failing, and I have given him the reins while I advise him on his decisions. He has done a good job," the proud-looking father said while looking at his son.

"What about Jacob?"

"He refuses to have anything to do with me or my company."

"Do you know if he works or how he makes a living?"

"No. But after Jacob went to the monastery, Joshua pleaded with me to set up a trust for his twin brother. I agreed. It made sense since I had to somehow pay for Jacob's time with the monks."

"When did you start the trust?"

"The trust went into effect when Jacob refused to see me or come home."

"Have you tried to follow his whereabouts?"

"Yes. I track what he is doing through the money he spends out of the trust. Every day I check to see where he is."

"Do you do that to see how much he is spending?"

"No. I gave him a very large trust. I will never let him go without money. I follow his whereabouts to see that he is all right."

"Do you know what your son does with the money?"

"He has spent the money while studying at the monastery and at various universities. He also appears to be an avid surfer because I see many of his purchases are about surfboards and surfing."

"Do you approve of his expenditures?"

"I am very proud of how he has managed his money. I just wish he would come home."

"Do you know if Jacob has committed any criminal acts?"

"No, I don't. But I wouldn't be surprised."

"Why is that?"

"He was always a very free-spirited young man, at times very confused and confrontational, at least in my opinion."

"Why do you have that opinion?"

"He blames me for his mother running off and leaving the three of us when the boys were six-years-old."

"Do either of the boys have any deep psychological problems because their mother left them?"

"Joshua responded well to counseling and accepted the fact he had to grow up without his mother. Jacob continues to resent me and his mother. According to psychiatrists I sent the boys to, Jacob has deep-seated emotional problems toward women, especially if they look or act like his mother, whom he believes was a whore who ran off with another man."

"Your Honor, I object. Hearsay," Farrat said as he rose to

make a speaking objection. However, the court silenced him. "No, Mr. Farrat. I want to hear this. Please sit down."

"Has Jacob ever hurt any woman?"

"Not that I know. But again, we haven't talked since he was fifteen years old."

"Has Joshua ever hurt or sexually acted improperly toward a woman?"

"He is not that way. Josh is a God-fearing young Christian," answered the father as he smiled at his son

"Sir, how a son and a woman interact is a personal thing that many parents never know about. So how do you know Joshua would never harm a woman?"

"He and I talk about the ladies he dates all the time. He brings them home for dinner and includes me in their dating lives whenever possible. He is a good boy who enjoys female company and always talks well about his dates. I have never seen Josh angry or upset with a woman. Most of his young ladies really adore him."

"Do you know if Joshua ever traveled to the United States?"

"Yes. He traveled with me to MIT to view the campus when Joshua was trying to decide where he would go to college."

"Did Jacob also visit MIT?"

"Not with me. Josh later told me he and Jacob met up while we were there and Josh took Jacob on a tour of the campus."

"Where did the boys go to college?"

"Josh studied and graduated from Oxford in England. Jacob has attended several universities, but to my knowledge he has never graduated."

"Did Joshua visit the United States after the MIT visit?"

"He went to Hawaii for a month after he graduated from college. That was about four or five years ago. I then asked him to attend a mining and mineral conference in Chicago, but he

DONALD E. MCINNIS

never got to the conference. He was arrested upon landing in San Diego, and that is why I am here."

"Do you know if Joshua met Jacob while he was in Hawaii?"

"I wouldn't be surprised. The boys have always been close. I know Josh always talks to Jacob, and I assume they meet from time to time."

"How do you know that?"

"When I ask how Jacob is doing, Josh always assures me Jacob is OK and not to worry."

"How do you know they meet?"

"When Josh travels for the company, I see that Jacob uses his trust money to either buy an airplane ticket to the same location or he has hotel bills at the same hotel as Josh."

"Mr. Wellington, are you sure Joshua has only been to the U.S. three times: the time he visited MIT, when he went to Hawaii, and his recent trip to San Diego on his way to Chicago?"

"Yes. I have always reviewed all expenses by both boys. Josh uses the company business card for everything. I taught Josh to charge everything to the company, even his personal expenses. My accountant, who is outside waiting to testify, would then separate personal from company expenses."

"Mr. Wellington, it is not unusual for a father to protect his child, even an estranged son. Are you lying now about Joshua in order to protect him? Is what you have said today the truth?"

"What I have said is the truth. To lie to protect even a loved one will bring only disgrace upon those who lie, but worse harm to the person one lies for. I swore to God to tell the truth and I have done that."

"I have no further questions. Thank you, Mr. Wellington."

"Your witness, Mr. Farrat," instructed the judge.

As Drew walked back to his desk, he observed out of the

- 201 -

corner of his eye members of the jury busy making notes. *I think the father was believable. I hope he stands up under cross.*

Farrat began his cross-examination. "Mr. Wellington, defense attorney Hawke asked you an interesting question. Would you, the father, lie to protect your son? Why wouldn't you shade the truth in order to keep the son you love from going to jail?"

"If I understand what this trial is about, you have charged Josh with crimes committed by Jacob. I have told you enough about Jacob to ensure that he is sentenced harshly. I swore to tell the truth and I have."

"So you wouldn't lie to protect the son you love, the president of your company, but the bad son, the one who disowned you at age fifteen, you would throw him under the bus."

A murmur went up in the gallery. Drew looked to the jury. All twelve jurors were intently watching the witness, waiting for the answer.

"Mr. prosecutor . . . "

"My name is Assistant District Attorney Jack Farrat."

"Mr. Farrat, no man will sacrifice a son, even for another son."

"But yet as a loving father you sent the two boys away to boarding schools. At what age, Mr. Wellington, did they leave?"

Mr. Wellington's face reddened but he calmly replied. "Port Hedland, Mr. prosecutor, excuse me . . . Mr. Farrat . . . is a very small town. Everyone knew about . . ."

Farrat, seeking blood, interrupted. "Too small, sir, to have an elementary or high school?"

"Too small, Mr. Farrat," the Australian's right hand noticeably shaking, "to shield my sons from their mother going to bars where miners go to pick up women for the night; too small to shield them from stories of her late-night carousing; too small to shield the boys from town rumors calling their mother a whore. A town where families refused to let their daughters and sons play with my boys. That is why I sent them away to boarding schools. Even to Hong Kong, where I couldn't see them for nearly a year at a time. That's why, at age ten, they went away, Mr. prosecutor!"

"So, you wouldn't subscribe to the murder of Able by Cain?"

"Sir! I don't know what you mean by that. But I am not God." James Wellington's voice quivered in anger. "And I have not favored one son over another as God favored the offerings of Abel over Cain's. Nor do I believe that one of my sons would ever do anything to harm the other. What I have said is the truth, Mr. Farrat."

Holy shit, Mr. Wellington, thought Drew. *Ha! 'Tis the sport to have the engineer hoist with his own petard.* Hawke looked to the jury and observed them all writing feverishly what he surmised was their judgment on the father's testimony.

But Farrat persisted with a note of disbelief, if not anger, in his voice. "Mr. Wellington, why did you establish a trust fund for Jacob?"

Seeming to calm down, the father responded, "After he refused to see me, I had to do something for the boy. He had obviously chosen to make his own way, and I didn't want him to lack any money in whatever endeavor he chose."

"Even if that endeavor, Mr. Wellington, were a life of crime, depravation, and the destruction of women's lives?" snapped Farrat.

The prosecutor's words seemed to shock Mr. Wellington. After a pause, "Mr. prosecutor, I know not what Jacob has done. I only know of your accusations."

"There, sir, sits Jacob Wellington, your son," Farrat said,

pointing to the defense table. "A man you have lied to this court about by saying he is Joshua when the evidence says he is Jacob."

With that the witness broke down and began to sob. Suddenly, he grabbed his chest and screamed.

"Dad," yelled Joshua as he started to go to his father, but was restrained from behind by a deputy who immediately cuffed the young man and moved him out of the courtroom as he screamed to let him go to his father.

Drew was already on his feet and rushed to the witness, who appeared to be unconscious, his body twisted between his chair and the railing of the witness stand.

"Quiet, please," yelled the judge as she pounded her gavel. "Deputies, call for medical assistance."

Drew and Deputy Castro pulled him from the witness box and laid him out on the floor. Joseph pounded his fist twice upon the chest of the witness and began chest compressions while Drew started to breathe into the man's mouth.

Turning to the jury, the judge ordered, "Please exit the jury box to your right; walk calmly to the far door on my left. The deputy at the door will take you to the jury room. Ladies and gentlemen, this court is adjourned. Cameras please terminate filming." Two more deputies entered and the judge directed them to remove the gallery from the room. Almost simultaneously two more deputies came from the hallway behind the bench with medical equipment. They took over the CPR and administered a defibrillator shock to Mr. Wellington's chest. They then administered a higher voltage and watched the monitor for a pulse.

"We got a pulse," yelled one of the two deputies. "We got a weak pulse but it is holding."

Shortly thereafter, two ambulance personnel entered and

took over. Three firemen followed with a gurney. The judge stood to the side, observing the heroic efforts to save the man.

Farrat, who had been standing by the jury box watching what was happening, looked up as Drew Hawke, with his fists at his side stepped aggressively toward Farrat.

Joseph Castro rushed between the two, but Drew pushed forward against the outstretched arms of the deputy. "No, Drew, it's not worth it." Finally another deputy pulled Drew back.

"Gentlemen," ordered the judge in a loud voice, "court is adjourned for the day. I want you two in my chambers tomorrow at 9:00 a.m. Do you hear me?"

Both attorneys answered yes. But Deputy Castro walked Drew over to the table, helped the still-tense defense attorney gather up his files, and escorted the him, Pat DeLuca, and Liz into the corridor, down the escalator, and to the street.

ooooo

As Drew, Pat, and Liz walked into the office, Debbie was on the phone. She immediately hung up and asked, "That nasty Farrat fella, did he kill Mr. Wellington?"

"I don't know, Debbie," Hawke answered. "I'm going to the hospital in a few minutes. He was weak but stable when they took him from court. How did you find out about what happened?"

"The Department Twenty-eight's court clerk called me."

"Oh, yes. I keep forgetting you used to work in the court clerk's office."

"This is a cursed case Andrew Jackson Hawke. A cursed case."

"It definitely has an odor of death to it, Debbie. Liz, thank you for helping. You can go home now. Debbie, please call the hospitals and find out which one they took Mr. Wellington to. Pat, let's talk."

In Hawke's office, the two sat down. "Pat, how do you think we've done so far?"

"You dismantled Margret Lange and Eve Bloch didn't hurt you. The victims just made the jury angry at the Sphynx rapist. Dr. Brown you shot down. But we were hurt by Dr. Okuda and Sergeant MacNeal. I think the jury now believes Joshua is Jacob. The father didn't help on that issue because the jury could believe he suffered a heart attack because Farrat called him out for lying about our client not being Jacob. So that's how I see things."

"I agree, Pat. But I will still put on the Aussie account, and then Dr. Rougtbeck to explain why Joshua has different-colored eyes. I don't see any other options. Once Farrat sprung the college records and Hawaiian driver's license on us, we were doomed. This chimera two-colored eye thing was always a risky defense from the beginning. Farrat just did an end run around it by offering new evidence Joshua is Jacob. Now I don't see any other option but to play out our hand as planned and hope for the best."

CHAPTER 24

Chambers, Friday, 9:00 a.m.

JUDGE SONJA GONZALES-BLACK sat erect in her chair, hands resting on the desk but tightly clasped as Deputy Joseph Castro escorted in Drew Hawke and A.D.A. Jack Farrat.

"Sit, gentlemen," she commanded as she gestured with her right hand to the two chairs in front of her desk. "Joseph, you may leave and close the door."

"Yes, ma'am."

Once the door was shut, the judge began. "Mr. Hawke, no matter how horrible the provocations may be, you *will* control your temper, in court and in public, for that matter." Her voice rose as if she were an army drill sergeant dressing down an errant recruit.

"As a lawyer you must adhere to a higher standard of conduct. Ours is a profession of reason and deliberation. Without lawyers, we have no justice. Once you follow your emotions, Mr. Hawke, you become judge, jury and executioner—a state of one. For two-hundred and forty-plus years this nation has fought to make it 'We the People' not a king or select group who rule as one."

"Yes, ma'am."

"Don't 'yes, ma'am' me," retorted the judge. "I am fed up with your inability to control your temper. I have half a mind to send a transcript of these proceedings to the California Supreme Court and recommend censure for your conduct."

Drew sat quietly looking at Judge Gonzales-Black, who was obviously at wits end with his conduct. Then she turned on Jack Farrat. "And you, Mr. Assistant District Attorney, your cross-examination of the witness James Wellington was abhorrent, frankly, to the point of inhumane. I would sanction you right now for your conduct but for the fact you have a right to aggressively cross-examine a witness, even one who was obviously sick with an ailing heart. Morally, I think you stepped over the line A.D.A. Farrat. Sir, don't do that again in my court. There are other ways of accomplishing your objectives without killing a witness."

Farrat started to say something but bit his tongue.

"Why do you two provoke such animosity within each other?" she said, shaking her head.

Hawke kept his thoughts to himself. *No way am I going to step into that one. Let Farrat open his damn trap—and reap the fury of the judge.*

After a minute of the judge looking at the two attorneys, the tension in her face began to relax somewhat. Slowly her entire demeanor seemed to ease.

"Gentlemen, do you remember Shakespeare's famous line in King Henry VI? The one where the scoundrel Dick the Butcher and the political rebel Cade are plotting to overthrow the state? 'First we'll kill all the lawyers.' Even in 1450, lawyers defended citizens against oppression, evil, and corruption. Simply put, we are the back bone of freedom. You, Jack Farrat, as prosecutor must prosecute all that is evil while never losing sight of the good in humanity. Jack, not all witnesses who come to the defense of a defendant are evil. I am very disappointed in you."

Turning to Drew, she said, "Hawke, what is the word on Mr. Wellington?"

"He is stable and resting well. The cardiologist early this

morning told me Mr. Wellington should change the heart medication prescribed by the Australian doctors. Once Mr. Wellington, wakes up the doctor will discuss this with him."

"Will he be able to continue testifying?"

"Judge, I have no further questions for my witness. You should ask Mr. Farrat if he would like Mr. Wellington back on the stand."

"Mr. Farrat?"

"Judge, I too am satisfied with the witness's testimony. Any further questioning by me would likely create more sympathy for the witness and cause the jurors to lose sight of my cross-examination's purpose."

"In that case, gentlemen, I propose I inform the jury that Mr. Wellington is convalescing in the hospital and you will not require him to testify further."

"Judge, couldn't we change the last part of your proposed statement and say 'Both attorneys agree they are satisfied with the testimony of Mr. Wellington and will not require him to testify further?' " Farrat asked.

"Mr. Hawke?"

"If such language would make Mr. Farrat look better, then I agree."

"Judge, I don't need to . . ."

Judge Gonzales-Black cut Farrat short. "Then we are agreed. I will use your suggested language, Mr. Farrat. Now about the trial, I told the jurors Thursday before they went home that because of the medical emergency we would not resume today. The trial will resume Monday. It is my desire to finish testimony by Monday afternoon or Tuesday at the latest. So, Mr. Hawke, have your witnesses lined up and ready to go. That includes your rebuttal witnesses, Mr. Farrat, if you intend to have any."

The two lawyers rose to leave, but the judge had one final admonition. "And gentlemen, remember, winning at all cost isn't everything. Doing the right thing is."

"Yes, Your honor," the two chastised attorneys answered in unison.

Drew got up and walked out into the hallway connecting all the judges' chambers only to be greeted by Joseph Castro.

"How did it go, Drew," asked the deputy sheriff. Before Drew could answer, the deputy directed Drew into the courtroom, where Pat DeLuca was waiting.

"A.D.A. Farrat will be escorted by another deputy to his office upstairs. The judge wanted me to tell you no more temper tantrums or it's off to jail. I believe she means it, Drew."

"I got the message loud and clear just a moment ago, Joe. Don't worry, the emotions of the moment got to me yesterday. It won't happen again." The two men shook hands and Pat and Drew walked out of the courtroom.

CHAPTER 25

Friday Evening At The Loft

DREW SAT IN THE DARK, looking out the large loft window into a luminescent night lit by the nearby high-rise condominiums and apartments. The judge's dressing down had been more cutting than he let on while walking out of the courthouse with his trusted investigator. Drew had brushed off what the judge had to say whenever Pat asked. But it still rankled.

My willingness to resort to fisticuffs is indeed a shortcoming. I have resorted too often to my cage fighting experience when I should be using my mind. But Farrat is such a weasel and an easy prey. I would love to rearrange his nose. Yet, the judge's words echoed in his mind. He mused a bit longer. Then he spoke out loud, "Maybe my fighting days are over?"

The deep self-reflection was interrupted by the vibration of his cell phone. The screen read "unknown," as had his previous late-night calls from his nemesis.

He sighed and answered. "Hello, Jacob."

Correct. Not one of your whores. How's the old man?"

"You know, Jacob, I try every day to find some redeeming quality about you but I fail every time."

"I love your humor, counselor. But how is he?"

"The doctors think he will live. I don't know. He looks really frail."

"I will say this about him Hawke—he did try to save his favorite son."

"You watched on TV?"

"Yes."

"Then you should have seen that he loves you both. It's time to put your long-standing grudge aside and wake up to the fact that he misses you and would love to see you."

"I didn't hire you for family counseling, Hawke. I hired you to save my brother. And it doesn't look that good. What are you going to do to turn things around? The old man was a flop."

"I told you dozens of times the issue is still the same. I've got to prove somehow that Joshua isn't you. Farrat has torpedoed every effort I've made on that point. The only thing I have left is your dad's business accountant and my biogeneticist.""Can't you put my father back on the stand and undue his poor performance?"

"And kill him?"

There was a long silence before Jacob answered. "Then what are you going to do?"

"Try my best, Jacob. My best defense witness refuses to cooperate."

There was another pause, then Jacob spoke in a slow and very strong voice. "Counselor, I told you before I'm not going to surrender myself. I'm not going to do it. Dude, live with the cards you've been dealt. Quit crying you may lose. Your ego isn't everything. Just do what you do so well. After that you and I will have to live with the bloody consequences. I know you, Hawke. I've known you since our time with the monks. You're one of those guys who will not stop trying even when it's a lost cause."

"Tell me, Jacob, is it Joshua you're trying to save or an

opportunity for you to seize the company your infirmed father would never let you have? After all, we both know Joshua will do whatever you say."

"You know, Hawke, sometimes you are too smart for your own good." After which the phone went dead.

You conniving S.O.B. Time does reveal the truth. You are exactly who and what I thought you were.

CHAPTER 26

Monday, 9:00 a.m.

ONCE AGAIN DEPARTMENT 28 was jammed. The local Sunday morning talk show had been full of debates over the trial's events of the last week, especially the collapse of James Wellington while on the stand.

Reporters had tried to interview the hospital medical staff on Wellington's condition, but the doctors refused to comment. One reporter tried to enter the sick man's hospital room only to be escorted out of the hospital with threats of arrest. Even the San Diego Herald newspaper had an editorial on the case, speculating as to whether this second Sphynx trial would be the end of Andrew Hawke's miraculous string of victories.

"All rise. Department 28 is now in session, the Honorable Sonja Gonzales-Black presiding."

"Good morning, ladies and gentlemen," the judge said, then turn to the jury. "Please note, the parties have stipulated they are satisfied with the testimony of witness James Wellington and there is no need for him to return. He is therefore excused. Mr. Hawke, please call your next witness."

"The defense calls Cadel Campbell to the stand."

In walked a stout man in his fifties, dressed in a dark tan suit, brown and green flowered tie, and white shirt, pulling what looked to be a wheeled airline suitcase with a long handle. After being sworn in he took the stand.

"Please state your name for the record."

"I am Cadel Campbell. Cadel is spelled C-a-d-e-l."

"Mr. Campbell, where do you work?"

"I am the Certified Practicing Account for Wellington Ore and Mining Pty."

"Who owns Wellington Ore and Mining?"

"W.O.&M. is a privately owned company. James Wellington is the owner."

"Who is the president of Wellington Ore and Mining?"

Looking to the defense table, he said, "Mr. Joshua Wellington, the gentlemen seated to my left."

"Your Honor, may the record reflect that the witness has identified my client by the name of Joshua Wellington."

"The record may so reflect."

"Mr. Campbell, has Joshua Wellington gone by any other name?"

"Why, no. His given name is Joshua Wellington."

"To your knowledge has Joshua ever used the name Jacob Wellington?"

"No, sir. Jacob Wellington is the twin brother of Josh."

"Mr. Campbell, did James Wellington ask you to bring any business records with you and if so what are they?"

"He did. They are the company financial records for the past five years showing all the business and personal expenditures incurred by Josh Wellington."

"Are Joshua's personal expenses kept separate from W.O.&M.'s business expenses?"

"You are correct. All of Joshua's expenditures are kept separate."

"Who told you to keep Joshua's expenses separate?"

"Since Josh returned from Oxford, he has worked for his father. James Wellington instructed me to keep all expenditures by the young man separate."

"Does Joshua receive a salary?"

"Not really. He has several company charge cards and unlimited access to the company petty cash for any of his financial needs. He need only provide receipts for any personal cash purchases or personal charges on the company cards."

`"Do you track and account for all cash used by Joshua?"

"Yes, sir. He must provide receipts or state what the money was used for in order for him to continue to draw money from petty cash. Anything over one hundred dollars must be paid with a company charge cards."

"Why did his father have such a financial relationship with his son, if you know?"

"I asked Mr. Wellington that same question several times over the years, since the system required extensive accounting procedures. His answer was always the same: 'I love my son, and I want him to learn to manage money. Giving him unlimited access to money allows me to see how well he does.' "

"Is that the only reason?"

"No. I know for a fact the money Josh spends allows Mr. Wellington to know exactly how Josh lives and what he spends his money on."

"Seems rather controlling?"

"Actually, Mr. Wellington is quite a generous father. I have never once seen him criticize the life styles of either of his two sons."

"Did Mr. Wellington do the same for Jacob Wellington, his other son?"

"Jacob has no access to petty cash or the company charge cards. Mr. Wellington tracks the whereabouts and activity of Jacob another way."

"How so?"

"When Jacob was fifteen, he wanted to live with Buddhists

in Thailand. Mr. Wellington agreed. Josh pleaded with his father to set up a trust fund for Jacob in order to pay for Jacob's needs at the monastery. When Jacob turned eighteen, the trust was turned over to young Jacob to run. Once Jacob had control, Josh again intervened and convinced his father to continue to fund Jacob's trust."

"How much is in the trust and who controls it?"

"Initially, it was one million U.S. dollars—two hundred and fifty in cash and seven hundred and fifty thousand in W.O.&M. private stock. Over the years that stock has split several times, and Mr. Wellington has added more company stock to the trust. It is now worth over three million U.S. dollars."

"So only Jacob decides how the trust money is spent?"

"Since he turned eighteen, Jacob Wellington owns and has total control. However, an Australian law firm administers the trust for tax purposes as required by the terms of the trust."

"Does James Wellington track Jacob's whereabouts and his financial activity through the trust attorneys?"

"Yes, sir. Since Mr. Wellington and Jacob had a falling out, James has tracked Jacob's life through the trust."

"In regards to my client, does Joshua have any sources of income outside of W.O.&M.?"

"The boy has no other access to money but through the company. It is an unlimited access, so why would Joshua have a need for another income?"

"The suitcase you brought to court . . . does it contain Joshua Wellington's financial records?"

"Yes."

"Are these records kept by you in the normal course of your employment with W.O.&M.?"

"Yes, Mr. Hawke."

"Would that be Exhibit Twenty-two?" the judge asked her clerk.

"That is correct, Your Honor," replied the clerk.

"Do you attest, Mr. Campbell, the method of keeping of these records is done in the normal course of your employment with the company and to your knowledge such records are true and correct?" asked the judge.

"Yes, ma-am. I created those records. They are exactly accurate down to the penny. I constantly review those records, and they are kept by me as part of my job at W.O.&M."

"Your Honor, I provided a duplicate copy of those records to the prosecution before this trial began, and I have a copy which I wish to now move into evidence. It should be noted that a summary sheet accompanies each month of the five years of records. These summaries are attached to the records as Appendix A. Is that correct, Mr. Campbell?"

"Yes, sir."

"A.D.A. Farrat, do you have any objections?" inquired the judge.

"No, Your Honor."

"Then Exhibit Twenty-two, the business records of W.O&M., are received into evidence."

"Mr. Campbell, did I ask you to provide a special accounting of Joshua's expenditures and whereabouts on certain days over the last five years?"

"Yes, sir. That summary is also attached to the records as an appendix. It is marked as Appendix B."

"Did I tell you what those dates were about?"

"No, sir. You just said to be accurate in all the details and that I was to show where, excuse me, show the locations where Josh spent money during a period of one month before and one month after each date."

"Does Appendix B show Joshua Wellington traveling outside of Australia on any of those dates?"

"On the dates you gave me, all of Josh's expenditures were in Australia except for two time periods. One occurred while Josh was signing contracts in Shanghai for the sale of our ore and other precious metals to a Chinese government company. The other was when he flew to Tokyo for the signing of a port contract for the receiving of our ore shipments and container ships. In each case, Josh returned on or slightly after those two dates."

"Your Honor, I proffer that the five dates I asked Mr. Campbell to research are the dates during which the Sphynx raped five women here in San Diego. I'm sure A.D.A. Farrat will so stipulate."

"Your Honor, I've reviewed Mr. Campbell's work and I agree the dates Mr. Hawke provided are when the rapes occurred here in San Diego," Farrat acknowledged.

"Thank you, A.D.A. Farrat. You may proceed, Mr. Hawke."

"Your Honor, I ask the charts with their supporting documents showing those five rape dates and where my client was at the time be shown to the jury through the court video system. Deputy Castro has a computer memory stick which contains the five charts with supporting documents for each of the dates the Sphynx attacked a San Diego victim."

"Very well. Joseph, please publish to the jury the charts." The deputy lowered the motorized screen, turned down the lights, and brought up the first chart for viewing by the jury, gallery, and TV cameras.

"Mr. Campbell, will you please explain to the jury what each chart shows and how you were able to track the whereabouts of my client on those days the Sphynx attacked women."

The witness went through all five dates of each rape, explaining where Joshua was at the time. Mr. Campbell explained how each chart showed what Joshua used the company credit cards for. The charts showed charges for gas receipts, lunch receipts, bar receipts, hotel statements, airplane tickets, cab charges or Uber fare receipts for a one-month period before and after each date of a rape. And, finally, the witness showed Joshua's cell-phone statements and the phone call locations corresponded to all the expense receipts' dates, thus confirming where Joshua was on the dates in question.

"Mr. Campbell, are you sure to a professional accountancy certainty that Joshua was in the locations you have charted out for the jury?"

"Yes, sir. There are just too many financial documents cross referencing his activities and matching his whereabouts on the dates of the rapes. This is especially true for his airplane flights both within Australia and out of the country."

"Do you have personal knowledge when Joshua was out of the country doing company business to China and Japan?"

"Yes, sir. I was the one who made his airplane and hotel reservations. In addition, I provided him with copies of the agreed-upon business contracts, supporting business records, and other information necessary for those meetings. I also talked to him by phone about the progress of each meeting while he was in China and in Japan. The Shanghai meeting was protracted as the Chinese wanted additional language changes to the contracts which Mr. Wellington and I worked on by phone and Zoom with Josh. Finally, I was the one who took him to the airport and picked him up on his return."

"Thank you, Mr. Campbell." As Drew walked back to the defense table, he turned to the prosecutor and said, "Your witness, Mr. Farrat."

Before Farrat could commence his cross-examination, the court interrupted. "Ladies and gentlemen, I need to return a call to the Presiding Judge regarding a scheduling problem. We will take a fifteen minute recess. My apologies."

As the judge rose from the bench, Joseph Castro stood and announced, 'This court is in recess."

"Deputy, may I have a word with my attorney?" Joshua asked.

"Absolutely, Mr. Wellington."

"Sir, how is my father," Joshua asked Hawke.

"Like I said earlier this morning, his doctors think he will recover. I haven't had any further updates. Look, Joshua, have you thought of anything else I should know about you and Jacob? We can't have any more surprises. For instance, are there any other travels outside of Australia you want to tell me about?"

"No, sir."

"OK. Go with the deputies, and don't forget to use the restroom."

Drew, Liz, and Pat did their normal walk down the hall, discussing how the testimony went. Liz felt positive. But Drew was leery of Farrat's coming cross. "Liz, depending on how much damage Farrat does to the accountant, I may have to put Joshua on the stand. I know the jury wants to hear from him."

"That could be risky, Drew," she replied.

Pat spoke up. "You'd better thoroughly prep the young man. Especially why he and Jacob have always swapped identities."

"Yes, I know. Depending on how much impeachment material Farrat has, it could be a disaster if Joshua crumbles under pressure."

CHAPTER 27

Court Resumed

THE JUDGE TOOK THE BENCH and looked toward the prosecution table. "A.D.A. Farrat, you may proceed with your questioning of Mr. Campbell."

Farrat rose from his seat and walked toward the witness. In his right hand he held a small folder.

"Mr. Campbell, how long have you worked for Wellington Ore and Mining?"

"Forty years. I started as a clerk in the Port Hedland office and once graduating from college with a business degree I worked in the accounting department. I now run that department," the witness said with a seeming air of pride.

"You are now a CPA?"

"In Australia I am referred to as a Certified Practicing Accountant. The certification is similar to the American Certified Public Account designation or CPA. But, Australia has certain requirements that American CPAs must adhere to before they can be certified by the Australian government."

"Would it be fair to say you have known the two Wellington boys since they were born?"

"Yes, sir."

"When was the last time you saw Jacob Wellington?"

"Oh, dear . . . when he left at fifteen to Thailand."

"You haven't seen him since?"

"This is true."

"Then you wouldn't know what his signature looks like?"

"W-e-l-l, that is not true," the witness said somewhat hesitantly.

Drew leaned over to Pat and said, "Hold your breath, Pat. Here he goes. Farrat is going for the jugular."

"If you haven't seen the man since he was fifteen, how could you know the manner in which he signs his name?"

"When I do my monthly reconciliation of the company books I review and create a separate report based on the trust law firm's monthly accounting sent to me. The law firm's reports show all disbursements and expenditures by Jacob. Amongst those documents are receipts signed by Jacob backing up all major expenditures. As requested by Mr. Wellington, I take those numbers and put them into various categories which tell Mr. Wellington where Jacob is living, locations of where he is spending the money, and what he spent the money on."

"But you have never gone to where this Jacob Wellington is living and seen or talked to him?"

"You are correct."

"Neither has the father, James Wellington?"

"Correct, except when the boy first got to Thailand. Mr. Wellington went to visit Jacob, but when they met the boy told his father to never come back. Since then the two haven't even talked."

"And of course you are familiar with the other son's signature, the man you call Joshua Wellington?"

"That is true."

"Do the two men have similar signatures?"

"Oh, no! Jacob's signature is bolder, more slanted, with a

somewhat, how should I say . . . with a flare, especially the first letters of his given name and his surname."

"Let me show you a copy of one of Joshua's signature." Farrat approached the witness, pulling from the folder he was carrying a sheet of paper with a signature written on it. "Does that signature look familiar?"

"Yes, it does. That is Josh Wellington's signature."

"Mr. Campbell, are you sure?"

"Of course. I've seen it a thousand times."

What is Farrat up to, thought Drew.

"I ask the copy of Joshua's signature I just handed to the witness be identified as People's Exhibit next in order. That should be Exhibit Forty-three."

"It is so ordered," the judge replied.

"Mr. Campbell, let me hand you five pages of signatures. The first page is the one you just said was Joshua's signature, Exhibit Forty-three. The only difference is this new page shows the charge-card receipt the signature came from. The other four pages show various charge-card receipts: a hotel registration in Tokyo, two lunch receipts in Shanghai, and one for a dance club in Tokyo. Do they look familiar?"

"Yes. These are copies from the records I brought to court."

"Your Honor, I ask that these five pages be marked Exhibit Forty-four, A, B, C, D and E."

"They may be so marked."

"Now, let me show you a copy of a signature purported to be that of a Jacob Wellington. Is that the signature of Jacob?"

The witness examined the signature for the longest time, then looked up. "No, that is not the signature of Jacob Wellington."

"Why is that?"

"The signature isn't slanted like Jacob writes. It has a smaller stature and the first letters of the given name and surname aren't large."

"I ask the court to mark as Exhibit Forty-five the signature purported to be of a Jacob Wellington, which the witness says is not by the Jacob Wellington he knows."

"So ordered."

"Mr. Campbell, please compare the signature in Exhibit Forty-five which you say is not that of Jacob Wellington to the five pages of Joshua's charge card signatures in Exhibit Forty-four."

After a few seconds the witness looked up with a somewhat confused expression.

"Mr. Campbell, doesn't the fake signature of Jacob Wellington, in Exhibit Forty-five, look like the five signatures of Joshua Wellington in Exhibit Forty-four?"

After another look at the signatures, the witness answered, "The five signatures appear to be similar to the handwriting style of Josh but I am not a graphologist."

"By graphologist you mean a handwriting expert?" asked A.D.A. Farrat.

"Yes."

"If I were to tell you a handwriting expert felt the writing styles in Exhibits Forty-four and Forty-five were the same, would you disagree?"

Drew held his breath, looking at the witness as the prosecutor prepared to literally tear apart his defense, leaving only puffs of dust to hang in the air for all to see.

Finally, the witness answered, "No, I would not disagree. The signature in the name of Jacob Wellington looks to be in the style of writing I recognize to be of Josh Wellington."

"Now let me show you where the Jacob Wellington signature in Exhibit Forty-five came from." Farrat went over to his table and picked up Exhibit Forty, the SDSU admissions folder, and took it to the witness. Campbell opened the file folder. The inside of the folder cover had a plain piece of paper taped over it.

"Mr. Campbell, what you are looking at is the application of a student for admission to San Diego State University. What is the name of that student?"

"It says Jacob Wellington . . . ah . . . Port Hedland, Australia," the witness said with a surprised look.

"Did you know Jacob was studying at San Diego State?"

"No . . . I'm sorry. . . but I do vaguely remember an airplane ticket to Los Angeles and another flight from L. A. down to San Diego three or four years ago."

"Do you know why Jacob flew to California?"

"I think . . . please don't hold me to this . . . but I believe it was for a surfing safari, something like that. The young man has flown all over the world, surfing."

"Do any of the trust fund records or your reconstructed version of those records indicate any housing or other expenses for Jacob showing he was living in San Diego or any part of California?"

"No, sir."

"Has the man you identified in court as Joshua Wellington ever studied at San Diego State?"

"No, he went to Oxford."

"Has the defendant to your knowledge ever traveled to California?"

"No, sir. None of my records indicate Josh has been to California except for his recent trip several months ago on his way to Chicago."

"Mr. Campbell, please look at the inside cover of the folder marked as Exhibit Forty. See the piece of paper taped over the inside of the cover."

"Yes."

"Please remove it." The witness complied by pulling the taped sheet off.

"Sir, what do you see under the white sheet you just removed?"

With an astonished expression the witness looked up and said, "A picture of Josh."

"You mean Joshua Wellington, the man seated at the defense table?"

"Yes," answered the accountant is a very low voice.

"And again, please look at the back of the admissions folder. Do you see an Australian passport and U.S. visa?"

"Yes, sir."

"Whose picture is on those documents?"

"Joshua Wellington's," answered the witness.

"And how did Joshua Wellington sign those documents?"

The witness stared at the signatures and then back to the pictures. After a pause, he said, "Josh signed them as Jacob Wellington . . ." His voice trailed off to near silence.

"Mr. Campbell, let me show you Exhibit Forty-one. It is a Hawaiian driver's license, or a certified copy of one. Does the Hawaiian license bear the picture of the defendant Joshua Wellington?"

"Yes," Cadel Campbell answered almost under his breath.

""I'm sorry, Mr. Campbell. Please repeat your answer, this time into the microphone so all can hear."

"Yes, it is a picture of Josh Wellington."

"What is the name on that license?"

The witness leaned forward toward the microphone. "Jacob Wellington."

"Finally, sir, I hand you Exhibit Twenty, the contract Jacob Wellington signed when he rented an apartment in Pacific Beach, the one raided years ago. What is the renter's name on the first page of the contract?"

"Jacob Wellington."

"Please go to the last page of the contract. How do you read the signer's name?"

"Jacob Wellington."

"Correct me if I am wrong. Isn't the name Jacob Wellington in the same writing style of Joshua Wellington? The same writing style you identified as Joshua's in the passport, visa, Hawaiian driver's license, and university application?"

"It appears so," Campbell answered in a strong voice.

"Mr. Campbell, you are very close to James Wellington aren't you?"

"Yes, sir. We are lifelong friends."

"Did you know the defendant was using the alias name of Jacob Wellington?"

"No!"

To your knowledge, does James Wellington know his son, the defendant, uses the alias of Jacob Wellington?"

"He has never told me this."

"Would he confide such a matter to you?"

"Oh, yes, sir."

"Your honor, I have no further questions."

The judge, who had been following the witness closely as he testified, turned to the gallery. "Ladies and gentlemen, it is time for our lunch break. We will recess and return at 1:30 p.m."

"This court is now in recess until 1:30 p.m.," announced Deputy Castro in a loud voice, trying his best to be heard over the din of voices talking about what A.D.A. Farrat had just pulled off.

Drew held his head low, his face ashen, as he struggled to grasp what had just happened. There he sat, frozen, as everyone exited the courtroom. In doing so, he violated his highest tenet—never show any reaction to anything the opponent does in court, even if it was devastating to his case. But this was a different feeling he had never experienced before.

My God, Farrat has done it. My defense is now the Titanic. It's just a matter of time. A knot welled up in his stomach so painful he winced as an acidic taste flushed his mouth. He first looked at Joshua, then to Pat as if looking for help, but they just stared back with blank expressions.

Deputy Castro tapped Joshua on the shoulder. "It's lunch, Mr. Wellington. Time to go." The deputy cuffed the young man and led him to the door next to the judge's bench and into the corridor behind the courtrooms to his cell.

Drew watched the twenty-four-year-old leave. *The young man does not know what has just happened.*

"Pat leaned toward the still-seated attorney. "Drew, are you all right? Would food help?"

"Hell no! I'm about to throw up as it is." Drew looked at Pat. "Well, sir, I finally know what defeat feels like."

CHAPTER 28

Lunch Hour

DREW, LIZ, AND PAT spent the lunch break hidden away from the reporters, near the restrooms at the back of the court building. No one said a word about lunch much less spoke as Drew appeared to be in deep thought. From time to time the young lawyer shook his head and mumbled something under his breath. And so it went for a good twenty minutes.

For the first time in years Pat DeLuca had no words of wisdom for this young man. Then Drew's phone vibrated. He pulled it out of his coat's inner breast pocket.

He answered in a soft voice. "Hello."

"Drew, it's Dr. Rougtbeck. You wanted me in court before one. I'm here, outside Department Twenty-eight. How's everything going?"

"Lousy."

"Well, I may have some good news. Where are you?"

"At the restrooms on the north end of the Courthouse. I'll send Liz to get you."

A few moments later, Liz and Dr. Rougtbeck turned the corner and walked up to the two dejected men.

Looking at Drew and his investigator, the scientist asked, "Who died?"

"My client," answered Drew.

"Really?"

"No, of course not. But he may as well be dead. We're getting our ass kicked."

"Then what I have to tell you may help."

Drew looked up, as if not believing.

"I broke the code on the greatly contaminated partial DNA in the last folds of the condom. They match the sperm DNA of the brother living in Mexico. Your chimera client has a different DNA in his sperm. That Jacob guy is the rapist."

Drew looked weak as he stood still ashen in the face.

"The prosecutor has my client identified as Jacob Wellington. Your testimony about this new evidence may . . . I don't know what the jury will think of it. The D.A. has everyone convinced my client is the rapist."

"But, Drew," spoke up Liz, "this is exactly what we're looking for—DNA evidence as to who the rapist is."

"You're right. But at this point I don't know if it's enough." Drew turned and walked past the surprised scientist, stopping a few feet away. *Come on man. You've gotten the crap kicked out of you before in cage fights and fought back and won. Jacob is right. Stop feeling sorry for myself. It's time to regroup.*

Turning to face his confused team, his face brightened. "OK. Here's what we're going to do. Doctor, I hope you have given me the key to winning. I'll put you on the stand. You explain the whole chimera thing, what your testing does, and how you were able to recreate the rapist's DNA. Then I will put on the Mexican lab witness and hope he holds up under cross. Where is Dr. Rojas?

"He's sitting in front of Department Twenty-eight."

"How'd you do the sperm match," asked Liz, again keying in on the most important question.

"By having Jacob's sperm sample, it allowed us to test

various snippet combinations in the PCR process until we matched Jacob's DNA. We were totally unable to find any combination of snippets that matched Joshua's sperm sample."

Drew spoke up and, with an air of confidence, said, "OK, guys, we're back in the game." After a pause, he added, "Just barely."

With the jury believing Joshua was the Sphynx, there will be no room for error, he thought. It's going to be scientific evidence versus all the D.A.'s physical evidence that Joshua was Jacob. I hope my two scientists hold up.

As the group walked toward the court room, Drew counseled Dr. Rougtbeck. "Listen to my questions carefully. Answer only the question. Don't embellish." The scientist nodded. "I just know Farrat is wrong. Our client is innocent," Drew added.

ooooo

Court Resumed After Lunch

"All rise. Department Twenty-eight is back in session."

Judge Sonja Gonzales-Black swiftly stepped onto the raised platform and into her chair. To her surprise Andrew Hawke was standing.

"Yes, Mr. Hawke, you want to be heard?"

"If it pleases the court, I have no questions for the witness Cadel Campbell."

"Where is Mr. Campbell?"

"He's outside, waiting for you to release him."

"A.D.A. Farrat do you have any further questions for Mr. Campbell?"

Farrat looked over at Hawke, who gazed straight ahead, refusing to acknowledge any look from the prosecutor. Farrat turned back to the judge. "I, too, believe Mr. Campbell has said all that needs to be said, Your Honor. The witness can be excused and make his way back to Port Hedland."

"Very well, the witness is released. Do you have another witness Mr. Hawke?"

"We call Dr. Lawrence Rougtbeck to the stand."

A small man about five feet, seven inches tall, impeccably dressed in a black double-breasted, pinstriped suit, entered the courtroom carrying a reddish brown flex folder full of papers. After being sworn in, the scientist walked to the witness stand. Once seated, he adjusted the microphone downward so he could see over it.

"Please state your full name," asked Drew.

"I am Dr. Lawrence Peter Rougtbeck. The last name is spelled R-o-u-g-t-b-e-c-k."

"Dr. Rougtbeck, what is your occupation?"

"I am the head of the California Forensic Laboratory at Berkeley, California. My specialty is biogenetics."

"What is biogenetics?"

"It is a field of study involving biology and genetics. My specific area of research is DNA codes, their detection, construction, replication, and the transmission of genetic traits through human DNA."

"By DNA you mean deoxyribonucleic acid, an essential component of all living matter and a basic material in the chromosomes of all human cell nucleuses?"

"Yes. But to be more specific, DNA contains the individual genetic code of all humans, and passes on such human hereditary patterns or traits from one generation to another."

"Doctor, have you ever been qualified as an expert witness by the Superior Courts of California?"

"Yes, over a hundred times. In fact, I have testified as an expert witness on DNA testing and identification in the San

Diego Superior Courts many times. Assistant District Attorney Farrat and I have worked together several times. Good afternoon, Jack."

A.D.A. Farrat acknowledged the witness's greeting with a smile and titling of his head. A gesture the jury fully observed.

Drew turned and looked at the jury while asking, "Doctor, are you familiar with a case involving the Sphynx rapist?'

"Yes. That is a serial rape case for which you and A.D.A. Farrat asked me to replicate a partially destroyed DNA sample found in the rolled end of a condom. We used our advanced PCR process to recreate the DNA."

"Were you successful in identifying the person the partially destroyed DNA sample belonged to?"

"Yes. With the help of Mr. Farrat, it was determined that the DNA sample belonged to a person by the name of Jacob Wellington."

Farrat interrupted. "Your Honor . . ."

"Yes, Mr. Farrat?"

"I will stipulate to the qualifications of Dr. Rougtbeck to testify as an expert in DNA."

"If the court has no objection, I will accept Mr. Farrat's offered stipulation that Dr. Rougtbeck is an expert in DNA research, testing, replication, and genome ancestry," stated Hawke.

The judge looked at A.D.A. Farrat, who nodded yes. "May the record reflect Mr. Farrat agrees to Mr. Hawke's stipulated designation of expertise. Dr. Rougtbeck, you are accepted as an expert in the field of DNA and genome ancestry."

"Thank you, Your Honor," replied the witness.

Hawke resumed his questioning. "Dr. Rougtbeck, did I ask you to again examine a condom that you worked on in a previous Sphynx rape case?"

"Yes."

"Did you also test the DNA of my client, Joshua Wellington?"

"Yes, it did."

"What did you find?"

"I discovered that your client has a rare form of DNA. He is known in the field of genetics as a chimera."

"How do You pronounce chimera doctor?"

"It is pronounced 'ky-mee-ra.' "

"What is a chimera?"

"Chimerism is a condition where a person has two or more distinct types of DNA. In simple terms, where most people have one DNA that is exclusively theirs, Joshua Wellington has two distinctly different types of DNA."

Hawked noted that all the jurors picked up their notepads and began writing. *I do think I have the full attention of the jury.* He walked over to the end of the panel next to jurors six and twelve, the end of the jury box closest to the witness and the judge, causing the witness to look in the jurors' direction. "Why is having two different types of DNA in one's body important in criminal law?"

"Being a chimera complicates the authorities' ability to accurately identify a suspect. For instance, if I have two types of DNA and you swab my cheek, you may get one type of my DNA. But if you test my blood, semen, or another part of my body, it may match my other type of DNA. It all depends on where the second DNA is located. Either one of those DNAs may match another person's DNA, such as a twin brother. In other words, the police may think they have a rapist or murderer because a suspect's cheek-swabbed DNA matches blood or sperm found at crime scene. But if you test the suspect's semen or blood, it won't match. There have been cases where an innocent person has been charged with a crime because the police didn't know about the existence of chimera."

"Are there any noticeable physical signs the average person can see which would tell us a person is a chimera?"

"A person with multiple DNA may have two different-colored eyes or different patches of skin color or hair, just to name a few noticeable signs."

"Does Joshua have any noticeable signs of different types of DNA?"

"Yes, he has two different-colored eyes and very significantly different colors of skin. He has a darker patch of skin which starts on the left side at his waist line and wraps around the waist and buttocks to the right side and down the back of his right leg to just above his inner knee. The rest of his skin is a lighter white. I took multiple skin samples from both colored skin areas. The darker skin had a DNA different from the lighter skin samples."

"Your Honor, I have marked photographs of Joshua and Jacob's unclothed bodies as Defense Exhibit Twenty-six and will move them into evidence at the end of my case."

"Any objection, Mr. Farrat, to them preliminarily being discussed during the trial until accepted by the court?" the judge asked.

"No, your Honor. Mr. Hawke provided us with copies of the pictures and sworn statements of witnesses he plans to call to authenticate when the pictures were taken and who the persons are in the pictures."

"Very well. Proceed, Mr. Hawke."

"Doctor, did you do any further testing of Joshua?"

"I also took a blood sample, prostate fluid, which is produced by the male prostate gland, and a semen sample from which I extracted sperm cells."

"I'm sorry, could you clarify for the jury the difference

between semen and sperm, and the process involved," Drew asked, still standing next to the jury box.

"Semen is the liquid in which sperm cells exist. It is the sperm cells that fertilize a woman's egg. Sperm cells carry the DNA of the male sex partner. Once I have extracted the sperm cells from the semen, I can then analyze the sperm's DNA. I also tested hair samples and the swabbed sample of Joshua's mouth for DNA. The DNA of the prostate and sperm samples matched Joshua's darker skin DNA sample. Joshua's blood sample DNA matched the cheek and light-colored skin DNA. There is no question that Joshua Wellington is one of those rare individuals whose genome is made up of two types of DNA."

A murmur spread through gallery. Judge Gonzales-Black gaveled the courtroom to order and nodded at Hawke to continue.

"Now, Dr. Rougtbeck, how about the condom that you tested years ago in the first Sphynx case?"

"Over the last three years my laboratory has been working to refine our revolutionary method for isolating and extracting DNA from mixed or multiple partners' DNA, or damaged DNA. We have also improved the PCR process we developed four years ago. Today our system of analysis is much more sensitive and accurate. We can now analyze very small DNA snippets and through our PCR process reconstruct enough of a DNA strand that we can identify who the DNA belongs to. Even DNA which has been damaged by a chemical as used by the Sphynx rapist."

"Doctor, would you explain what a DNA snippet is?"

"DNA snippets are small portions of the DNA chain or strand found within human cells."

"And what is a DNA chain or strand?"

"A DNA molecule consists of two long polynucleotide strands interlaced in a swirling chain. We normally refer to the two strands of DNA as a double helix, which is similar to a twisted step ladder. Now, each strand is composed of four types of nucleotide subunits. The two DNA strands comprise an individual's genetic makeup. That DNA makeup is usually specific and unique to each person."

"Was your reconstruction of the DNA in the first Sphynx rape case successful?"

"Yes. Our first DNA reconstruction led to the matching of a DNA swab taken from a Jacob Wellington by the U.S. Citizenship and Immigration Services. Our findings were confirmed when the police raided Jacob Wellington's apartment, where the police found physical evidence tying the man to many different rapes."

"Have you been able to confirm your findings in the first Sphynx case in another way?"

"I reran the small DNA snippets we still had in our laboratory using our new extremely sensitive PCR process. We were able once again to reconstruct a full DNA chain that matched the DNA of Jacob Wellington. In fact, Dr. Ethan Brown used our latest process to confirm again the Sphynx rapist's identity. I believe Dr. Brown testified earlier in this trial about his successful DNA match."

"Did you try to match the rapist's DNA found on the condom to the sperm and prostate samples taken from my client Joshua Wellington?"

"We did. They did not match. The condom was not used by Joshua Wellington."

"Dr. Rougtbeck, what is a fraternal twin?"

"Fraternal twins occur when two of a woman's eggs are each fertilized by two separate sperms, producing two zygotes within that woman's uterus."

"And what is a zygote?"

"A zygote is formed when a woman's egg is fused with an individual male sperm. If a second egg is released during the same ovulation, and it too is fertilized by another sperm from the same man, a second zygote is formed and you have the makings of fraternal twins. Each of the two fertilized eggs grow within their own placenta. Since each fraternal twin carries a different DNA from the father's two sperms, the twins will have different features, some not noticeable, others very noticeable. These different features could include one twin having curly hair while the other twin has straight hair; or the twins have different nose shapes, eye colors, and other differing features."

"When you say eye colors, do you mean one twin may have two eyes of different colors?"

"Oh, no, not at all. Each twin's eyes will both be the same color, just different from the color of the other twin's two eyes. Each of the twin's different features are determined by the genetic heritage carried in each of the father's two sperms. As a consequence, the two fraternal twins will have similar but different features."

"What are identical twins?"

"Identical or biological twins occur when a mother's single egg is fertilized by a single sperm, forming a zygote which later divides into two cells which later develop into two embryos. The two embryos have the same exact DNA because they come from a single sperm that fertilized a single egg, and both embryos are receiving their blood within the same placenta."

"Thank you, doctor. We now understand how twins,

whether fraternal or identical, typically occur," Hawke said. "Now, please explain to the court, how does an atypical chimera or people with multiple DNA, occur?"

Dr. Rougtbeck nodded and glanced at the members of the jury, who sat transfixed. "There are many ways a chimera can occur. If a person received a bone-marrow transplant, the bone marrow will produce DNA from the donor which will be different from the recipient's original DNA, unless of course the donor is a biological twin. Also, a blood transfusion can introduce another person's DNA into a recipient's blood. There is disagreement on how long the blood donor's DNA will stay within the recipient's body. Another instance is where fraternal twins exchange DNA while in their mother's womb. Yet another way two types of DNA can occur is when a woman has a previous pregnancy and her fetus's DNA enters the genome of the mother, who later passes on that DNA along with her own DNA in a subsequent new pregnancy. The mixing of the mother's original DNA with a prior fetus's DNA is called microchimerism. But that is not how Joshua's chimera was formed."

Walking over to the defense table, Drew picked up a notepad and asked, "How so?"

"While the mother was with the boy's father, she had only one pregnancy. This information was provided by the father, James Wellington. The father also told us neither boy had any bone-marrow transplant or blood transfusions. Further, the medical records provided to me by the father indicated the Australian doctor's sonogram of Mrs. Wellington showed two boys, each within their own amniotic sac in one placenta. In other words, Joshua and Jacob were to be born identical or biological twins. However, our genetic testing of the DNA obtained from Joshua indicates two types of DNA. Fortunately, we were able to test the other twin's DNA. Jacob Wellington's DNA showed only one genetic DNA. That DNA matched Joshua's blood, cheek, and lighter-colored skin DNA."

A.D.A. Farrat shot to his feet. "Objection, Your Honor."

"Gentlemen, approach for a sidebar."

Farrat continued. "The prosecution was not told about—"

"No speaking objections, Mr. Farrat. We will discuss your issue at a sidebar," ordered the judge.

When at the side of the bench, Farrat exploded. "This is ridiculous! When did this supposed twin become available and why isn't he on the witness list? Is Hawke intentionally hiding him from us? If so, he is harboring a criminal. Hawke should not be able to introduce his DNA evidence without the twin's availability as a witness. I move to strike the testimony of Dr. Rougtbeck."

"Mr. Hawke?"

"I knew Dr. Rougtbeck was going to test Jacob, but he didn't inform me of everything he would say. The doctor just arrived thirty minutes before we reconvened court. He told me he had new test results but didn't elaborate except to say he tested the samples collected in Mexico from Jacob, and the results were positive for Joshua. What the doctor meant by 'positive' I didn't have time to get into. Besides, I'm surprised A.D.A. Farrat would object to last-minute evidence since he dropped bombshell evidence all day yesterday."

"I told you, Mr. Hawke, not to make this personal between the two of you," the judge admonished.

Hawke sighed. "What I am trying to say, Your Honor, is you denied my motion for a mistrial, and said you wanted the appellate courts to have all available evidence, if and when this case goes up on appeal. I believe Dr. Rougtbeck's information is vital to this court getting to the truth."

"You twist my words, Mr. Hawke, and I do not appreciate that."

Farrat jumped in. "Judge, I think Mr. Hawke should be . . ."

The judge interrupted Farrat with a wave of her hand. "I don't need your help, Mr. Farrat. Silence is all I want to hear from you!"

Drew's face contorted in a pained expression. *Oh, no. Gonzales-Black looks like she's going to blow a gasket.*

After a few seconds, the judge glared at the defense attorney. "I know, Mr. Hawke, this is a difficult case. In some respects I find it very interesting. I even applaud the two of you for your aggressiveness. But we really have to proceed with some order here. Andrew Hawke, do you have any further surprises you wish to inform me about? Before you answer, think and proceed cautiously. Tell me now or bear the harsh consequence of me denying any further last-minute evidence."

"Your Honor, I am not trying to be a wise ass . . ."

"I don't know about that judge," piped up Farrat.

"Silence! I told you I don't need your assistance. Farrat, I am not above holding an A.D.A. in contempt. Be quiet until I ask you to speak."

Farrat sheepishly stepped back and folded his arms.

Hawke continued. "As I was saying, ma'am, I am only trying to defend my client. I take to heart your criticisms of me." The judge's biting words echoed through his mind like the constant peals of a church bell. "To answer your question, my expert did mention he had done tests on James Wellington when the father first arrived here in San Diego three days ago. I don't know the results of that testing. I know of no other surprise evidence this witness may come up with. Much will depend on what Mr. Farrat asks and what doors he opens on cross-examination."

"Very well. Your objection is denied, Mr. Farrat, and the witness may continue to give evidence regarding the twin Jacob Wellington. The prosecution will have as long as you may need to consult with your expert Dr. Ethan Brown to plan your rebuttal of Dr. Rougtbeck's testimony." The judge paused, looking from one to the other of the men standing before her. Gentlemen, one more thing. As I stated before, I want only formal objections. You know the procedure—'objection, hearsay,' 'objection, leading,' 'asked and answered,' et cetera. I do not want you embellishing your objection with commentary that will influence the jury. I'm sure you get my point."

Both attorneys nodded and the judge then turned to jury. "Ladies and gentlemen, we will take our afternoon recess."

CHAPTER 29

Court Resumed, 3:00 p.m.

As Drew Hawke approached his witness, Dr. Lawrence Rougtbeck, he noticed the jurors lean forward with notepads in hand. *I do believe they are truly interested in the doctor's testimony. I hope this goes well.*

"Dr. Rougtbeck, before the recess we were talking about your testing of Joshua's twin brother, Jacob Wellington. Does Jacob have two types of DNA?"

"No. Jacob has only one type of DNA."

"How could a biological or, as some say, an identical twin not have the same DNA as his other twin?"

"The condition is called semi-identical twins. There are many mysteries that exist about what happens during conception and pregnancy. We are now discovering that chimerism is one such mystery."

"Doctor, could the father, James Wellington, be a chimera himself—a man who has two types of DNA—and passed on the chimera trait to one of his sons?"

"No. I tested Mr. Wellington for this. He has only one DNA. Therefore, he couldn't have passed on a chimera trait to the two boys. But there are two ways Joshua most likely came to have two DNAs in his genome."

"What are those?"

"The first is when James Wellington had sex with his wife,

two of his sperms fertilized one of her eggs. The fertilization of her one egg could have occurred yet another way. If the wife had sex with a second man shortly after she had sex with Mr. Wellington. In this scenario, each man's sperm would have fertilized the mother's single egg."

"Were you able to verify if another man did have sex with the mother and thus fertilize the mother's egg at or near the time Mr. Wellington had sex with his wife?"

"No. The mother's whereabouts hasn't been known for over fifteen years. But we did discover one indicator that there may have been another man involved. In running a genealogical search of Joshua's two-DNA genome, we found something interesting. Joshua's darker-colored skin's DNA was traceable to an Australian aborigine DNA. Specifically, the Yidinji people. The father and the twin Jacob had no such aboriginal DNA in their genomes. But for a genealogical search to be accurate, we need to test the potential second male or an ancestor of that second man to see if their DNA has any aborigine DNA. We don't know who that man might have been. So we can't do such a test."

"Correct me if I am wrong doctor, what you are saying is we don't know exactly how Joshua is a chimera?"

"That's correct."

"Doctor, I am still confused about how the male DNA contribution is determined in a chimera."

"Mr. Hawke, may I explain further?"

"Yes, please."

"Normally, a child will get half its DNA from the mother and the other half from the father when his single sperm impregnates the mother's egg. However, if her egg is again fertilized by a second man's sperm, then when the mother's egg divides you get two growing cells within the same placenta, just as biological twins do. Except each developing embryo will have a different percentage of the two men's DNA. This is so because each sperm has its own unique DNA genome mix.

The witness turned to the judge. "Your Honor, I have a slide presentation that illustrates how chimerism can occur with biological twins. May it be shown to the jury?"

"Mr. Farrat, do you object?"

"No, Your Honor."

"Mr. Hawke?"

"Absolutely not."

The witness handed a USB memory stick to Deputy Joseph Castro, who dimmed the courtroom lights as the screen motored down.

Dr. Rougtbeck introduced the presentation, saying he created a series of slides that illustrate what probably happened to create a chimera twin. "First, let me go back to the structure of DNA. A DNA molecule consists of two strands of twenty-three paired chromosomes. As a consequence, each living cell in our bodies has 23 pairs of chromosomes. Slide one shows a DNA molecule, which consists of pairs of chromosomes that wind around each other like a twisted step ladder. As I said earlier, a double helix of two twisted strands. But how does this double helix come about?"

Dr. Rougtbeck turned from facing the screen to face the jury and smiled. "That is the miracle of conception." He paused for a moment, then continued, facing the screen. "Let me go to slide two. When an egg is formed, the twenty-three pairs of chromosomes of the double helix divide so the egg has twenty-three single, unpaired chromosomes. The same occurs when the sperm is formed."

Again, he paused and faced the jury. :This next bit is critical, so please listen carefully." Several of the jurors nodded, and the scientist resumed. "When the chromosomes divide and become unpaired during the formation of the egg and sperm, there is some mixing of the DNA segments so each egg and sperm has a unique sequence of genes different from the mother and the father." He added emphasis to the words "each" and "unique."

He paused to let that sink in before continuing. "Now, slide three shows what happens when the sperm penetrates the egg. The sperm's twenty-three individual chromosomes combine with the egg's twenty-three individual chromosomes to form a new, paired, twenty-three-chromosome double helix.

"Now to slide four. When two sperms penetrate a single egg, then the 23 unpaired chromosomes in the egg mate with a random assortment of chromosomes from the two sperms. Small segments of the DNA from the second sperm, such as those encoded with eye color and skin pigmentation, can join complementary trinucleotide binding sites of the egg's DNA. Once the egg splits to create twins, the collection of DNA can segregate unequally, giving the ensuing twin's cell lines slightly different genotypes, which can lead to different-colored eye irises and patches of skin. That is how one or both of the twins can have more than one type of DNA. The result is semi-identical twins."

"Thank you, Dr. Rougtbeck," Hawke said. "Your Honor, may be please have the lights turned up again?"

"Yes. Joseph, please."

Hawked resumed his questioning. "Doctor Rougtbeck, has science confirmed this is one of the ways a twin can have two different types of DNA in his body?"

"Like I said earlier, conception is a mysterious event in many ways. What I have shown you is exactly how the egg chromosomes mate with one or more male sperm chromosomes. This is how chimerism comes about. What we are unable to explain at this time is how, when the fertilized egg divides, one new twin egg will only have one type of DNA and the other twin egg has multiple types of DNA. We believe the two-sperm mating process with an egg is totally random, as is the normal pairing of the egg with a single sperm. This randomness, by the way, is how the human species survives. It explains how the immune systems of certain people can survive or provide total protection against HIV and other viruses. What we know for sure is that chimerism is a documented fact in biological, supposedly identical, twins."

"Is what you have just explained how Joshua Wellington came to have two different types of DNA in his body?"

Yes, this explains why Joshua has eyes and skin of two different color. Even Joshua's hair, though blond like Jacob's, is of a different texture, waviness, and color. Obviously, this can get very confusing to a lay person. But the point is, our supposedly identical twins, Joshua and Jacob, are not biologically the same. Each has a distinctively different genome ,even though each came from a single fertilized egg."

"Doctor, could the Australian doctor have interpreted the sonogram wrong and the boys are really fraternal twins?

"I doubt that. If the twins were truly fraternal twins, they would have their own separate placenta. It's pretty hard to miss two placentas on a sonogram."

"However, I have to emphasize this again. We don't know exactly how Joshua developed two DNA strains because the mother is missing. The important point is not how Joshua became a chimera, but that he carries two sets of genomes, or DNA, part of which is similar to his brother, Jacob. Thus, it is easy to think Joshua is Jacob when a cheek swab shows the same DNA as our reconstructed DNA from the condom and

Jacob's swabbed check. What the authorities have not done is test Joshua's sperm. If they had, the police would have found it did not match our reconstructed DNA from the condom."

Hawke raised a hand, signaling his witness to pause. "Just to be clear, you did test Joshua's sperm DNA?"

"Yes. It is different from the DNA found on the condom. Again, to be clear, the DNA on the condom is not Joshua's."

Drew paused his questioning so the jurors could complete their note taking on what the witness had just summarized. He then asked, "Did you test the sperm of Jacob, the twin in Mexico?"

"Yes. His sperm matched the sperm found in the rolled end of the condom we previously tested, which led to the raid on the rapist's apartment."

"So your conclusion is that Joshua is not the Sphynx rapist?"

"Correct. Jacob is the rapist, not Joshua."

Hawke turned to face the judge. "Your Honor, I have no further questions of Dr. Rougtbeck."

Farrat quickly rose and walked toward the witness. "Dr. Rougtbeck, how did you get all those samples of the defendant's body. I have a copy of the jail's visitor log, and I don't see your name or your laboratory's name on it."

"I did not see Joshua in person. A local San Diego laboratory collected the samples and sent them to my laboratory in northern California."

"And Dr. Rougtbeck, how do you know that the twin who is not here in court is Jacob Wellington?"

"I believe Jacob is hiding in Mexico. But he did agree to provide bodily samples for testing to a renowned Mexican laboratory."

Farrat laughed. "Please, doctor. Are you telling me some

guy walked into a Mexican laboratory and said he was Jacob Wellington and gave body samples?"

"Not just somebody, Mr. Farrat. The Mexican technicians video taped him giving his samples. I have viewed those digital recordings and the subject looks like the defendant, Joshua Wellington. Visually, the only difference is the color of the subject's eyes and skin. Jacob's eyes are both dark blue and his skin is all one light, white color. After the laboratory collected the bodily samples, Javier Rojas shipped them to my laboratory by special currier where I tested them."

"Your Honor," offered Hawke, "the witness has a digitized video copy of Jacob's examination for A.D.A. Farrat."

"I object, your Honor," Farrat said. "If I need Mr. Hawke's assistance, I will ask."

The judge gestured toward the defense table. "Mr. Hawke, please sit down. Proceed A.D.A. Farrat." But Farrat looked confused as he stood before the witness, who pulled out a CD and offered it to the prosecutor.

"Mr. Farrat would this be a good time for a recess?" the judge asked.

Farrat looked at the judge. "Yes."

"Ladies and gentlemen, we will take a ten minute recess."

The ten minute break turned into thirty minutes after Farrat asked to meet with the judge in chambers.

With Hawke present, Farrat asked for the continuance the judge had earlier promised. She was not anxious to have another delay but agreed she had promised time to the prosecution to rebut any new defense scientific evidence. The judge sent the jury home until 1:30 p.m. the next day.

CHAPTER 30

The Following Day

WAITING FOR COURT TO RESUME, Drew, Liz, and Pat sat at the north end of the courthouse by the bathrooms watching the Channel 12 Noon News with anchor Larry Snowden on Drew's iPad.

"We interrupt our normal Noon News broadcast to give you an update on the second Sphynx trial," Snowden said. "I have with me criminal defense attorney Mitchel Jones. Mitch, what do you think of the events unfolding in the Sphynx trial?"

"Attorney Andrew Hawke has made a stunning recovery from the withering attack of A.D.A. Farrat's cross-examination of the defense's witnesses."

"How would you summarize the trial to date."

"It would appear, Larry, the prosecution and defense are on separate tracks in this second Sphynx trial. A.D.A. Farrat is attempting to prove defendant Joshua Wellington is Jacob Wellington, and defense attorney Andrew Hawke is saying the defendant's twin brother, Jacob Wellington, is the rapist."

"Are you saying, Mitch, the jury must decide who is the real Jacob Wellington?"

"That's right, Larry. More importantly, will Andrew Hawke call to the stand the black-sheep brother in order to prove his client isn't Jacob Wellington? The answer to this question will, in my mind, decide the outcome of this trial. If he doesn't, I think the defense's chances of a favorable verdict are low."

"Why is that Mitch?"

"As I see it, the jury must decide between a scientific theory, which few have ever heard of, and the A.D.A.'s hard-core proof Joshua Wellington uses the alias, Jacob Wellington. If Hawke produces the twin in Mexic,o and he testifies he gave his DNA for testing, then the defense wins. But without such affirming testimony the case looks strong for the prosecution."

Drew closed the iPad and turned to Liz. "Too bad we can't force Jacob to turn himself in." Liz and Pat both nodded in agreement.

ooooo

Court Resumed Testimony, 1:30 p.m.

Dr. Lawrence Rougtbeck was back on the stand and A.D.A. Farrat approached the witness, holding a CD.

"Sir, would you agree a picture is worth a thousand words?"

"In this case, A.D.A. Farrat, I would say yes."

"Doctor, I noticed the video you submitted as evidence yesterday was from an Apple cell phone. Am I correct?"

"I don't know how the filming of Jacob Wellington was done."

"Are you aware that anyone can purchase a digital camera capable of producing prints whose quality is indistinguishable from a thirty-five millimeter negative?"

"Mr. Farrat, I am not a film expert."

"Then you wouldn't know that some cell-phone cameras can produce digital images, even movies, approaching thirty-five millimeter quality?"

"Again, I am not a film expert. I am an expert in DNA and genetic ancestry."

"And yet you produced this CD video for what purpose?"

"To show how the samples were obtained and from what parts of Jacob's body."

"Are you aware, sir, digital-manipulation software is readily available to the average Joe?'

"No."

"So you have no way of knowing if the images on your CD have been changed. Even to the point of changing the person who provided the samples?

"No."

"Dr. Rougtbeck, are you aware that DNA evidence can be falsified?"

"Yes, I have heard of that."

"You are aware then one can centrifuge blood to remove its white cells which contain DNA?"

"Yes."

"Since the remaining red cells have no DNA, you now have a vehicle to which you can add another person's white cell DNA, correct?"

"In theory, yes."

"Another way you can falsify DNA is by cloning DNA where you put together tiny DNA snippets from various pools of DNA, am I correct?"

"To do that you would have to have a very large library of DNA snippets and the original DNA sample to copy."

"Doctor, you said the DNA samples were collected by a laboratory in Mexico, did you not?"

"Yes."

"Ever been to that lab?"

"No."

"Have you ever worked with that lab before?"

"No."

"Do you know how much the lab was paid to collect the samples?"

"No. But I did ask them if they were adequately paid."

"And what did they say?"

Dr. Rougtbeck paused and looked at Drew. "The man said extremely well."

"By extremely well did he mean five thousand dollars?'

"I don't know."

"A hundred thousand dollars or two hundred thousand dollars?"

"Sir, he never said how much."

"Let's see if I understand your testimony correctly. You believe that the person providing the samples to the Mexican laboratory is Jacob Wellington, correct?"

"Yes, sir."

"But you have never met Jacob Wellington have you?"

"No, I have not."

"And you are sure the samples sent to you have not been fraudulently tampered with or cloned, am I correct?"

"I do not believe the samples have been tampered with or cloned."

"Sir, I am not accusing you of tampering with the DNA evidence you have opined on. But it seems you have relied upon other people to collect the samples from the person you call Jacob. In doing so, isn't it true you have no way of being sure that the evidence sent to you by currier hasn't been compromised, or in the case of this Jacob guy, you can't even be sure the samples came from him?"

"A.D.A. Farrat, I have confidence in the laboratory that took the samples, if that is what you are asking."

"No, Dr. Rougtbeck, I am not asking if you are confident. I

am asking if you are absolutely sure? Sure to the standard of scientific certainty."

The witness started to answer, shaking his head. "Mr. Farrat, no scientific finding . . ." when . . .

"Objection, Your Honor. A.D.A. Farrat is badgering the witness. He has already answered the question."

"Your Honor, I think the jury totally understands the witness's testimony, verbal or otherwise, and to avoid an argument with Mr. Hawke I will move on," Farrat conceded.

"Very well. Proceed."

"Doctor, when did you collect the defendant's body samples for your testing?"

"I didn't."

"Who did?"

"A San Diego laboratory."

"Doctor, have you ever worked before with the laboratory that took the samples from the defendant?"

"No, sir."

"So you have never worked with the Mexican lab that sent you the samples nor have you worked with the San Diego laboratory before, correct?"

"Correct."

"Dr. Rougtbeck, how much have you been paid by Mr. Hawke to give your testimony?"

"Nothing yet. I have not prepared my bill."

"Thank you, sir, you have been very patient."

Farrat turned and as he slowly walked back to his desk he gave a knowing look of confidence to each and every juror. Watching what Farrat was doing Drew hesitated to say anything, fearing that it would only amplify the impression Farrat was apparently attempting to convey.

Turning to the jury, the judge said, "This would be a good time for us to take a short recess. Please feel free to use our juror facilities during the recess." As the judge rose, Deputy Castro announced, "This court is in recess."

Drew, Liz, and Pat once again walked toward the rear of the courthouse, discussing the status of the case. Once seated, Drew asked, "Pat, did you talk to the president of the Mexican lab?"

"Yes, but you will not like what he told me."

"Why?"

"They are the largest in Mexico. They do DNA research, including removing DNA from blood, saliva, and other areas of the body."

"Oh, no. Does that mean they then insert that DNA into other cells?"

"I asked him that and he said yes. He also added that he can clone DNA."

"Oh shit, Pat."

"And that's not all, Drew. Since the Mexican government has just started a comprehensive DNA bank of suspects or arrestees, the government relies heavily on our witness's huge bank of identified DNA samples."

"I bet Farrat knew this or else he wouldn't have asked the questions the way he did," Drew said, looking at Pat, who had a worried expression on his face.

"Pat, I think Farrat is baiting me to put the Mexican on so he can get supporting testimony about the lab's ability to manipulate DNA."

Pat added, "I thought at first such capability would make our Mexican witness look really good but not now after Farrat's line of questioning."

"Christ. What am I to do Pat? Put the guy on and have Farrat magnify what he has already planted in the jurors' minds or just rely on the credibility of Dr. Rougtbeck?"

Drew's trusted investigator just shook his head and replied, "That's a tough call. You will have to decide."

Liz added, "I think you should put on the gentleman since he is already here. Besides, if you don't, Farrat will berate you for hiding a witness who may give negative evidence. Evidence the jury I am sure wants to hear."

"Yup. You're right, Liz."

After a pause, Hawke said, "Liz you will do the direct with Dr. Javier Rojas. Keep it simple. Establish credibility of his lab and the type of work they do. Then have him describe what samples they took from Jacob. Then sit down. Let Farrat fumble around in his cross. He may forget to ask some damaging questions."

"Got it."

"Now, guys, the other thing is do I put Joshua on the stand? If he blows up, we lose for sure."

Pat shook his head. "Drew, you know Farrat will go right for the jugular and ask Joshua why he impersonates his brother. Worst yet, the dad and the account both said he hasn't been to California before he was arrested. But here he is registering at San Diego State for his brother. And if Joshua admits to knowing where Jacob is in Mexico, why is our client helping his brother to avoid arrest?"

"Yup. And from there it's all downhill. Especially if Farrat asks Joshua if he knew about Jacob raping women. Damn! I don't see much benefit in putting Joshua on except the jury will want to hear from him and will wonder why he refuses to testify."

Liz injected, "Drew, if he doesn't testify, you can argue Jacob put the admissions file together to help Jacob get admitted to San Diego State, not knowing of course what Jacob was up to? That might help negate Farrat's argument that Joshua is really Jacob."

"Uh-huh. But that still doesn't explain why Joshua is forging so many of Jacob's signatures."

ooooo

Court Resumed

Hawke addressed the court. "Your honor, at this time my co-counsel, Ms. Elizabeth Bernquist, will call the next witness."

Liz rose and stated, "The defense calls Dr. Javier Rojas."

A tall, slightly built gentleman with straight, combed-back, black hair, dressed in a gray suit, entered the courtroom. After being sworn in, he took the stand.

Liz approached the witness. "Sir, what is your name and occupation?"

"I am Dr. Javier Rojas, president of Texacoco Genetic and Ancestry Laboratory located in Mexico City, Mexico. We are internationally known as the Texacoco Laboratories and are part of the Universidad Nacional de Mexico," answered the witness in English, but with a thick Mexican accent.

"What does your laboratory do?"

"We are the primary bio-genome research facility in Mexico. Texacoco Laboratories are involved in extensive studies decoding genes and specifically tracing the genetic heritage of the Mexican people."

"Does your laboratory examine the human body and take samples for testing?"

"Naturally, that is part of our work which we do every day. We are a genome research facility. We test and trace the Mexican population to its ancient beginnings. We are constantly comparing the Mexican genome to ancestral skeletons found in our excavations of ancient burial sites throughout Mexico. We are also the leading DNA research facility in Mexico."

"Did you have an occasion to take specific samples from a person by the name of Jacob Wellington?"

"Yes. An Australian by that name presented himself to us with a list of body samples he wanted us to take from him. He also asked us to film his nude body, especially his eyes."

"And did those samples include his semen and sperm?"

"Yes."

"Did Jacob Wellington ask you to send those samples somewhere?"

"He did. Mr. Wellington told us to send the samples and film to the California Forensic Laboratory in Berkeley, California."

"Did you talk to anyone at the Berkeley laboratory before sending the samples?"

"Yes. I talked to Dr. Lawrence Rougtbeck. He told us what samples he wanted us to take. He also told us how to package the items and which currier service to use."

"How did you identify Mr. Wellington?"

"He presented his passport for our inspection. We also filmed the passport and included that film in the package we sent to Dr. Rougtbeck."

"Thank you, sir. I have no further questions." Liz turned and walked back to the defense table. As she sat down, Drew leaned over and whispered, "Nice job. Straight and to the point."

"A.D.A. Farrat you may cross-examine," advised the judge.

"Thank you," he replied. "Dr. Rojas, had you ever met the man before—the one who said he was Jacob Wellington?"

"No, sir."

"Was he Caucasian and what color hair did he have?"

"Yes, he was white skinned and had long black hair as is shown in the pictures I took."

"Did he speak with an Australian accent?"

"No. He spoke fluent Spanish."

"Did he have any other forms of I.D. on him other than his passport?"

"I did not ask for any other identification."

"Sir, how much do you normally charge for the collection of body samples for examination?"

"We normally examine volunteers, in particular college students at the university. We only charge for testing if we do familia or ascendencia research."

"I'm sorry, doctor, but what is that in English?"

"Ancestry research."

"Sir, does your lab due DNA cloning?"

"That is not a word that would accurately describe our work. A better word is sintesis."

"I assume that is a Spanish word. What does it mean?"

"I believe the best way to describe sintesis as it applies to our work is the combining of DNA parts so as to form a whole. As we excavate an ancient burial site, we attempt to reconstruct genetically the people who were buried there."

"So in essence you are cloning ancient civilizations."

"Not really, since we do not attempt to bring to life such genetic reconstructions as others have done with sheep, dogs, and other mammals. If you look at our website, you will see pictures of early occupants of the Americas. Through our research we render computer images of these people based on our reconstructed DNA."

"In other words, doctor, you remove DNA from a cell, replace it with a reconstructed DNA that is derived from snippets of DNA you have found in the remains at ancient burial sites, correct?"

"That is a crude way of saying what we do and somewhat

inaccurate, but in a very vague sense, I guess one could say yes. A better choice of words would be that we do genetic genealogy."

"Thank you. Did you examine the man called Wellington for free?"

"Yes." After a brief pause, he added, "There were the packaging and currier charges but we absorbed those charges. Dr. Rougtbeck offered to pay for these incidentals, but we said no."

"Let me be more specific. How much money was exchanged between you and this Jacob Wellington fellow?"

"If you put your question that way, Mr. Wellington was very appreciative and gave us a donation of twenty thousand U.S. dollars to our institution."

"Really, just for taking a few hair, skin, and blood samples and, oh, yes, photographs?"

"Well, he also provided sperm and prostate samples."

"Yes, of course. That too," spoke the A.D.A. in a sarcastic tone. "Did you question why such a man would ask you to provide all these samples?"

"Yes. He said they were for research at the California Forensic Laboratory."

"Did you question why he would give you such a generous donation of twenty thousand dollars?"

"Yes, and he said he was most impressed by the work we do and he wished to know more about our program. He was most interested in contributing to our future work. I thanked him and asked him to contact us at his earliest convenience."

"Did he indeed contact you later regarding your work?"

"No."

"Do you know that passports and other forms of identification can be forged?"

"I am not familiar with such work."

"Then you do not know if the passport shown you was a forgery or real?"

"I just assumed it was authentic since the samples were to be sent to a California laboratory of such renown. I also talked to Dr. Rougtbeck, who confirmed that Mr. Wellington would be asking for such sampling."

"Did you know that a person by the name of Jacob Wellington," pointing to the defense table, "is charged with multiple felonies for several rapes in San Diego and that he uses multiple forged passports?"

"Objection, Your Honor," Hawke said as he rose to speak further.

"Objection sustained. Please be seated."

"No," answered the witness.

"Dr. Rojas, you needn't answer a question when there is an objection," instructed the judge.

"Sorry," replied the witness.

"Sir, I have no further questions," Farrat said.

Liz rose for further direct, but Drew touched her arm and whispered. "No. Do not ask any further questions."

Liz leaned close and said, "I want to have the witness tell us whether Joshua looks like the man in Mexico."

"No. Sit down."

"Does the defense have any further questions for this witness?" asked Gonzales-Black.

Drew rose and answered no.

"Very well. Dr. Rojas, you are excused. Mr. Hawke, I see you are still standing. Do you wish to call another witness?

"At this time, Your Honor, I ask that all exhibits used by the defense but not previously moved into evidence be so admitted."

Farrat jumped to his feet and, in an almost joyous expression, queried, "Is the defense resting?"

Ignoring Farrat, Drew added, "I also move all exhibits earlier stipulated to by both parties, including those exhibits regarding the raid on the rapist's Pacific Beach apartment, and the exhibits from Mexico be admitted into evidence."

"Any objection, Mr. Farrat?"

"Again, Your Honor, is the defense resting?"

Drew ignored the question and looked straight at the judge, who said, "Mr. Farrat, the decision to rest is Mr. Hawke's. He will do so when he wishes. Do you object to the admittance of any of Mr. Hawke's requested exhibits?"

"No."

"That would include the samples and pictures taken by Dr. Rojas?" queried the judge.

"They may come in your Honor," replied Farrat, still looking at Drew.

"Then all exhibits used by the defense, including the evidence collected by Dr. Rojas, are hereby admitted into evidence."

"Thank you, Your Honor," Hawke said. "At this time the defense rests."

"Mr. Farrat, do you wish to put on any rebuttal evidence?" the judge asked.

Farrat looked down and after a few seconds answered, "No. However, I move all exhibits used by the prosecution into evidence."

"They are so received."

"The prosecution also rests, Your Honor."

"Then ladies and gentlemen, this concludes the presentation of evidence in this case. Counsel and I will use the remainder of the afternoon to go over jury instructions."

Turning to the jury, she said, "We will resume tomorrow at nine a.m., at which time counsel will make their closing arguments. Thereafter, I will instruct you on the law and how you are to deliberate as twelve judges of the facts. For now, let me say this: Do not discuss this case with anyone, including your loved ones. You are to keep an open mind and listen to the attorneys and their closing arguments. My instructions tomorrow will help guide you in your deliberations. Mr. Hawke and Mr. Farrat, please join me in my chambers."

Judge Gonzales-Black stood and gaveled the court into recess.

CHAPTER 31

The Next Day, 9:00 a.m.

"Good morning," the judge greeted the courtroom. Everyone replied, "Good morning."

"A.D.A. Farrat, are you ready to give your closing argument?"

"Yes, Your Honor."

"Then proceed."

Farrat rose from his chair and walked over to the jurors. "Good morning." The jurors acknowledged his greeting. "You twelve chosen jurors are the trier of fact—the sole judges of what evidence you choose to believe and what evidence you choose not to believe. Your job is a serious one. Unlike some judicial systems in the world where a judge decides what is true and what is not true, our tradition is to let the people, through you twelve jurors, decide what evidence is to be accepted as true. The judge, after I and the defendant's attorney are done talking to you, will tell you how to evaluate the evidence and then how you should use that evidence, along with the law, to render your decisions. So let's go over the evidence you have heard during this trial."

Farrat paused for a moment, scanning the faces of the twelve jurors. "In preparing for this morning, I find that there are two types of evidence you have heard over these last several days. The first type of evidence is factual, supported by physical documents and testimony as to the accuracy of such evidence, but most importantly, testimony by the person who collected that evidence or who was responsible for keeping safe such evidence.

"The other type of evidence you heard had one very important flaw. The presenter of the evidence could not produce the man who provided the evidence or verify the authenticity of such evidence. In fact, you heard no testimony as to how such evidence was kept or protected from being tampered with. In legal terms, there was no reliable chain of evidence that was documented and verified. In other words, the witness could not say if the evidence was true or not. I believe one witness said "I am confident" about the evidence. I submit to you, being confident is not the true test. We believe evidence when the person from whom the evidence was obtained testifies; we believe evidence when the person who collected the evidence testifies; and we believe evidence when the person who is responsible for maintaining such evidence secure testifies. Most importantly, we believe evidence when there is direct testimony from a person who has knowledge that the evidence had not been manipulated nor was it fraudulently created."

"You know what evidence I am talking about. The evidence Dr. Lawrence Rougtbeck said came from a wanted criminal, Jacob Wellington, a person he has neither met or knows. The evidence in question was collected by a laboratory in Mexico, which Dr. Rougtbeck had never been to or worked with before. The whole premise of his testimony was based solely on some anonymous person who said he was Jacob Wellington. He didn't even speak English."

Farrat's voice rose as if in disgust. He slowly walked in front of the jury box, then pause to look each juror in the eyes as he spewed his disdain for Hawke's defense of the young man Farrat believed was the Sphynx rapist.

Drew sat motionless at the defense table. His stomach again churning as each word of the A.D.A. tore apart his DNA defense.

Farrat turned and looked at Hawke with a look of accusation and continued. "And when Dr. Rougtbeck was asked if the body samples had been tampered with or scientifically altered, what was Dr. Rougtbeck's reply? 'I have confidence in the Mexican laboratory.' "

Turning back to face the jury, Farrat said, "I am sure the good doctor believed the evidence hadn't been tampered with. But believing without a factual foundation is not enough. You have every right to disregard such evidence—not even include such evidence in your deliberation of innocence or guilt." After pausing, Farrat again turned and looked at the defense table and added, "Especially when such evidence is bought for twenty thousand dollars."

Drew did not react, and Farrat resumed his closing argument. "Do the citizens here in court and those watching across the country believe such evidence? I doubt it. Does Mr. Hawke believe such evidence? Well, he will have his chance to say so and why he believes such evidence can be trusted when he is up next. I for one don't and you shouldn't either."

"So what evidence should you believe? You should accept the admissions folder from San Diego State University with copies of documents with the defendant's picture on them and a signature by the defendant in the name of Jacob Wellington. You heard Mr. Cadel Campbell say he has known the defendant since Joshua was born, and the signature on the admission forms were in Joshua's handwriting style.

Further, you heard that very same witness, who has seen the defendant's signature thousands of times over several decades, say the signature on the passport, Hawaiian driver's license, and the Pacific Beach apartment rental contract were in the style of the defendant Joshua Wellington's handwriting—all such signatures in the name of Jacob Wellington. The Australian accountant, who is also intimately familiar with the signature of Jacob Wellington, said the signatures on the passport, driver's license, apartment contract, and university admissions forms were not by Jacob Wellington. Again, I emphasize he said they were by Joshua Wellington, the defendant,"

Farrat's voice rose again as he pointed to the defense table. "I ask you, how long has the defendant been living two lives? A life where his father says the defendant is a good boy, a son who the father made president of his company, and a life of a depraved serial rapist who tortures his victims with chemicals after 'he got what he wanted from me,' as victim Eva Bloch said."

"I submit to you that in the face of such compelling evidence Mr. Hawke has desperately tried to construct a tale of fantasy. He asks us to believe the defendant is some rare species who has two types of DNA. He and Dr. Rougtbeck ask us to believe in some mysterious new procedure that identified one of the defendant's DNAs as not matching the DNA found on the condom of the rapist. Did you hear any explanation about how such a mysterious procedure—the new PCR technique—works? No. Yet, you are supposed to believe the word of Dr. Rougtbeck. I am just not a person who accepts such testimony with confidence. If Mr. Hawke had confidence in the technology, he could have taken as much time as he needed to explain the machine and its scientific wonders to you. But he did not. Hawke had the witness here who could have enlightened us on its marvels. The defense instead chose to leave us in the dark."

"And what about the samples taken from the defendant while he was in jail? Did the good doctor observe the samples being drawn from the defendant? No. Had the doctor ever worked with the San Diego laboratory that drew the samples? No. Had the good doctor ever seen the defendant before taking the stand in this court? No. Once again you are being asked to accept as true evidence that has no factual foundation. Only evidence the good doctor said he has confidence in. Again, you are left in the dark wondering, how can I accept this evidence? If I were to come to you with such evidence and ask for a conviction, you would throw me out of court. What's good for the goose is good for the gander. I say, throw Mr. Hawke's evidence out and not accept it in your deliberations. It just can't be trusted."

He paused to catch his breath and again looked each juror in the eye. "Finally, the only substantiated evidence presented to you is that the defendant is Jacob Wellington. Evidence that says he is the Sphynx rapist—the man who raped and tortured five young college-age women. What facts you may ask supports the conclusion that the defendant is the Sphynx rapist? I say the evidence found in the raid on his Pacific Beach apartment. When his apartment was raided, pictures of many young women were found, including pictures of the rape victims. Also found were chemicals used to destroy the rapist's DNA and to torture his poor victims, along with the carpet tape and nylon rope used to tie them up. Further, the sadistic animal took as trophies the driver's licenses and underwear of his rape victims, which I am sure he later lusted over. Oh, there is no question about it—Jacob Wellington is the Sphynx rapist. And there is no doubt that Joshua Wellington is Jacob Wellington, an alias he has used for his deprived needs. Such a personal disguise is just another way for him to continue his lust for women. Just as the defendant used torturous chemicals to try and kill his DNA."

Farrat turned and pointed at Drew, raising his voice again. "The shame of Mr. Hawke's defense is that if the wayward brother is alive or really is the Sphynx rapist, why wasn't he produced? Where is Jacob Wellington?"

Farrat's voice echoed in the courtroom as he turned and walked toward the defense table. "He is there seated to the right of his slick attorney." Pausing for effect while still pointing at the defense table, he added forcibly, "He is Joshua Wellington aka Jacob Wellington, the Sphynx rapist."

Drew, holding the young man's hand under the defense table, squeezed it gently and whispered, "Steady. Show no fear."

Farrat faced the jury once again. "Ladies and gentlemen, I ask you to find the defendant Joshua Wellington, also known by the alias Jacob Wellington, guilty of two counts of rape and two counts of torture. I would have put the other victims on, but their trauma has prevented them from confronting this animal rapist. To show you that I have hid nothing from you, let the record reflect that the other three victims also could not identify the defendant. But fear not. I have proven exactly who the defendant is."

Drew rose and calmly stated. "Objection. Counsel is talking about evidence not presented to the jury in this trail. As such, his statements should be struck and the jury admonished," stated Hawke.

Liz looked at Drew with a puzzled expression. As Drew sat down, she leaned over and asked, "Drew, why did you object? His comment was favorable to us. They couldn't identify Joshua."

"Liz, I want to appear impartial and law abiding. My objection legitimizes everything I am about to say to the jury."

"Then why didn't you object to his use of 'animal'? The judge admonished him not to during his opening statement."

Drew nodded. "This is different. The court allows greater latitude during closing arguments—"

The judge issued her ruling. "I agree, Mr. Hawke. . . . Mr. Farrat, you will reframe from introducing facts, whether true or not, into your closing argument which have not been introduced as evidence in this trial."

Turning to the jury, she instructed, "Ladies and gentlemen, you are to ignore the last statements of the prosecutor. You are to only consider evidence that you have heard during this trial. Nothing in this trial supports Mr. Farrat's claims about the other victims." Looking at Mr. Farrat with an extraordinary stare, Judge Gonzales-Black ordered, "Don't do that again, sir. Mr. Farrat. Proceed."

Farrat walked toward the jury. "In closing . . . to you jurors I say, do your job, and listen to the judge's forthcoming jury instructions. In particular, listen to that instruction which states you may accept any evidence you feel is true and reject that which you do not believe."

Hawke noticed that Gonzales-Black continued to stare at Farrat. *The judge obviously doesn't like Farrat's last remarks either, as they appear to comment on the ruling she had just made. I could object but that would only emphasize what he has said.* He continued to sit with an expressionless look on his face as Farrat proceeded.

"Ladies and gentlemen, justice now rests in your hands. Give the traumatized victims what they demand. Convict the defendant." Farrat turned and walked back to the prosecution's table and slowly lowered himself into his seat.

"Mr. Hawke you may now give your closing argument," the judge instructed.

"Thank you, Your Honor." Drew rose and deliberately walked slowly to the side of the defense table and rested himself against its edge. He looked up and moved his gaze slowly from one juror to the next. Assured he had their full attention, he finally spoke. "When we first talked, I told you there were two questions you as citizen judges would have to answer. The first, who is Jacob Wellington? The second, is my client Jacob Wellington? Through this entire trial I have tried to give you the facts to answer those questions."

"Let's take the first question: Who is Jacob Wellington? I believe the evidence shows he is a man who was abandoned by his mother when he was a very young boy; a boy whose father was a strict disciplinarian, or should I say a father who wielded a thick leather belt; a boy who, after trying to protect his brother from rape, was brutally beaten for his actions and ran away from his father to a foreign country. In doing so, Jacob left behind the only person he loved—his twin brother."

"I believe the evidence shows Jacob Wellington little understands the anger, indeed the rage, deep within him from the loss of his mother and the brutal punishment of his father—things he was too young to understand. A rage . . . a rage," Drew repeated in a forceful, rising voice, "which has consumed him and which he takes out on women; a man who is a serial rapist; a man who knows how to love but one person—Joshua—the only person who has loved him back. The only person who would do anything for Jacob, including signing admission papers and passports so his tormented brother could enter the United States and get an education. Only God knows what else Joshua did out of love for his twin brother."

Drew pushed himself up from the table and slowly walked toward the jury box, intentionally looking at those jurors who had siblings. "Twins are close," he said, nodding. "Twins do many things they shouldn't do for one another." Pausing so the jurors could reflect on his words. Drew then continued.

"Twins have a bond they can not ignore. A bond they see every time they look in a mirror."

Turning away from the jurors and walking over to the front of the defense table, Drew paused and looked at Joshua. "Now that we know who is Jacob Wellington. I go to the second question: Is my client Jacob Wellington?" Looking back toward the jurors, he said, "How, you may ask, can I prove Joshua is not the tormented rapist twin when the real monster wanted by the police is hiding in Mexico and refuses to come and save his loving brother? That is a dilemma I have pondered since I first decided to defend Joshua. My job has been made doubly difficult by the prosecution's belief that Joshua is indeed Jacob Wellington. To buttress the prosecution's belief, A.D.A. Farrat has introduced college admission forms with Joshua having forged his brother's signature and a picture of Joshua posing as Jacob, and the same for the passport and Hawaiian driver's license. When I challenged the purpose for such documents, what does the A.D.A. say? Joshua lives two lives: one as Jacob and one as himself. A real Dr. Jekyll and Mr. Hyde!"

Slowly walking back to the juror box, Drew continued. "But if you listened closely to the testimony of those who know Jacob Wellington, they all said his eyes are dark blue. Even the victim witnesses said they were both dark blue. Joshua's has one dark-blue eye and the other light blue. Why does Joshua have two different-colored eyes? I tried to answer that question by bring in a bio-Genetic expert, Dr. Lawrence Rougtbeck, a scientist who our very own prosecutor has used many times to explain DNA and help convict criminals. How does the prosecutor react to my using an expert he has relied upon to convict hard-core criminals? He accuses me of falsifying evidence the expert scientist used to come to his conclusions about chimera and about Joshua not being the Sphynx."

Hawke spun around and pointed at Farrat. "Does he have any evidence that the evidence presented by the defense was falsified? Absolutely not. If he did, you would have seen it. Rather, he is trying to plant falsehoods in your minds."

He turned back toward the jury. "Think, ladies and gentlemen. Think about the evidence you have viewed yourself and remember the words of the good doctor —Joshua's uniquely different eyes and skin has only one explanation—chimerism."

He paused for effect, looking each juror in the eye as if challenging them to find a reason to disagree. "Oh, before I forget. Remember Sergeant Anthony MacNeal's testimony? In the raid on Jacob Wellington's apartment, they found several passports. Those passports are in evidence. Look at them closely while you deliberate. They all have a picture of Jacob Wellington—not Joshua—and yes, both eyes in those passport photos are dark blue. Jacob Wellington even has black hair in one of those passports seized in the raid. Compare those photos to the images taken by the Mexican laboratory of the man saying he was Jacob Wellington. The eyes are both the same color. The very same dark-blue eyes the two rape victims said their attacker had. Again, not my client's light-blue and dark-blue eyes. I ask you to compare those passport photos to the pictures of my client on the college admission forms, including the passport and Hawaiian driver's license my client signed as Jacob. His eyes are light blue and dark blue. You were even given an opportunity here in court to view Joshua's eyes up close."

Hawke paused as he glanced toward Joshua, seated at the defense table. The eyes of jurors followed his.

Hawke regained the jurors' attention by raising his right arm. "Now, about our scientific testimony. Dr. Rougtbeck— after testing Joshua's blood, skin, hair, prostate fluid, semen, and sperm—found two types of DNA in my client's genome.

How could this be? After all, we grow up believing we are all unique individuals. Television shows—CSI, FBI, Law & Order, even the news programs—tell us that humans have but one DNA. Then Dr. Rougtbeck told us about chimera. He went on to explain how having two types of DNA can mislead the authorities—a mistake that can even lead to the prosecution of an innocent man."

He pointed toward Joshua. "Just like my client." He waited for the jurors to glance at Joshua before returning their collective gaze toward him. "The fundamental mistake the police made was swabbing only Joshua's cheeks. The defense went one step further. We analyzed his sperm DNA and found it did not match the sperm DNA in the rolled end of the condom. That same condom test which led the police to the rapist's liar. How could the police make such a mistake and misidentify the wrong twin, especially in a rape case where the best evidence is the rapist's own sperm? Is it laziness? Or is it just over confidence in a DNA science they don't fully understand? I say it is the later."

"What is the A.D.A.'s response to chimerism and my client's misidentification? He accuses me further of intentionally not asking the doctor to explain the advanced science Dr. Rougtbeck's laboratory has developed to identify the real rapist's twin."

Still standing before the jury and without pointing an accusatory finger at Farrat, Hawke, in a steady, soft voice simply stated, "If such scientific procedures were so important and questionable as to their accuracy, why didn't the prosecutor challenge our scientist or the prosecution's own expert, Dr. Ethan Brown, to defend the advanced DNA methods and their results? Remember, even Dr. Brown used the same equipment himself and praised its efficacy."

Drew walked over to the defense table, picked up a bible, walked to the end of the jury box, and stood in front of the witness stand. Hawke placed the bible on the witness stand railing and, with his hand on the bible, stated, "I submit to you the reputation of Dr. Rougtbeck's testimony given under oath is untouchable, as is his laboratory's work."

Leaving the bible on the witness stand railing for all to see, the young defense attorney walked back in front of the jury. "Believe me, if either I or the prosecution thought the credibility of Dr. Rougtbeck was in question, we would have addressed it. Has our esteemed prosecutor left any stone unturned in attacking me or my case? No. But when our A.D.A. couldn't attack my expert's laboratory and its work, what did Mr. Farrat do? The prosecutor instead said Dr. Rougtbeck didn't personally take the samples from Jacob and Joshua. Therefore, the samples couldn't be trusted."

Hawke shook his head, an expression of amazement on his face. "What an interesting argument against the validity of Dr. Rougtbeck's method of scientific work. It just doesn't make sense. If part of Joshua's two DNAs matched the DNA of the man who gave the samples in Mexico, how can Farrat say he wasn't Jacob. How could the man in Mexico know Joshua was a chimera or that he had two types of DNA, or for that matter which of my client's DNA would match his, and specifically match or not match the DNA of the rapist's sperm?"

Turning toward A.D.A. Farrat, Drew said, "I have a question for our esteemed prosecutor which he should answer when he rises to rebut what I say. 'Mr. Farrat, how many times has Dr. Rougtbeck, who lives in Northern California, flown down to San Diego to collect evidence from a crime scene or take samples from a person of interest in cases the D.A. hired the doctor as an expert? I believe the answer will be none.

That's because expert labs don't do that. The evidence is sent to them, just as Dr. Javier Rojas collected and sent Jacob's samples to Berkeley."

Drew stepped back from the jury box and walked several feet away so he could see all the jurors at once. "Remember, ladies and gentlemen, you have the right to consider what questions were not asked and what evidence was not presented by the prosecutor when you are deciding reasonable doubt regarding whether the prosecution has presented a case proving the defendant guilty. Questions unanswered are a burden the prosecution must explain, since the defendant is presumed innocent by law. Under our system of justice, a defendant doesn't have to put on any evidence or even testify if the state has not proven its case. I say to you . . ." raising a hand and his voice once again, "Prosecutor Farrat has not proved his case."

He pointed at Farrat. "Now this prosecutor has thrown up one more smoke screen, trying to prevent you from finding my client not guilty. He has continually inferred, indeed said, why don't I bring the wanted felon, Jacob Wellington, into court to exonerate my innocent twin? Ladies and gentlemen, I am not the state. I do not have unlimited power, money, and resources like the District Attorney's Office of San Diego County. That power rests in the hands of A.D.A. Farrat. Nor does my young client have such power. This twenty-four-year-old can't snap his fingers and send officers to Mexico to locate, arrest, and extradite Jacob Wellington. Only the district attorney has such authority and ability through its access to the courts and the United States-Mexico joint law enforcement task forces."

"Finally, let me add. Judge Gonzales-Black will soon read you several instructions to aid you in your deliberations." Walking over to the defense table, Drew picked up the California Judicial Council's book on Criminal Jury Instructions.

Turning to a marked page, he continued. "One such jury instruction I believe is crucial to your arriving at a just and fair verdict is the instruction on reasonable doubt. It reads as follows: 'The fact that a criminal charge has been filed against the defendant is not evidence that the charge is true.' "

Drew paused for emphasis and then continued reading. " 'You must not be biased against the defendant just because he has been arrested, charged with a crime, or brought to trial.' "

Looking at the jurors, Drew added, "The judge will instruct you further: 'A defendant in a criminal case is presumed to be innocent. This presumption requires that the People prove a defendant guilty beyond a reasonable doubt.'

"Whenever I tell you the People must prove something, I mean they must prove it beyond a reasonable doubt. Proof beyond a reasonable doubt is proof that leaves you with an abiding conviction that the charge is true. Yes, ladies and gentlemen, the judge will tell you, 'proof that leaves you with an abiding conviction that the charge is true.'

"The jury instruction continues: 'The evidence need not eliminate all possible doubt because everything in life is open to some possible or imaginary doubt. In deciding whether the People have proved their case beyond a reasonable doubt, you must impartially compare and consider all the evidence that was received throughout the entire trial. Unless the evidence proves the defendant guilty beyond a reasonable doubt, he is entitled to an acquittal and you must find him not guilty.'

"In going over this instruction, I was struck by the words 'Proof beyond a reasonable doubt is proof that leaves you with an abiding conviction that the charge is true.' What does 'an abiding conviction' mean? Well, I went to the dictionary and found that abiding meant 'lasting.' Frankly, I don't favor the word 'lasting.' Nothing in life lasts forever."

Farrat started to rise to object but then sat down as Drew continued. "I think you should interpret 'abiding' to mean that the twelve of you had come to a unanimous decision that Joshua is Jacob Wellington and that decision is without doubt. Not that you think he might be Jacob, or that the evidence could be interpreted to mean he is Jacob. Otherwise you must find Joshua not guilty.

"Throughout this trial I have noticed you taking vigorous notes. During your deliberations, please refer to those notes and discuss the evidence given you. Do not let criticism from your fellow jurors or, worse yet. emotions, deter you from the task of thinking clearly, logically about the evidence you have heard. In the end come to your own individual and independent decision. Do not just go along with the herd. When this trial is over you must be able to look back and say, 'I did come to my own independent decision.' I am counting on your ability to do this. Joshua is counting on this. Josh and I . . .'"

Drew paused, obviously affected by the emotions of the moment. He then slowly looked at each juror. "Ladies and gentlemen, this is the only way my young man can have a fair and just trial. Thank you." Drew turned and walked to the defense table and sat down. The bible still on the witness stand railing.

Turning to the jury, Judge Gonzales-Black said, "At this time we will take a ten-minute recess to allow everyone to stretch and, if needed, use the courthouse facilities. During this break do not discuss the case. All discussions about this case are to be done in the jury room when all twelve of you are present."

Deputy Castro announced, "This court is in recess."

Drew observed Farrat walking out of the courtroom with Chief Assistant D.A. Eric Washington, who had been seated in the gallery. They appeared to be having a serious conversation.

Drew turned to Joshua. "After the prosecutor does his rebuttal argument, the judge will instruct the jury and then the jurors will start their deliberations. While we wait for their decision, you and I will talk about the trial and what has happened."

"Do you think we will win?" asked the young man.

"Joshua, I never try to predict a verdict. There are too many variables that affect a panel of twelve jurors and how they decide a case. But I hope you believe I have tried my best to protect you."

"Yes, sir. You have. I thank you for everything."

CHAPTER 32

Court Resumed

THE JURY WAS SEATED; the defendant and lawyers were in place.

"A.D.A. Farrat, you may make your rebuttal," Judge Gonzales-Black advised.

Farrat rose, walked to the jury, and began. "Ladies and gentlemen, you have sat attentively through this trial, and I am sure you wish to begin deliberations. So I will not bore you with further rhetoric. Meaningless rhetoric such as Mr. Hawke has spoken. But I will warn you not to be swayed by a slick attorney's smooth manipulation of the evidence. Nor will I be bamboozled into answering questions posed by defense counsel. What he and I say is not evidence. The evidence you must consider is that which witnesses have given you from the stand and under oath. However, that evidence must be accurate. Not just a witness's assumption that it is true. Your decision must be based on things that you can touch and see, and testimony that is substantiated by a witness who can say, under oath, 'I observed and know exactly where the samples came from and my work on those examples was accurate.' And why such work was accurate. That evidence will lead you to one conclusion: Joshua Wellington is Jacob Wellington, the Sphynx rapist. Follow such evidence and find him guilty as charged. Thank you." The prosecutor turned and took his seat at the prosecution's table. The judge picked up the jury instructions, turned to the jury, and began reading.

"As judge, it is now my duty to read you the law which you will apply to the evidence you have heard."

As Judge Gonzales-Black read her jury instructions, Drew ran over in his mind

Farrat's rebuttal and whether the defense witnesses and their evidence would be sufficient to acquit Joshua. Again and again Drew came back to the same thought, *If only Jacob had the guts to surrender and save his brother, I would not be seated here, worrying about the future of Josh.*

The more the judge read the jury instructions, the more Drew felt uncomfortable about the success of his defense. *I swear, Jacob, we will meet again, and this time you will do the right thing by your brother.*

At the conclusion of the judge's instructions on the law, the jury retired to deliberate. All exhibits and a copy of the jury instructions were sent into the jury room. The prosecutor and Hawke were ordered to be on phone standby.

ooooo

Late the next day, Drew was seated outside the Barleymash Café when his cell phone rang.

"Hello."

"This is Debbie. The jury has a verdict."

"At three twenty-five? Debbie, that's not good. It's only been nine hours of deliberation."

"Actually, Drew, a little less than eight hours. The judge said she will not take the verdict tonight. Farrat and all of the D.A.s have gone to some big shindig at the Hotel Del Coronado. Because it was agreed the media would attend the verdict, she sent the jury home. They will be back at ten a.m. tomorrow morning."

"OK. Thanks, Debbie. Now go home."

"Go home? What's you talking about. I got work to do."

"OK, Debbie. See you tomorrow."

Thoughts about the case and his DNA defense once again rambled through his brain. Doubt about his trial decisions grew with each analysis. *Two short days of deliberation. That's not long enough for a defense verdict. Or is it?* His stomach began to growl. Drew decided to get dinner. He went inside and asked for a table. An hour later his phone rang again.

"Hello."

"Where are you? I'm at the elevator, but you don't answer."

"Silvia?"

"Yes."

"I didn't know you were coming."

"What did you expect? The news says the jury has reached a verdict but because of the late hour the verdict will be read tomorrow. Any idea how the jury will find?"

"No. It's a crap shoot. It's a question of whether or not the jury thinks Joshua is Jacob. I just don't know. The D.A.'s arguments were very strong." He heard a muffled sound and then Silvia spoke again. "Jacob wants to talk to you."

"Put him on."

"He's in Mexico, stupid. Go back to the loft and I will call him again from there."

"I've just finished dinner. Tell Jacob I'm about thirty minutes away. I'm up in Carlsbad."

"Well, get here."

"On the way." Drew smiled. *The only way to ensure victory is to bring in Jacob. I know he is here. He's not in Mexico.* Drew scrolled through his cell phone apps, stopping at cameras. He opened the app and brought up all four loft cameras. One of the loft's parking lot cameras he had changed so he could see the street and buildings west on 7th Avenue. He saw nothing. Not even Silvia on the other cameras.

ooooo

Twenty minutes passed and then another fifteen minutes. Silvia, waiting outside the elevator, began to pace, then sit, then up again pacing. Little did she know she was being watched remotely through Drew's cameras. She tried calling Drew again but got no answer. Finally, Silvia headed out of the parking lot and turned north on 7th. Drew watched from his car as she crossed over Island Street. Shortly after, Island she ducked into a small opening between two buildings where she met a man in a dark hoodie. They talked for several minutes, then her cell phone rang. She stared at the phone's screen, which showed it was Drew, then answered. "Where are you?"

"Sorry, I nearly got my car towed. I'm about three blocks away. Be there shortly to let you in." The phone went dead as Drew hung up. Silvia headed back to the loft, accompanied by the man wearing the hoodie. Five minutes later, a voice yelled, "Hey, punk. Are you afraid of me?"

The man in the hoodie said, "Oh, shit" and turned, looking to his right. There stood Drew. "You got to be kidding me. I'm not going to fight you, Hawke."

"Good. Then we can go peacefully to the cops. I'm afraid the jury will convict Joshua. This is the only way to free him."

"You know I'm not going to turn myself in."

"Then let's get it on."

"Bullshit, Hawke. Josh needs an attorney who's alive and hasn't had the crap kicked out of him."

"Don't make excuses, chickenshit."

"Damn you, Hawke." Jacob pulled off his hoodie, threw it to the ground, and stepped out with his fists up. The two circled on the sidewalk and then came at each other, throwing rights at the same time. Both punishing blows struck home, followed by lefts that missed. Both men staggered back, feeling each other's strikes.

"Damn," Drew muttered, clinching his teeth from the pain. *Think. Let him come to me.*

But Jacob didn't, so Drew snapped a quick kick to the side of Jacob's left knee. The blow caused Jacob's leg to buckle slightly. He stepped to the right and tried to kick Drew's left leg the same way, but he was flat footed and the extra step took too long. The attorney just stepped back and quickly retaliated, kicking as hard as he could against the same exposed leg. This time he hit the soft back of the knee where the nerves run down the leg. Jacob's left leg buckled badly. His knee almost touched the ground before he recovered his balance.

Drew could tell by the pained expression on the man's face his kick had struck one of the nerves behind the knee. *Wait. Don't rush in. Jacob could be feigning injury just as he did in our first fight. Remember Sullivan's warning. 'Let the Aussie come to you.'*

Drew stepped back and smiled as if gloating over the pain his kick had inflicted. Jacob moved aggressively to his right and in. Drew tucked his chin against his left shoulder and raised his fists as if he was going to charge in again to strike. The hurt Aussie responded with a roundhouse kick to Drew's head, but the attorney was already a step in, snapping a powerful thrust kick straight forward. His body and foot turned to the left, arms up to deflect Jacob's kick. The heel of his right foot struck squarely into the center of the Jacob's torso.

Drew could hear a cracking sound and felt his heel bury itself deep into the solar plexus. *I've struck him exactly where I wanted—right into the two sensitive bundles of abdominal nerves that radiate throughout the body.*

The force of the kick doubled Jacob over as he staggered back and dropped to the ground. He lay there, gasping for air. Drew jumped on top of the man and pounded his face with a flurry of fists. Jacob grabbed the back of Drew's head and slammed the crown of his head into Drew's face. Drew was stunned but continued to wildly strike with both fists. The wounded Aussie rolled to slightly to the right, trying to avoid the bombardment of blows while still gasping for air.

Still leery of the trained fighter, Drew stood and instinctively wiped blood from his nose, blinking to clear his eyes following the head butt. He attacked again, this time with a vicious kick to the back of Jacob's head. The man's chin was driven into his chest as he gave a mournful cry. Jacob rolled squarely onto his back and held both hands to his head in a fruitless effort to protect himself. Drew kicked again, this time to Jacob's left side, striking squarely into the kidney. He could hear an audible moan. Keeping his distance, Drew stepped further to the right side of the man and kicked him in the head again. The hard strike forced Jacob onto his left side, with his arms wrapped around his head. The Aussie, totally defenseless, rolled onto his back and attempted to bring his legs up into a defensive ball. Drew immediately mounted Jacob again, forcing the man's legs flat with the weight of his body and started pounding Jacob's face as hard as he could with both fists. *If this was in the octagon, a referee would have stopped the fight a long time ago. But this is a street fight. The first one to become defenseless pays the ultimate price. There is no rematch. The only rule is life or death, and it's not going to be my death.*

Drew kept pounding away as the man tried to protect his face with both arms. Then the Aussie flexed his hips upward, pushing Drew upward, and turned his head and body to the right. Drew's fists were bloody, and his left hand hurt so bad he couldn't hit with it. Jacob was almost on his stomach, with his arms covering his head, allowing Drew to go for a chokehold. Drew reached his right hand around to the front of Jacob's neck, forcing his arm between the man's neck and forearms. With his right arm squeezing against the neck, Drew took his left arm and anchored it against his right forearm, pulling as hard as he could against Jacob's neck squeeze the right carotid artery.

Jacob grabbed his attacker's wounded left hand and attempted to pull it away from his throat. Drew wanted to scream and let go, but he knew if he did Jacob might recover and kill him. Jacob continued to pull against the grip around his throat, trying to lessen the pressure. The man twisted his head to the left in an effort to breathe, and with his right leg pushed himself almost on top of Drew. To keep the weakening man from twisting away, Drew brought his right leg up against Jacob's right side and wrapped his left leg around the struggling man's abdomen, slamming his left heel twice into Jacob's groin. Drew could feel Jacob quiver from the pain of the kicks, then Jacob's arms started to go limp, and he ceased to struggle.

Suddenly, there was a loud explosion near Drew's head. "Stop it," yelled a voice. "Stop choking him or I'll kill you."

A second explosion went off, this time the hair on his head seemed to move as something went by his head and smashed into the sidewalk behind him. This snapped Drew out of his animal rage to kill. Opening his eyes, he saw Silvia standing a few feet away with a gun in her outstretched hands.

"Damn you, Hawke," Silva shouted. "I will blow your head off if you don't let him go."

Silvia turned her head slightly to the right, closing her right eye as she attempted to steady her aim.

"Don't shoot. Don't shoot. I've let go of him," shouted Drew as he pulled his right arm away from Jacob's neck and further shifted himself under the limp man for protection.

"Is he dead? Is he dead? Did you kill him?" she demanded still pointing the gun at Drew as she moved to the right for a better angle.

Drew held his wounded hand to the man's mouth and nose. "He's OK. He's breathing. I just choked him out. He will live Silvia. Jacob is going to be all right."

"Get away from him."

Drew pushed Jacob off of him.

"You stay on the ground," she commanded. "Roll over on to your stomach—now."

Drew rolled to the left and onto his stomach as ordered. *Crap. What have I gotten myself into?* he wondered, then spoke out loud. "Silvia, Joshua needs me. Don't shoot."

"Shut up. Spread your hands out to the side so I can see them," screamed Silvia. "You make one move, and I will kill you, you son-of-a-bitch."

Drew complied and in doing so turned his head toward Silvia as stinging sweat and the swelling blister under his left eye blurred part of his vision. He could hear the sound of sirens in the distance. He blinked both eyes in an effort to clear his vision, barely making out the image of Jacob trying to stagger to his feet. Silvia grabbed Jacob's left arm, pulling him up. She wrapped her right arm around the beaten man's waist and the two staggered south on Seventh Avenue, disappearing into a building on the right.

ooooo

Drew lay there, breathing ever slower as his adrenalin lessened and he began to feel an excruciating pain in his left hand. With a blaring siren behind him winding down, a man ran up, shouting, "Police, put your hands behind your head. Now!"

Drew slowly put his right hand on his head, which the officer cuffed. Then he slowly moved his extremely painful left hand onto his head. The officer then grabbed it, slapping the other handcuff around his wrist. Drew's scream echoed off the building walls around him. As the officer ratcheted down tight the cuff on his left hand, Drew screamed again.

"How does it feel, punk?" barked the officer.

"Aaaah, please, I think the hand is broken," Drew pleaded between short, shallow breaths as he writhed in pain. The officer ignored the plea as he rolled Drew over onto his back, pinning his left hand against the cement. The pain was so intense Drew clinched his teeth, biting his cheek in the process.

"Hawke? Andrew Hawke, is that you?"

Another uniformed man said as he walked into Drew's blurred vision, a gun in hand. A second siren whirred down as another police car pulled up, followed by two more squad cars.

Then Drew heard a familiar voice. "What have we got here? What's this about gun shots?"

Drew opened his eyes. Standing there was an indiscernible image of a man looking down at him. "Oh, shit, not another fight," said the familiar voice.

"Tony, is that you? I think my hand or wrist is broken."

"Get him up. No, just sit him up and, Davies, remove those damn cuffs," Sergeant MacNeal ordered. Two officers pulled Hawke into a sitting position and Officer Davies undid the cuffs. "Get me some water. There's a bottle on my front seat."

Davies ran to the sergeant's squad car and returned with a bottle of water. Sergeant MacNeal poured the water over Drew's head and face, then gently wiped the flowing water around his Drew's face.

"Tony, I'm fine. I just broke something bad in my hand."

Looking at the welt under Drew's blackening left eye, MacNeal asked again, "Who'd you fight?"

"Jacob Wellington—the Sphynx."

"Again?"

Drew gave a half smile to his old friend. "I did better this time."

"Does DeLuca know you're out here playing vigilante."

"Nah, Pat doesn't know. This was my idea."

MacNeal lifted Drew's left arm and examined his hand. "Drew, when are you going to realize you always need a back-up when cornering a bad guy, especially one like the Sphynx?" Looking at two rookie cops, he said, "You two carry him over to my car and set him in the passenger seat. Davies, call for an ambulance. And I want to see you when this over."

"Yes, sir."

Once in the car, MacNeal gave Drew some water to drink and asked, "What happened?"

"I had him choked out when Estrada shot at me and ordered me to stop."

"The TV reporter Silvia Estrada?"

"They went that way and into a building on the right," pointing south.

The sergeant ordered two officers to check out the building Drew had pointed out, then turned to Officer Davies, who was still talking with dispatch, asking for an ambulance.

"We've got a fugitive on the run," MacNeal said. "I want all cars that are near the Gaslamp area. Now! Tell dispatch that

Jacob Wellington, the rapist, and Silvia Estrada are on the run, and they're armed. Approach with caution. Then get your ass after your partner and the other officer in case they find him." The sergeant then looked at Drew.

"Tony, I'm OK," the injured man said. "It was the handcuffs digging into my wrists. They were killing me."

"Damn new officers. I've got to yell at them all the time."

"Tony, I'm OK."

"Yeah, yeah, I hear you. Just sit there. The paramedics are on the way."

While MacNeal talked to dispatch through his shoulder mic, an ambulance, followed by a fire truck, showed up.

MacNeal spoke to the paramedics as they approached on the run. "He's got an injured hand or wrist. The left eye is battered, but it appears to be just a blood blister. I gently touched the area around the eye socket and he did flinch."

After examining Drew's hand, the lead paramedic said, "I think you've broken some bones in your hand, maybe the wrist? We'll take you to a hospital."

The paramedics walked Drew over to the ambulance, opened its back doors, and helped him step inside for treatment.

"You got anything for the pain," asked Drew.

"No. You got to wait until you're at the hospital."

Another ten to fifteen minutes passed as the paramedics took vitals, talked to the on-duty doctor, and applied a splint on the injured hand in preparation for transport. The only holdup was where to take the patient on an especially busy night. Then a call came in over the police radio.

"MacNeal. Sergeant MacNeal, excuse me, this is Officer Davies. Thorn and I think we have the two suspects cornered on the roof of the Horton Grand Hotel on Fourth and Island."

Just then the sound of a gunshot and a voice could be heard over the radio. "Shit, she shot at me."

Sergeant MacNeal pulled the mic on his shoulder closer to his mouth. "Shots fired, shots fired. Officers need assistance at the Horton Grand Hotel. Two felons cornered on the Grand's roof," yelled MacNeal. as he bolted toward his squad car.

Drew stood and stepped out of the ambulance onto the pavement. The paramedic yelled, "Hey, what are you doing?" as he tried restrain him.

"No I'm going with the sergeant. Tony wait for me."

"Sir, you can't," replied the lead medic.

"Bullshit!" yelled Drew as he ran to the squad car, his left arm slack at his side. The sergeant slammed the driver's side door shut and started the engine. Drew jumped into the passenger seat. "Let's go, Tony."

MacNeal looked at him and asked, "What about your hand?"

"It will survive."

"Kid, you're either stupid or you got a lot of guts. I don't have time to figure out which."

The Sergeant sped south on Seventh, lights flashing and siren blaring. He turned right onto Island, heading west toward the Horton Grand Hotel.

Christ," MacNeal said. "It had to be that old 1887 Victorian hotel. There are dozens of small corridors and blind corners in the Grand, the perfect place to hold off my men. You said they were armed?"

"Yeah," replied Drew. "But I think they have only one gun. It was Silvia's. I don't know the type so I can't say how many bullets they have."

Tony again called dispatch. This time the lieutenant on

duty, Connie Stewart, answered. "Sergeant, what you got? I heard shots fired."

"Lieutenant, I need the Swat Team and the captain on duty over here immediately. Suspects are on top of the Horton Grand. Looks like a barricade situation. I don't know if they have any hostages."

"Tony, I already requested Swat. But right now you will have to handle this one on your own. All the brass is at the Hotel del Coronado, celebrating the chief's thirtieth year on the force."

MacNeal silenced the mic. "Shit! This mess is now in my lap." He pushed the talk button again. "OK, send me some more officers. I need at least ten more. If I already have all you can spare, ask the sheriff for assistance. We're going to have to shelter in place a lot of people. The suspects are in the heart of the Gaslamp and the place is full of tourists and revilers. And lieutenant, send sharpshooters. Tell Swat of my need."

"Ten four."

As the car approached the intersection of Fourth and Island MacNeal killed the siren and lights, and stopped about twenty feet from the intersection. He pulled out of the glove compartment his new SiOnyx night-vision monocular.

"What the hell is that, Tony," asked Drew.

"My new toy," he replied as the sergeant scanned upward.

"The rooftop looks clear. There's no one looking down on us. Hold on, Hawke, I'm going to gun her through the intersection." The sergeant accelerated through the intersection, then pulled up the emergency brake, which caused the old squad car to spin around, coming to rest on Island, facing at ten o'clock to the front of the Horton Grand Hotel.

Both men kicked open their doors and crouched behind

them. Again MacNeal scanned the roofline of the hotel with his monocular.

"Drew, on my command run, to the south side of the street and stay up against the brick wall of the hotel," ordered the officer as he held his service revolver at the ready.

"What're you gonna to do?"

"Once you're safe, I'll move around to the trunk and get a rifle."

"Tony, grab me a handgun." The sergeant paused as if to say no.

"Tony, you need backup. I have one good hand."

"Go, kid. Go now," MacNeal yelled.

Once Drew reached the wall under the overhang of the hotel, MacNeal ran, crouching, along the side of the car to the trunk and flipped up the lid for protection. Just as he reached in for his ArmaLite AR-15, he heard a shot, and then another round went off.

"What the hell is going on up there?" demand MacNeal yelling into his shoulder mic.

"She was going to fire down on the street, so we took a chance and fired."

"Well, stop it until I get up there."

"Yes, sir."

With the trunk lid still up, MacNeal ran along the passenger side of the car for cover and over to Drew clutching his rifle and a hand gun.

"Damn rookies. They'll shoot at anything. He should have yelled something instead of shooting. He just made negotiating ten times more difficult."

The two ran along the north side of the hotel toward Fourth Avenue until they reached the hotel's floor-to-ceiling glass entrance. MacNeal took a peek into the lobby. It was empty except for Officer Nguyen Dinh crouching next to the stairs leading to the upper floors. Officer Dinh motioned for them to come in.

"Officers Davies and Thorn got everyone on the first two floors out. The guests are now in the dining room, sheltered. Don't know about the third and fourth floors. But Davies and Thorn are on the roof," Nguyen said.

"I know, they've already fired at the suspects. I want no one to shoot until I give the order. Do you hear?"

"Yes, sarge."

Still looking at Dinh, MacNeal said, "I thought you were supervising Davies and Thorn."

"Yes, sir."

"Well, how in the hell did they get over to Island and Seventh?"

"Don't know, sergeant. I had them on crowd control down on Fifth Avenue."

They heard a tap on the front window of the hotel. Four more officers signaled with their hands if it was safe to come in. MacNeal motioned gestured for them to come in low and quick. He sent one officer toward the dining room so he could cover the lobby and protect the guests.

"Here's what we are going to do," MacNeal said. "Officer Ernst, you stay here by the stairs. If the suspects on the roof get past us, you stop them. If necessary, retreat to the dining room and protect the guests with the other officer. As more officers, arrive send them south to the Horton Theater next door. Have them secure the roof so the suspects can't retreat south over the roofs. You two men are going to check the upstairs floors and evacuate any guests there. Whoever you find, have them walk slowly and quietly down to the dining room."

The sergeant reached out and grabbed one of the officer's

arm as he started toward the stairs. "We don't know if there are any accomplices. Be careful. Officer Dinh and Millis, you come with me up to the roof. Drew, you stay here."

"Hell, no. I know them both. I may be able to get them off the roof without killing anyone."

"OK, then the four of us will join the rookies. Turn your radios to low. Let's go."

Once on the roof, they joined the two rookies, taking shelter behind some mechanical equipment. MacNeal peered over the equipment using his night-vision monocular, which had been hanging from his neck. "Looks like the guy is down. Did you shoot him?"

"No, sarge, we just fired in the air."

"Great, now you're raining bullets down on the public." The two rookie officers look at one another sheepishly. MacNeal again raised the monocular and scanned the roof a second time. Jacob was lying on his back, with Silvia bent over his torso as if she was protecting him.

MacNeal shouted to the pair of fugitives. "This is Sergeant MacNeal, San Diego Police. Wellington, are you hurt?" When he got no response, he asked again, "Jacob Wellington, are you injured?"

"Jake can't breathe well," yelled Silvia.

Still looking through the monocular, MacNeal asked, "What the hell did you do to him Hawke? He just spit out a big chunk of blood."

"I kicked him in the chest pretty hard. I might have broken a rib or two. "

"Well, if he's spitting blood, one of those ribs may have punctured his lung.

"Hey, it was him or me. He swore he would kill me."

"What else did you do?"

"I kicked . . ."

"Forget it. I don't want to know." Still looking at the two suspects, he said, "I think the guy's hurt badly. He keeps coughing up blood." The sergeant leaned over to Davies. "Call for a couple of ambulances. Tell them it's a hostile situation and to park on Third Avenue, just north of Island until we tell them to come in."

The sergeant addressed the fugitives once more. "This is Sergeant MacNeal again. Put the gun down, Silvia. It's no use. You are surrounded."

The man raised his head with the help of his girlfriend. "Back off or we'll shoot," he yelled, then coughed. Blood trickled from the side of his mouth.

"Throw the gun toward us and we'll get you medical help. I've got an ambulance around the block."

"I'm not going to get locked up. I'd rather die," yelled Jacob.

Drew stood up and yelled, "Jacob, it's me."

"Hawke, you son-of-a-bitch. You surprised me. You were just as good as the young guy I admired . . .," he coughed again and he spit out more blood. ". . . back with the monks."

"Come on, Jacob, this is not the way to end this."

"Hawke, I'm not going to be sent away again like Dad sent me to that damn Hong Kong school of butt-fuckers and bullies."

"It won't be that way. You're going to be sent to a prison hospital for treatment for your sex offenses."

"Don't bullshit me, Hawke." He paused to take a bunch of shallow, quick breaths which caused him again to spit out blood. "We both know I will sit in prison for . . . the rest of . . ." Again he started to cough and moaned as he did so. ". . . the rest of my life."

"Jacob, living is better than dying. You still have Silvia and Josh. Prisons allow conjugal visits."

"Stop it, Drew. We both know what's happening," Silvia screamed. "Leave us alone. All of you. We will end this our way," she added while waiving the handgun around.

"Come on, Silvia talk to him. I know you love him. Make the love of your life want to live."

Unbeknownst to Drew, a snipper had reached the rooftop of a taller building directly across Fourth Avenue and to the east of the Horton Grand Hotel. He had a commanding view of the entire hotel roof. Another one was on the sixth floor of the same building, but further south. Both had a good view of the four-story hotel roof. Both rifles were trained on the suspects. They asked permission to fire.

"You've got it, if either one makes a hostile move," replied Sergeant MacNeal.

Silvia kneeled next to Jacob and kissed him, then held the gun to his head. Two almost simultaneous shots rang out. One high-powered round struck the back of Silvia's head and the second shot from the other sniper went through her throat as her body jerked forward. Bone fragments, brains, and blood flew everywhere. She twisted to one side and fell onto Jacob. Drew ran to the two as MacNeal followed, kicking away the hand gun that had fallen. Drew pulled Silvia off and knelt by Jacob as he gasped for breath, coughing up blood with each attempt.

"You selfish fucker! You God damn miserable animal," Drew yelled as the sirens of ambulances arriving could barely be heard over the lawyer's condemning words.

Within minutes medics, breathing hard from running up four flights of stairs, arrived and took command. They ordered Drew away and immediately pronounced the obvious—Silvia was dead and Jacob was dying.

Drew turned and looked at MacNeal. "What a shitty way for her to die."

"You're right, a total waste of life."

As they watched the medics, Jacob appeared delirious, muttering incoherently while going in and out of consciousness. Tony turned to Drew. "I don't want to criticize, but what possessed you to beat the man so viciously?"

"He's evil, pure evil. If he'd been given the chance, I would look like that," Drew answered, pointing to Jacob. "Don't feel sorry for him, Tony. He used everyone in his life for his own needs. He even used me. He raped for the pleasure of raping; not one concern for his victims and how he tortured them. He manipulated his brother at every turn. He got Joshua to talk their father into establishing a trust fund. He used Joshua to create false identifications so this beast could go about his rage against women. Once Joshua was arrested, Jacob only tried to help his brother in order to keep the family company running. A cash cow Jacob thought he would need in the future. He knew Joshua would do anything for him."

"You really have a disgusting opinion of this man."

As Jacob was being strapped to a spinal board in preparation for the approaching medical helicopter, Drew responded, "He's an animal who lacks any human compassion. He even used Silvia. He wooed her instead of raping her because she was a journalist who could make him famous. Jacob manipulated her with his supposed tragic life of abuse by his father and the heartbreak abandonment by his mother."

Tony grabbed Drew's arm and walked the angry man toward the hotel's stairs, away from the noise and prop wash of the hovering helicopter. As they descended the stairs to the lobby, Tony asked, "You really believe that?"

"Hell, yes," Drew responded, turning to the obviously shocked sergeant. "I would have killed the son-of-a-bitch if Silvia hadn't shot at me. He is the worst in human kind—an extremely selfish, violent, sadistic person who would torture and kill at will."

"So you think he's mentally deranged?"

"You know, Tony, it may be comforting to think inhumane, selfish, irrational behavior or a desire for infamy, are simply rooted in mental illness. But in my short life span on this earth, I've found that's not the case. A minority of such antisocial behavior is due to psychologic turmoil. No, such traits have been with us since the dawn of our species. Jacob Wellington is just an animal and, like a mad dog, he needed to be put down."

"You may be right, but one thing is for sure, he was a selfish coward who couldn't take his own life."

"Your right Tony. Jacob convinced Silvia to kill him and probably take her own life. Instead, she dies and he lies on the roof, still breathing. I hope he dies on the operating table."

MacNeal didn't say anything but was obviously disturbed by Hawke's rant, no matter how much he agreed with the young attorney's insight into the character of Jacob. Once they reached the lobby, the sergeant put a hand on Drew's shoulder. When Drew turned to look, Tony put his right hand on Drew's other shoulder. He squeezed both shoulders hard with his big hands, which commanded Drew's full attention.

"It's time we talk man to man. Drew, I don't care how bad a person may be. He could be the damn devil. You are an attorney. An officer of the court who is expected to set an example by always following the law. You are not supposed to be charging off into a physical confrontation and in the process endangering others. That's my job. We're trained to do so. You are not a self-appointed crusader for public good. Your actions tonight caused the death of Estrada and probably Wellington. Worse yet, you endangered your own life, mine, and my fellow officers by your vigilante antics."

"But Tony . . ."

"No buts, Drew. It's time for you to realize you are no longer a twenty-something kid cruising the Gaslamp, picking up drunk women and fighting guys like a dog marking his territory. You should be ashamed of what you've done tonight and how it endangered so many.

Drew stood there, staring into the man's glaring eyes. He wanted to say something but couldn't find the words.

MacNeal took a step back and broke the silence. "When's the last time you talked to Father O'Connor?"

"What? . . . What do you mean?"

"You've got to come to grips with what happened tonight. Why not see Father O'Connor? He's always been there for you in the past. A talk with the man might do you good."

"But I . . . I don't know. . ." Drew stammered, his face showing a pained expression of confusion. MacNeal reached toward Drew, this time gently placing a hand atop his shoulder in a reassuring manner. "Oh, all right. It's been a tough night. Just think about it. If you want, we can talk later. Right now I've got a mountain of paper work to complete and a lot of explaining to do about how a friend of mine caused this bloody mess."

MacNeal turned and walked toward the hotel doors. Drew stood motionless. Once the sergeant got to the doors, he turned. "Come on, kid, you need to go to the hospital." MacNeal waved for Officer Nguyen Dinh to come over. "Drive Mr. Hawke to the hospital and then make sure he gets home. That's an order."

Drew tried to protest.

"You heard the sarge. I have my orders," Officer Dinh said. "Or would you prefer I put the cuffs on you?"

Drew stepped backward, a look of horror on his face. "No, anything but that."

CHAPTER 33

The Following Day

A BATTERED AND BRUISED attorney Hawke walked into Department 28, his hand wrapped in a splint, his arm in a sling, and his broken noise taped.

"Jesus, Hawke what does the other guy look like?" asked Deputy Joseph Castro.

"Worse," responded Drew, squinting through his left eye.

"What happened?"

"It's a long story. Tell the judge the Sphynx rapist is in custody. Farrat and I should meet with her as soon as the A.D.A. gets here."

Just then Farrat walked in with Chief Assistant District Attorney Eric Washington. "Beat up again, eh, Hawke?" Farrat said with his usual nasty smile.

"The Sphynx rapist is in custody," Drew said, looking to Chief Assistant D.A. Washington and ignoring Farrat.

"Yes, we know," replied Washington.

Deputy Castro entered from the back hallway. "The judge will see you now."

The three followed the deputy back to chambers, where Judge Gonzales-Black sat at her desk, holding up the San Diego Herald newspaper, the front page screaming "Sphynx Rapist Captured." Below, the subhead said, "Reporter Silvia Estrada Killed." The judge, still reading the four-page story, complete with past photographs of the Horton Grand Hotel, Silvia Estrada, and the previous night's crime scene, finally put down the newspaper.

"Good morning, gentlemen. I see, Mr. Hawke, you also do police work," said Judge Gonzales-Black with a smile. "The paper is saying the love story of Jacob Wellington and Silvia Estrada will now join that of the card-cheating gambler Roger Whittaker who in the 1800s was gunned down while hiding in room 309 of the Horton Grand. And some psychic is predicting Silvia's spirit will make haunting appearances to the guests of the hotel as Roger Whittaker and the Stingaree brothel madam Ida Bailey do now. I'm sure, Drew, you will be mentioned in this lore as well."

Drew looked at the judge, not sure what to say, Sergeant MacNeal's words still foremost in his mind. Slowly he replied, "I guess everyone knows about last night's events?"

"You're the talk of the courthouse, Drew. I had Joseph pick up a stack of newspapers so all the judges and court staff could read about your exploits."

Drew could only stammer out, "So . . . Your Honor . . . what now?"

"The jury is waiting with the verdict. I haven't seen it."

"At this time, Your Honor, the prosecution wants a recess to interview Jacob Wellington," Washington said.

"No way, Your Honor," Hawke responded. "Jeopardy attached when the jury was sworn in. The Fifth Amendment against double jeopardy applies. A continuance is bullshit. My client wants to hear the verdict now."

"I'm sure it has been a long night, Drew, and you look tired and . . . in pain . . . but let's refrain from swearing."

Hawke nodded in acknowledgment and took a half step back.

Turning to the two prosecutors, she said, "Gentlemen. I asked the court reporter to sit with us in chambers so we may discuss—on the record—last night's events. I thought it easier to resolve the issue of the supposed rapist and his capture in chambers."

Judge Gonzales-Black motioned for all to sit. "Joseph, please close my door." Pointing to the court reporter, she added, "Gentlemen, state your presence for the record."

"Chief Assistant District Attorney Eric Washington and Assistant District Attorney Jack Farrat for the people."

"Andrew Hawke for Joshua Wellington."

"Thank you. Mr. Washington, the defense has a point," the judge began. "The defendant has indeed been placed in jeopardy. Further, the evidentiary portion of this trial has closed, you both have rested, and the jury is waiting with their verdict. At this time, I see no misconduct by the prosecution or the defense during the trial that would cause me to consider a mistrial. Given that, it seems the district attorney's office can either ask me for a directed verdict of acquittal, you dismiss all charges, or see what the jury has decided. Either way, the Fifth Amendment against double jeopardy comes into effect and Joshua Wellington can never be tried again on these charges. If the jury's verdict is one of guilty, Mr. Hawke will appeal the verdict if, in fact, last night's man is the rapist. Now, if the verdict is not guilty, the People have spoken and Joshua will never again see the inside of a California state court on these charges. No matter what your office does, it seems to me the only person left to prosecute is the man just arrested, if he is indeed the rapist."

"Judge, this is an extraordinary situation. My office has found no precedence addressing a set of facts as we now face.

We would like a recess to interview the arrestee," responded Washington.

"Mr. Washington, the Channel 12 news this morning said the arrestee is being operated on and the hospital doesn't know if he will survive. Do you know when he will be well enough to interview if he does survive the operation?"

"No, Your Honor."

"Mr. Hawke, do you and your client ask for a mistrial or continuance based upon the arrest of last night?"

"I met with Joshua earlier this morning. I explained if we asked for a mistrial and you grant it, double jeopardy will not apply because we are the one making the motion. He insists on hearing the jury's verdict. Joshua told me he has sat through this trial hearing things about himself and his mother that will haunt him forever, and he wants resolution. We do not ask for a mistrial nor a continuance."

"Mr. Washington, does the district attorney's office ask for a mistrial?"

"Yes, we do."

"On what grounds?"

"That new evidence has been found by the capture of the man last night."

"And what is that new evidence?"

"At this time, we don't know other than the police think he is the real rapist."

"And how do they know that?"

"Ah, we don't have the police reports yet, but Sergeant MacNeal briefed me on the roof standoff this morning. The sergeant said Hawke told him the guy's Jacob Wellington, the rapist."

"Is that all?"

"No. The sergeant said the man, while surround by the police yelled, 'I would rather die than go to jail.' "

"Mr. Wellington, isn't that what many defendants say when cornered by the police at gun point?"

He did not reply.

"Mr. Hawke, why do you think the man is Jacob Wellington?"

"I believe the arrestee is the same man I talked to several times over the phone. He also looks similar to Joshua."

"Mr. Washington, let's assume this guy is Jacob Wellington, the man Mr. Hawke claims is the real rapist. Did your office make an effort to find this man before deciding to prosecute Joshua? Before you answer, let me caution you. Neither of you should attempt to mislead this court or invite a charge of prosecutorial misconduct by admitting you charged Joshua Wellington when you knew about his twin or that Joshua was innocent. Everything your office has done to date says you didn't know about a twin brother of the defendant. This is especially true since once you learned Hawke's defense was that the real rapist was Joshua's twin, you then proceeded to prove Joshua was Jacob."

She paused as Washington opened his mouth as if to protest.

Judge Gonzales-Black held up a hand. "No, Mr. Washington, I am not inclined to grant you a recess or a mistrial. Jeopardy has already attached to Joshua Wellington, and we have a jury with a verdict waiting. If you don't know what the new arrestee will say, do you have any other evidence as to the hospitalized man's true identity or evidence linking him to any of this case's rapes?"

Both prosecutors looked at one another. Chief Assistant D.A. Washington answered, "No."

At which point Drew spoke up. "Your Honor, there is an attorney, Mr. Randy Wright, already at the hospital. I believe he intends to represent the man under arrest. If so, I doubt the man will agree to give a statement to the police."

"This whole set of events puts the court in a difficult position. I see no grounds for a mistrial. And, if I grant a continuance there is no way to keep this jury from finding out what happened last night. They, in fact, may already know since this story is all over the news. Under such circumstances, if I grant a temporary recess or a longer continuance, I see no way we can continue with this jury. What keeps us from wasting all our work is that the verdict was sealed last night before I sent the jurors home. To be honest, I don't want to waste a jury nor do I want to waste the hours we have spent on this trial by granting a recess of the proceedings on an assumption by Mr. Hawke and the newspapers that the man in the hospital is the rapist."

"Mr. Washington, I again ask, what do you want to do?"

After a few moments of thought, the Chief Assistant D.A. replied, "The People wish to proceed to hear the verdict."

"Joseph, as soon as everyone is in the court, bring in the jury."

"Yes, ma'am."

ooooo

Department 28 was packed, standing room only, with more than a dozen local and national reporters. Every local television station, even CNN, had cameras at the back of the courtroom. After the judge took her seat, the jury entered and was seated.

"Ladies and gentlemen of the jury, have you chosen a foreperson?"

"Yes, Your Honor," responded juror number six, who stood. "I am the foreperson."

"Have you reached a verdict?"

"Yes, we have."

"Deputy Castro, would you please accept the verdict from the foreperson and bring it to me."

Everyone in the court was riveted by the formality of the passing of the verdict from twelve citizen jurors who have rendered judgement on a fellow citizen. The judge took the verdict and read it.

"Mr. Foreperson, is this the unanimous verdict of the jury?"

"Yes, Your Honor."

"Madam clerk, would you please take this and announce the jury's verdict."

The court clerk, seated to the right of the judge, rose and took the verdict from Joseph. She turned toward the packed court room and announced, " 'In the case of the People of the State of California verses the Defendant Jacob Wellington, otherwise known as Joshua Wellington, we the jury find the defendant not guilty on all counts.'

Upon hearing the words not guilty, Joshua collapsed head first onto the defense table, sobbing into his hands. A pronounced murmur spread across the gallery. But this time the judge did not demand silence.

The clerk then turned to face the judge. "Your honor, should I read the individual charges and the jury's finding on each?"

"No, Susan," replied the judge, "that will not be necessary, unless Mr. Washington desires each juror polled individually, but first, ladies and gentlemen of the jury, are you unanimous in your verdict?"

In unison, the jury members answered, "Yes."

"Does the prosecution wish the jurors polled?"

Mr. Farrat stood. "No, Your Honor."

"Mr. Joshua Wellington, please stand."

Drew and Liz both helped the shaken man rise.

"The jury has found you not guilty. Joshua Wellington, you are free to go."

The court room erupted into roaring applause. Drew shook Joshua's hand and gave him a hug, whispering in his ear, "Joshua you are a free man. Jacob is very happy for you."

Before Joshua could say anything, Liz grabbed him and held the young man in the longest embrace. Those seated in the front row reached to congratulate Drew, some just to touch him. From the back of the gallery, someone shouted, "Way to go, Hawke! What a stunning victory."

Reporters and camera crews rushed out to the corridor and jostled for position to interview Joshua Wellington and his lawyers as they exited the courtroom. With his hand around the shoulders of Joshua, Drew, followed by Liz, headed toward the courtroom doors where they were joined by Pat DeLuca. With Pat's help, the joyful crowd parted as the three escorted the Joshua into a blur of camera lights and shouts from reporters. Amongst the noise of a dozen shouted questions came a familiar Aussie voice, "Josh, Josh."

From the crowd emerged Cadel Campbell. The two embraced, with Joshua

collapsing into the man's arms.

Drew whispered to Cadel, "stay with Joshua while I answer reporters' questions." After a good twenty minutes he announced, "Come on, guys, I am out of things to say except this was a great victory. It shows the prosecution is susceptible to mistakes. In our system of law, it is the defense attorney's duty to expose such failings. Have a good day. I will watch your broadcasts and look forward the Herald's coverage in tomorrow's paper. I hope the media does today's victory justice."

The five then walked toward the elevators. Once out of the hearing of the media mob,

Drew stopped and asked for a private moment with his co-counsel. Pat, Cadel, and Josh walked a few feet farther and stopped. Cadel and Josh hugged again and began talking with Pat DeLuca.

Once they were out of earshot, Drew looked into his associate's face said, "Liz, you did a great job on this case. I ask you not to leave us. You are a valuable part of the firm. I couldn't have won without you. Joshua wouldn't be free if you hadn't done everything I asked so well. Let's work out our personal relationship later. Right now, I'm dealing with some really tough personal problems. Problems where some powerful people are messing with my life. I just . . . I don't know how to handle them."

"Drew, I didn't know. Who are these people? That female judge?"

"No, I ended that. I don't want to get into what's going on. I just need you to continue to help carry the load as you have done so far. And I need you to have patience with me and stay. What do you think?"

"I'm not going anywhere, Drew. Just don't ignore me or make sarcastic comments about what I say."

"Fair enough."

CHAPTER 34

SAINT JOSEPH CATHEDRAL was dimly lit this night, empty except for a lone man kneeling near an alcove before the statue of the Blessed Virgin Mary. Four rows of small, rose-colored candle holders, their flames flickering, provided a comforting glow. The perfect place to pray for guidance and understanding. The only other light was a solitary beam shining from the cathedral's tall, ornate ceiling onto the altar, illuminating Jesus on the cross.

A shadowy form walked along the side of the church and paused next to the confessionals. After a while, the cassock-dressed figure slowly walked up and knelt next to the man. After a few moments, the man looked to his right.

"Hello, Father."

"You seem in deep thought, Drew. Has the week's events bothered you so that you seek the help of the Lord?"

"Yes. I . . . I . . ." After a pause, he went on. "It appears I may have caused the death of Silvia Estrada and nearly killed Jacob Wellington."

"Come, let's sit," the priest said.

They stood up and moved the nearest pew, where Father O'Connor continued. "Inflicting pain on another is very disturbing, especially when your own hand causes death. But, Drew, I don't think you were the sole cause. Those two set a series of events in motion that you had no control over."

"But Father, I nearly beat a man to death and in the process placed Jacob and her in a position where they intended to commit suicide, only to be stopped by sharpshooters' bullets killing Silvia. I believe Sergeant MacNeal was right. I should have called the police instead of challenging the rapist to a fight."

"And if you had called the police, how would things have ended? The police would probably have cornered the two, and one or both would have died. You must remember, Drew, people control their own destiny by the choices they make. Some of these choices set in motion events they cannot control. Many times, those choices end in death. When well-intentioned people are drawn into such swirling sets of events, these well-meaning people can't control the outcome. That's what happened with you."

"But Father O'Connor, I myself have made some wrong choices. I just can't control my temper. I threaten to resort to violence, even in court, if things don't go my way. I believed I was losing the Wellington case and had to take Jacob to the police in order to save my client."

"It's not unusual for the young to become emotional and rush ahead. Even resort to violence. The young are idealists and want immediate results. But you are a highly educated man who must make prudent and cautious decisions. Your actions affect not only you but many others, including your clients. Sergeant MacNeal is right. It is the job of the police to handle the violent. It is your job to make sure justice is done. To achieve justice, you must rely on your legal training and your God-given talents of reasoning and persuasion. You losing control hurts your cause and the power of your argument."

"That may be so, Father O'Connor, but I was losing the case and knew no other way to bring in Jacob Wellington."

"You personally bringing in Jacob may have seemed the most expedient way to save your client, but in hindsight you now know there was another way. Learn from such challenges. And never forget—our citizen jurors have more common sense then we give them credit for. I watched the foreman of the jury being interviewed on Channel 12. He said the verdict turned on the credibility of Dr. Lawrence Rougtbeck and the fact that A.D.A. Farrat had enough confidence in the doctor to use him in other prosecutions. Your argument that the man named Jacob in Mexico didn't know whether Joshua's sperm DNA would or would not match the rapist's sealed your win. So common sense prevailed and the jury did the right thing for Joshua. Now, Drew, it is time for you to start doing the right thing also."

Drew remained silent. The priest sat still, sensing there must be more troubling the young man.

"Father . . ." Drew turned to look at the priest, a painful expression on his face. "I wanted to kill the man. I was in a blind rage. My whole body was uncontrollable. I didn't want to bring Jacob into the cops. I intended to do nothing but kill him."

Drew looked shamefully away and, in a soft voice, went on. "Father O'Connor, I just wanted to kill him. I don't know if it was because of the prior fight, or how he manipulated me to represent Joshua in this trial. It may have been my own damn ego. I don't know. What I realize now is that I just wanted to choke the air out him and send him to Hell."

The two sat next to each other for the longest time, saying nothing. Finally, the Jesuit priest spoke. "When I served as a chaplain in the United States Army during the Iraq War, many young soldiers came to me emotionally destroyed. They too suffered guilt, magnified by the horror of reliving through nightmares what they did to Iraqi soldiers—even innocent Iraqi citizens. I tried to sooth them, even take unto myself the horrible burdens that haunted them."

Drew looked at his priest, surprised he would share such intimate thoughts.

The priest continued. "But I learned that in war there is a base animal instinct within us, some would say an evil. We know it is wrong, yet we allow such evil to overtake us and even control us in the heat of conflict. At first I thought it was the instinct to survive. But as time went on, I saw that some soldiers just enjoyed killing other humans. Even now, when I counsel police officers after a shooting, or do my monthly rounds of confessions at Donovan State Prison, I am shocked that some find a rush, for many almost an addictive exhilaration, when they harm others."

"But Father, that's not me. I just couldn't control my rage."

"I know." The priest waited a few moments more, then he asked, "Drew, in college did you study the Greek philosophers?"

"Yes, sir. I thoroughly enjoyed my studies in Aristotelian logic and in particular the writings of Plato."

"Do you remember Plato's The Republic wherein he discusses what he calls the three elements of the mind and how they interreact with each other?"

"Yes, sir." Drew paused. "Plato deduced there were three parts of the mind: reason, emotion, and desire."

"Not quite, but yes, in a sense. In The Republic, Plato has Socrates gathered in the house of Cephalus with some well-known Athenians. These Greeks are discussing what the ideal polis or city-state would be. In doing so, they try to understand the human mind of those who will comprise such an ideal state. I refer to Plato because he attempts not to explain the different parts of the mind. I believe he is talking about human morals. Plato tells how Socrates concluded that being good means never letting desire dominate a man in such a way he is controlled by his desires. The same with emotions. Socrates deduces that reason must always be in control of what a man does. Some say this is how man lives a good life and avoids the evil within us. But life has shown us that humans can justify through reasoning whatever they do. However, by God allowing the sacrifice of his only begotten son on the cross for our sins, I believe the Lord showed us the power of forgiveness. We learn forgiveness through a nurturing and forgiving love, first from our parents, and later as we learn to live with our fellow humans and forgive their transgressions. Just as the Lord forgives our sins. This, I believe, is how man learns, through his power of reasoning, to control human desires and emotions. Reasoning must always have the moral guide of tolerance and forgiveness. If it does, then I believe Plato's goal of the perfect citizen can be attained."

The priest paused as he saw Drew bow his head as if in deep thought. After a period of silence, the young man looked up. "Thank you, Father. I miss our talks together. You always give me so much to think about."

"I, too, miss our talks. Does this mean I will see you at Sunday Mass again?"

Drew laughed. "Yes, Father. I think I need to get off this merry-go-round I am on and confront the very real problems I am having with Judge Brian O'Shea and his persistent efforts to control my life."

"Ah, yes, Brian O'Shea. A very troubled soul. Once you are ready to talk about Brian I may be able to shed some light on what motivates him and his desires toward you."

"You know what's going on?"

"Yes. But this is a subject you must resolve within your

heart. I can't tell you what to do. When you are ready, we will talk more about Brian. In the meantime, why don't we pray to God and ask him to help guide you when confronted with terrible choices and give you the strength and confidence to let reason control your emotions."

"You mean my temper?"

"All your emotions, including *sesso e amore*."

"You know, Father, I don't speak Italian, or was that Latin?"

Ignoring the question the priest continued. "One step at a time, Drew. One step at a time. True happiness does await you. In the meantime, remember, God is not done with you. You have more good work to do and many more perils to face. Let us pray."

EPILOGUE

Wednesday, 11:00 a.m.

A BLACK BMW CONVERTIBLE sped north on Fifth Avenue, slowed, and came to a stop across the street from the Ace parking kiosk in front of the Geo. J. Keating Building. A. J. Hawke glanced into the rearview mirror, brushed his hair back with both hands, and exited the double-parked car.

"Morning, Mario," he said as he flipped the car keys to the parking attendant running toward him.

"Hey, jefe, lookin' good. Congrats on stuffing it to the man," Mario said. "Been worried about you though."

"No worries. Just a few days off to let the swelling go down," Drew replied as he held up his left hand and nodded at the cast.

Mario sheepishly attempted a smile in return while staring at the yellow-and-black skin surrounding Drew's still slightly puffy left eye.

"You'ze one tough hombre, amigo."

Drew smiled, turned, and headed across the street towards the Keating's double front doors. As he ran up the flights of stairs, his body ached, reminding him of the brutal fight five days earlier. At the top of the landing, he glanced at the brown-and-gold lettered wooden sign on the wall in front of him. It read "Attorney at Law" with a hand's index finger pointing left down the long hallway. "It's nice to be back," he muttered as he strode down the long hallway, his Allen Edmond shoes echoing softly off the old building's floor.

Debbie raised her head as the sound of familiar steps approached. "He's here," she announced and stood as the office door opened.

"Good morning, Debbie," Drew greeted her and smiled as he shut the office door. There was no response as his devoted office manager looked shocked at the appearance of her young lawyer.

"Morning, boss. Nice to have you back," Matt added as the beaming surfer rose to greet the man he admired and hoped to be like.

"Morning, Matt. Nice to see you, too, and yes, I am alive and well."

Debbie and Matt attempted a smile at the apparent effort to distract themselves from his obvious appearance. Liz stepped out of the conference room and gave the battered lawyer a hug. "You're looking handsome as ever," she said, producing a round of forced laughs.

"OK, guys, enough affectionate ribbing. How about we all go into the conference room and discuss what's been going on."

The team followed their lawyer into the room and sat as Drew stood at the head of the long table. "Let's address the obvious. I look a mess. I'm a little sore but I'm healing and am good to go. Most importantly, I finally look close enough to my old self so we can attend the celebration party this noon at the Tipsy Crow. The Gang of Five have been calling me every day about when I could attend. Talk about persistence." Turning to Matt, he continued. "I see you're dressed for the event with your red, yellow and blue flowered Tommy Bahama shirt and, oh, yes, white Bermuda shorts. And I shouldn't forget the bright red Vans. You must have a girlfriend—you're almost color coordinated."

"Ready to part-e-e, boss."

"Now to business. Liz, you will have to continue making all court appearances until my eye looks better. Other than that, where are we in the SMA Construct Fab matter and the deposition of C.T.I.'s CFO, Douglas Chandler." Drew stopped for a second. "You know our client's name is a little awkward. From now on let's just call it SMA Construct. OK?"

Everyone nodded.

"Now, Liz, why don't you summarize what's happened while I was recuperating."

Liz was describing recent events and the postponement of the deposition when the office door opened and in walked a stunning petite woman in a blue business suit, her long blonde hair pulled back and rolled into a French twist behind her head.

"What's she doing here?" snapped Liz, glaring at Drew.

Debbie looked at Drew, who was fixated on the petite woman. "Drew, she's been calling constantly for the last few days," Debbie explained. "I told her you were out, but she demanded to see you. Something important," she added, glancing forlornly at Liz.

Drew turned and walked over to Judith Hudson, gently grasped her left elbow, and walked her out of the office, pulling the door shut behind him. A few minutes later Drew returned, his expression somber. He entered the conference room and sat down at the head of the table, gesturing to Liz to retake the chair next to him. She remained standing and near tears.

"Please sit so I can explain," Drew said.

The obviously distraught woman reluctantly sat but at the opposite end of the conference table.

Drew glanced at each of his associates. "Judge Hudson just informed me that Jacob Wellington agreed to cooperate with the police and has confessed to the rapes."

"That's fantastic," Matt responded.

"Not really, Matt," Drew replied. "Jacob also told the police he bribed the Mexican laboratory to falsify his DNA so as to exonerate his brother. He claims I encouraged him to do so. Presiding Judge Brian O'Shea somehow has learned about this and intends to file a complaint with the state bar and the California Supreme Court. He will recommend I be disbarred for conspiring with a wanted felon in order to acquit Joshua. In addition, the judge will allege I unethically withheld evidence from the district attorney and failed to disclose such evidence until late in the trial. To make himself look good, Judge O'Shea will also accuse A.D.A. Farrat of failing to timely disclose evidence to the defense. It appears the judge is going after my license to practice law and, at the least, demonstrate his power and ability to control me and my practice."

"Boss, that is not good. Can O'Shea do that?" Matt said.

Unable to control himself further, Drew slammed his good fist on the table and yelled, "I hate the son-of-a-bitch." The young lawyer rose and walked out of the room and into his office, slamming the door behind him.

All joyful thoughts of the recent victory and coming celebration were crushed by the revelation of such a blatant and apparently vindictive exercise of power by the presiding judge.

Liz hung her head and began to sob softly. Matt turned to Debbie, "What do we do?"

"We carry on," replied the stout Black woman. She lifted herself from the chair and ordered Liz to go to the ladies' restroom and fix her face. "When you get back, start preparing for the Chandler deposition. Matt, make yourself busy. We have a law office to run. I will talk to Drew. Now move, you two. He needs our love and support. The best way to show that is to carry on as if nothing has changed." As she walked toward Drew's office she softly said to herself, "With the grace of God, we just carry on."

She paused at Drew's door and listened. Not a sound. She knocked softly. Then a little bit louder. Finally, she heard a "Who is it?" Not waiting to reply, she opened the door and stepped in. Before her sat her attorney slumped in a chair behind his desk.

"Not now, Debbie."

"We have to talk, Andrew," Debbie stated in a soft voice as she closed the door and sat herself down in a side chair in front of Drew.

"About what? How you were right? That the Wellington case would bring nothing but pain and sorrow?"

"I may be demanding at times, but that doesn't mean I'm always right. You did the right thing and in doing so acquitted an innocent man."

Drew looked up at his most demanding critic with surprise.

"Success always has a price. And when the devil comes to collect, you got to fight back. If not, that nasty man will own you."

A long pause followed as Drew looked at her big round face and those loving dark eyes. Debbie's words, indeed her entire posture, was the reassuring confidence Drew needed to hear. A confidence, however, that was shattered when she asked, "Did you cheat?"

"No, Debbie. I would never. How could you think that?"

"Well, then, get up off your ass and quit acting like you did.

And don't think about how you will suffer if that judge gets away with his outrageous claims. Fight back. Every young lawyer in town will feel the boot of O'Shea if you don't prove him wrong." Debbie ordered as she rose from her seat.

"I've never seen you so demanding, Debbie."

"Am I right or not?" she retorted, glaring at her young man.

Drew thought for a moment before answering. "You're right. Besides, what have I got to lose?"

"Good. Now it begins this noon with your friends at that cow place. Before you start celebrating your victory you tell them exactly what is going on and how you did no such thing. You hear me?"

"You're right, Debbie. Why wait for O'Shea to make everything public."

"That's right."

"But, Debbie, only on one condition."

"What do you mean?"

"You have to come and be there when I tell them," Drew said with a slight smile.

"Andrew Jackson Hawke, you know I don't go into no such places."

"Well, it's about time you did. Besides, I need your support."

"Oh, you are one incorrigible young man. But," she added, "the Wellington Victory was great and this attack by the judge has to be denied publicly, now."

"Then it is settled. You will come with Liz and Matt. Stay long enough for me to tell everyone what O'Shea intends to do and how it is false."

"Yes, a show of unity is best. Besides I want to see what goes on in this cow place any way."

"Thank you Debbie."

ooooo

As the four walked across the street to the Tipsy Crow, Drew was in deep thought. I wonder what everyone's reaction will be when I tell them? Should I let everybody party for a while or kill the festive atmosphere with the bad news right off?

Suddenly, the two doors to the bar opened with Randy and Chad each announcing, "The conqueror has arrived. Enter. O mighty dragon slayer."

"Ha, ha. Very funny, guys."

"Let the party begin," Chad added as the four walked into the bar. Music and laughter could be heard in the upstairs room. Drew suddenly felt nauseous at the thought of having to ruin the celebration.

"What have you guys done? It sounds like a crowd."

"Just a few friends," Randy said as Chad led the way upstairs.

At the landing, Drew stopped abruptly as a huge crowd gave a loud cheer and pressed forward to congratulate Drew and his staff.

"Hey, guys," Drew greeted the crowd. Turning to Randy he asked, "What have you done dude?"

"You're a hero, Drew. Enjoy the moment."

As the crowd pressed forward, the stunned attorney didn't know what to do. One after another shook his hand or slapped him on the back. Women gave him huge hugs. It appeared as though every young lawyer in town was present.

Finally, Randy announced, "OK, OK. Everyone give me your attention."

But no one responded. He couldn't be heard over the noise of the crowd's vociferous congratulations to the victorious warrior.

Randy raised his voice and yelled again. "All right everyone, give the man some room. After all, our valiant gladiator appears battered enough as it is."

The crowd roared in laughter as they stepped back and chanted, "Speech, speech."

Finally, Drew raised his hand and the beaming crowd grew quiet. "I don't know what to say, guys."

Someone yelled from the crowd. "That would be a first." More laughter followed.

"I see you are ready to party," Drew replied, producing another rise of laughs and cheers from the gathering of young attorneys.

Again, he raised his good hand. "Yes, it was a great victory. No one felt more relieved than our client, Joshua Wellington. Josh demonstrated a stamina and courage I have never seen in such a young man. "And . . ." again he was interrupted as the crowd cheered. ". . . none of our success would have been possible without my staff. He pointed to office mates. "Mrs. Deborah McCaleb, my trusted friend and office manager; Ms. Elizabeth Bernquist, my associate and co-counsel at the trial; Patrick DeLuca, the best private investigator a lawyer could have. Pat couldn't be here because he's on vacation in the Cayman Islands. And last but not least, I have to thank our avid surfing file clerk and general 'go for it, man,' Matt Van Dryden. Where is the dude?"

Several voices shouted out, "Here he is."

Drew looked to his right. "Step forward, Matt. There he is, that's Matt, the fashionably dressed partier with the white shorts."

The whole crowd responded with applause and a few catcalls.

Drew smiled. "Without these people I could never walk

into court, much less walk out with a victory. How about a hand for them." A loud cheer went up, followed by applause.

After a few seconds Drew raised both of his hands. "You obviously are here to party, but before we begin . . ." Drew hesitated to collect himself and keep his emotions in check. In a strong voice, he continued. "The good news is we won. But with every great gamble there is a price to pay. And this was indeed a gamble. We had to overcome the powerful evidence of DNA. And don't forget the dogged attacks of a relentless D.A." Again, the lawyer had to wait for the crowd's vocal affirmation amongst themselves about Drew's brilliant DNA defense.

"But, I'm now aware that a vengeful claim is going to be made against our successful defense. In my case, it's going to be personal. The presiding judge has decided to report me to the state bar and the California Supreme Court for supposedly colluding with my client's twin brother. That twin brother of my client, as you know, is the Sphynx rapist. I stand here today to tell you nothing the president judge claims is true. I did not collude with the wanted felon, nor did I falsify or hide any evidence."

In a rising voice, he elaborated. "In fact, I fought the asshole rapist in order to bring him to justice and insure my innocent client's acquittal. I will do everything in my power to prove the judge is wrong. The jury reached the right decision. In the coming days, if any of you have any doubts about me or how I conducted the trial, please come to me. I will gladly answer all questions and present the appropriate evidence to prove what actually happened."

The crowd of young lawyers stood there in stunned silence. Then a loud, slow clap from the back echoed in the silent room, followed by another and then more applause until the entire room was applauding and yelling their support.

After a minute or so, Drew once more asked for silence. "Now, my fellow lawyers and friends, the lesson to be learned is this . . ." He paused so his words could be heard by all. "If you tweak the nose of the man, he bites back." The room erupted in laughter.

Again, the young lawyer waited for the crowded room to quiet. Then added, "For us today there is only one thing to worry about, and that is, how much fun can we have together in order to dispel this terrible cloud of vindictiveness. Folks, the bar is open, as is the lunch menu. Feed yourself well. Everything is on me. So . . . let's party on."

The room erupted in applause and yells of support, with many coming forward and telling Drew not to worry. Others said they believed in him. Many offered to help with research and any legal assistance needed. Drew thanked them all. As he walked among them, however, he felt a churning in his gut. His words of bravado were only a cover for the deep fear gnawing at his insides.

ABOUT THE AUTHOR

Donald E. McInnis is a California liti-
gation attorney and the author of three
books: the true-crime account of the
Stephanie Crow Murder Case and the
first two novels in the A. J. Hawke legal
thriller series. He specializes in trying
cases involving criminal law, business
law, personal injury, wrongful death,
medical malpractice, and civil rights.

Early in his career, Mr. McInnis served as a Research Attorney for the California Superior Courts. Later he became a
Deputy District Attorney for two different counties in Northern California and a Deputy Public Defender in San Diego
County.

He has also served as a Superior Court Judge Pro Tem, has
been an arbitrator for the American Arbitration Association,
and a referee/arbitrator for the California Superior Courts.

Mr. McInnis has handled more than a hundred jury trials
and negotiated hundreds of settlements. He is admitted to try
cases before all state and federal courts in California.

Mr. McInnis is Of Counsel to the Law Offices of Hamilton
& Associates, APC, serving all of Southern California with offices in San Diego, Orange, and Riverside counties.

AWARDS AND RECOGNITIONS
- Who's Who in American Law
- Who's Who in California

- Member of the Mexican Academy of International Law, Mexico City, Mexico
- Bachelor of Arts Degree, San Jose State University
- Juris Doctorate Degree, Santa Clara University Law School
- International Law Diploma in European Integration Law, Europa Institute, University of Amsterdam

BOOKS

- *She's So Cold: The Stephanie Crowe Murder Case—A Defense Attorney's Inside Story,* Second Edition (true crime, J & E Publications, 2021)
- *The Sphynx Murder Case*—A. J. Hawke, Attorney at Law (fiction, thriller, J & E Publications, 2022)
- Return of the Sphynx—An A. J. Hawke Legal Thriller (fiction, thriller, J & E Publications, 2022)

LEGAL TREATISES:

The Initiative Process:
Money & Politics, Citizens Initiative: Who Shall Govern, Santa Clara University Law Review, Volume 59, Issue 1, Fall Edition (2019). Also available at: https://digitalcommons.law.scu.edu/cgi/viewcontent.cgi?article=2868&context=lawreview

Criminal Law:
The Evolution of Juvenile Justice, From the Book of Leviticus to Parens Patriae: The Next Step After In re Gault, Loyola Law Review, Volume 53, Number 3, Spring Edition (2020). Also available at: https://digitalcommons.lmu.edu/llr/vol53/iss3/1/

Children and the Law: Time to Fulfill the Promises of Miranda and Gault, The Dartmouth Law Journal, Volume 19, Issue 1, Spring Edition (2021). Also available at: https://dartmouthlaw-journal.org/article/28217-children-and-the-law-time-to-fulfill-the-promises-of-miranda-and-gault

AUTHOR'S NOTE

The Greeks Had It Right: CHIMERISM

The Greeks like, many early cultures, assigned human characteristics to their supernatural gods. Today's more familiar Greek gods are Aphrodite, the goddess of beauty; Apollo, the god of the arts; Athena, the goddess of wisdom; and Zeus, king of the gods. Greek mythology also talks about a lesser-known Greek god, a fire-breathing monster made up of multiple types of creatures: a lion's head and a goat's body, with a dragon rear end and tail. This creature they called Chimera (pronounced ki-mer-a). It is therefore not unusual that scientists would adopt the name Chimera for conditions where humans displayed mixed body parts and features.

What's more, with the development of DNA research, scientists discovered a new phenomenon—humans with more than one DNA. This, too, would be called chimera. In its simplest terms, a human chimera is an individual who has two different genomes found amongst the 3 billion base pairs of deoxyribonucleic acid (DNA). A condition long thought impossible.

At first, researchers believed that chimerism occurred when two separate sperms fertilized two separate eggs. The theory went that the two fertilized eggs would fuse together into one fetus, thereby mixing the two male sperms' DNA into one embryo. The result being a human with two different types of DNA. They called this occurrence the "Vanishing Twin," where two twins become one resulting in a single baby with two types of DNA.

Following the same logic, chimera occurred when the two fraternal twins, while still in their separate placentas, exchanged DNAs through their mother's mutually shared blood. That resulted in two fraternal twins, each with a portion of the other twin's DNA or two fraternal twins with the same DNA. Researchers believed neither of these phenomena could happen to biologically identical twins who came from one egg, which divided and occupied one placenta.

Then it happened. Two identical twins in one placenta were born. However, one of the biological twins was a boy and the other was a girl. This was an impossibility since biologically identical twins come from one fertilized egg that divides in the womb. Therefore, both twins had to be of the same sex. Yet, here the Australian mother gave birth to two babies from the same placenta but of different sexes. Once the Australian doctors tested the babies' DNA, they found the twins had slightly different DNA, including X and Y chromosomes, which accounted for the different genitalia. This finding led other scientists to randomly test the DNA of biologically identical twins and the discovery of more twins with two types of DNA.

Researchers named the new findings 'semi-identical' twins—or biologically identical twins whose cells are not genetically the same. It is now believed two or more male sperms can impregnate a single egg, resulting in biological twins' having a different mixture of DNA. This fertilization of one egg by multiple male sperms can come from one father, or from two or more different men, when the woman has sex during the early stage of her ovation cycle.

With the discovery of semi-identical twins, scientists are now conducting further testing of identical twins—humans as well as other species—for a better understanding of chimerism.

For further research see:

- "Semi-identical twins discovered," John Whitfield, Nature News, https://www.nature.com/news/2007/070326/full/news070326-1.html

- "Doctors confirm new type of twin born from one egg and two sperm," Gene Emery, Health & Pharma, February 27, 2019, The New England Journal of Medicine, February 27, 2019, https://www.reuters.com/article/us-health-reproduction-mosaic-twins-idUSKCN1QG2YH

- "A man's Unborn Twin Fathered His Son Thanks to Genetic Chimerism," Tom Hale, IFLScience, April 1, 2021, https://www.iflscience.com/a-mans-unborn-twin-fathered-his-son-thanks-to-genetic-chimerism-59233

- "The Impossible Crime (Unless You Know About Chimeras)," Jonathan Jarry, Office of Science and Society, McGill University, June 2, 2022, https://www.mcgill.ca/oss/article/critical-thinking/impossible-crime-unless-you-know-about-chimeras

- "Chimeras: Double the DNA-Double the Fun for Crime Scene Investigators, Prosecutors, and Defense Attorneys," Catherine Arcabascio, Akron Law Review, Vol. 40, 2007, Nova Southern University, Shepard Broad Law Center, https://papers.ssrn.com/sol3/papers.cfm?abstract_id=2734747

A. J. Hawke Returns

LOOK FOR THE NEXT CHAPTER in the life of A. J. Hawke as the young attorney faces yet another legal challenge and the realities of life.

www.ingramcontent.com/pod-product-compliance
Lightning Source LLC
Chambersburg PA
CBHW051135030726
47504CB00004B/880